Kenworth D 17

Dianne Nelson 1975
(Indiana)
Tucson

Anatomy of a Diesel

TRUCKSTOP

TRUCKSTOP

INDIANA NELSON

ST. MARTIN'S PRESS/NEW YORK

Any similarities to actual persons
or places which might occur in this book
are purely coincidental.

813.54
N426t

Library of Congress Cataloging in Publication Data

Nelson, Indiana.
   Truckstop.

   I. Title.
PZ4.N426Tr [PS3564.E464] 813'.5'4 79–16540
ISBN 0–312–82052–6

This story is for Hazele, my friend.

PART ONE

CHAPTER 1

Out back behind a truckstop, at the edge of a rubble heap full of crank shafts, diesel engine parts and burnt-out, defeated dragsters, surrounded by a chain-link fence and drooping mauve roses, there was a trailer parked in a grove of cypress trees. These trees are a rare sight in such a lonely place. Beyond the trailer and as far as the eye could see, there was nothing but wasteland and tumbleweed. Except for the cypress trees you couldn't find a more desolate spot.

Three people lived in that trailer: Mabel Jenks, who planted the cypress trees (even when no one in those parts had ever seen such a thing before), her husband Orville and Orville's brother Ralph. They owned and operated the garage next door.

Jenks' Diesel was the garage where they worked on the diesel breakdowns. Sagging, metallic, the garage balanced in disjointed harmony with the land, its west wall agape, waiting for the trucks to come. Even when the garage was empty, the inner space was swollen with greasy remnants of the trucks: hoses, crank shafts, wires, barrels, blow torches, decapitated engines oozing inky juices.

Orville worked the day shift in the garage while Mabel and his brother Ralph slept. Then, late at night while Orville slept, Mabel did the books and Ralph ran the night shift unless he had a game going. Ralph shot pool with people from Detroit and Moline, like Harry the Horse and Three Fingers Brown. When he won he would take Mabel over to the best department store in town and buy her a diamond ring. She had a diamond from every big win and wore them all at the same time, in clusters.

When the nights were slow, Ralph and Mabel would go over to the Truckstop Cafe for pie and coffee, and no one who saw her there, holding court in the big corner booth, could help but wonder who she was. A year or so ago, Mabel was about fifty and still the most fascinating woman in town. There was not one single thing about her person which was unusual. Yet there was nothing about her that wasn't special and rare.

Ovoid and slightly wobbling, her body was presided over by an impressive tower of platinum blonde hair. All this tapered down into short fat feet usually shod in glassy backless mules a size too small. Pale shrewd eyes, comprehending and slightly wicked, were set off by glasses. Winged and of a pale deceptive color, abalone or opaline, these glasses were edged in a spray of tiny, shimmering pinkish stones. A fine set of big healthy teeth gave her a witty, greedy mouth.

She had a wonderful face. All things at once, it was powdery and soft, shifting, feminine, irrepressibly greedy, dainty and yet tough. Mabel's favorite color was mauve, and when her time finally came she was buried in a mauve coffin.

A woman of high standards, Mabel hated living near the Truckstop. East of town, on the old Southfork Highway, out where Mabel lived, there was not much left to see. When the new highway came along nothing survived but a seedy sprawl of machine shops, trailer courts, a few seatcover kings, and one or two cowboy bars. Some rundown motels remained—Bucky's Lucky Lariat and the Mary Jo Motor Court. Next to the Mary Jo there was a small pink shack with a sign on it saying, "Beauty by Pocahantus, by Appointment Only." These were the only places left.

The Truckstop, situated as it was at the junction where the old highway meets the new, was well known around these parts. Some of the people from town with nothing to do on a Saturday night

3

came out to eat at the Truckstop and see the sights. Late at night the highway came alive. The day places would be lit up by the lurid blink of silent rhythmic signs, and in the shadowy Southern Pacific yard night trains came and went, loading freight. Travelers going to far-off places stopped to refuel, and the low mournful horn of a rig bound for El Paso would blow out past the far edge of town. Along the horizon at the edge of the desert a red neon sign flickered the message "TRUCKSTOP EAT TRUCKSTOP EAT" over and over again.

For the highway people the Truckstop was the center of life out in the desert. Things happened there that brought people together. Once a year a well-fed man wearing custom-made cowboy suits would appear at the Truckstop. This man, Billy Crum, was the traveling truck dealer. He could sell just about anything to anyone. A caravan of shiny new trucks would be set up under a circus tent on a revolving fur-covered platform. There were free apples, Seven-Up, a hurdy-gurdy and sometimes Lady Wrasslers out back in a tent. One year he brought a two-headed calf, dead, from Montana. You had to pay fifty cents to get a look under the blanket. Families came out from town and in from the ranches for the show and the men stood around talking in groups. On his last night in town Billy Crum would bring the Rodeo Queen and her Princesses over from nearby Tucson for an appearance at the Truckstop.

Rising up out of the barren desert scraggle, the core of the Truckstop was a low brick building with plate-glass windows overlooking the fuel pumps. The central building was surrounded by fuel islands, tire and grease bays and an enormous dirt field where sometimes as many as seventy rigs were lined up side by side in slumber, waiting out a layover. Off to one side of the parking field there was a steaming, hissing barn called the Truck-O-Mat where the rigs got washed. Next door to the Truck-O-Mat was Jenks' Diesel and beyond that, Mabel Jenks' trailer.

Mabel knew everything that went on in the garage, even though she only set foot in there under dire necessity. If a trucker came in looking for trouble, if a tool was missing or one of the mechanics moved slow on the job, not fifteen minutes would pass without Mabel's calling over to the shop on her house phone.

Mercilessly uncanny, she loomed large albeit invisible over the garage, and there was nothing more terrible than Mabel Jenks when she divined, from within her shuttered bastion some fifty yards away, a treachery, an offense against her code. Some nights, sniffing evil in the air, she called the shop every half-hour.

"What's going on over there, boys?" she demanded.

"Things going jes fine, Miz Jenks. Slow but fine," Dickey, one of the mechanics, would answer, his eye fixed to the trailer which he could just see—low to the ground, curtained tight against the night—through the garage doors.

"Hah!" he heard her snort. "You tell that Parker fellow there he'd better clear on out if he knows what's good for him, you hear? If he don't like the bill he don't have to come back . . . tell him I'll be waiting for him if he do. And there's a line wrench missing out there. Find it." And she hung up. Dickey glanced back at the trailer. Not a curtain had moved. It spooked him. There wasn't a man in the shop, however begrudging he might feel about the way Mabel ran things, who called her anything but Mrs. Jenks. That is the way she wanted things and that is the way they were.

On busy nights the men worked long shifts. Dawn came and went uninvited, a timid guest, and it wasn't until later when the first heat of the day bore down upon them, a silent rider on the hot trucks coming in from the desert with engines boiled and fuming, that the men remarked night was gone. On those nights four and five tractors with long hauls trailing would be lined up nose to nose in the garage and the cavernous inner space shuddered with engine roar. Thick with road dust and matted bugs, their heads slumped forward and innards bared, cast-iron entrails disemboweled, hoses coiled like snakes on a carcass, the trucks—their engines left on idle—awaited service.

Waiting for the trucks to come is the lonely part of the job. Some nights no one comes. On a dead winter night it can get down below freezing, and for warmth the mechanics huddle around the smudge pot, a foul-smelling diesel fuel burner, in the hollow light of the empty garage. Finally, there is the low-gear rattle of a truck pulling their way, and through the late-night dust a great limping rig appears.

It was on just such a night, when things felt slow and weary, that two old-timers pulled into the garage for repairs: Sly Fox and Tommy Buffalo. They had been driving together for so many years they had come to look like brothers, although Sly Fox was indignant about the idea and scorned any kinship with Tommy Buffalo.

Both men were angular and stooping, tall and very thin with small thin noses, mild eyes, frugal mouths and immaculate grey clothing of the serviceable unobtrusive sort. Texans, they each had a similar economy of speech. The words came out measured with a farmer's prudence, a disdain for waste. You don't see many truckers like that. They could have been Presbyterian ministers. Sly Fox had been driving a truck for forty-one years and Tommy Buffalo had been his sidekick for twenty-seven of those years. The rig, a Kenworth Cab over Engine, belonged to Sly Fox. He was the boss.

Sly Fox and Tommy Buffalo went over to the Truckstop Cafe where they found Mabel and Ralph in the corner booth.

"How do, Miz Jenks." Sly Fox stood with his hat under his arm until Mabel asked them to sit. Next to mechanics, the thing Mabel hated most were the truckers. Scum of the earth she called them and yet, there were one or two truckers, exceptional people, whom she spoke to. These special few had been pulling into the Truckstop for over thirty years; for them she made allowances and held a wary esteem sprung up not so much from friendship as from the endurance of time alone.

"How you boys doing?" Mabel slid several inches further into the booth. Lorraine, the waitress, flew past.

"What'll it be tonight, fellows?" she hollered, passing by fast with a ladder of plates stacked like bracelets along her arms, flat-topped volcanoes of mashed potatoes sliding sideways into pools of gravy. "There's a special on barbequed ribs and the beans is local," she hawked, her eyes everywhere else, on her way back.

"Biscuits and gravy," called out Sly Fox.

"Two," echoed Tommy Buffalo.

"How long since you two eat a decent piece of meat?" demanded Lorraine, coming to a standstill. Crabby-faced, she eyed the two grey men. There wasn't a trucker on the road who could out-talk or outsmart Lorraine. Stringy and sour, a little redhead of about sixty, Lorraine pushed great hulking truckers around by hissing at them, and on occasion she'd been known to pinch a man in the heat of battle. She wore short white vinyl boots. They brought her good luck, she said.

"Spare ribs'll put hair on them puny ole chests," she continued and then, turning with a hiss of disgust, she darted off to get their biscuits and gravy.

"There was a real bad accident," began Sly Fox when he'd wiped his plate clean.

"Trucker," put in Tommy Buffalo. "Going through Coffee Pass up in Oregon."

"That's right." Sly Fox waited for Lorraine to fill up his coffee. He could drink as many as fifteen cups a sitting.

"Happened at night. Man fell asleep behind the wheel doing about seventy-five. Rammed into the mountain. The whole durned engine got shoved back into his lap."

"They had to cut off his legs to git him out from under that engine. But he lived, just the same," said Tommy Buffalo, allowing his fork to circle a heaping mound of hot apple pie with soft vanilla ice cream.

"Go on, eat," snapped Mabel, her eye caressing the ice cream as it expired onto his placemat. She couldn't bear thin people who abused the whole ceremony of a good dessert.

"There's a truckstop over in Sparks, Nevada," said Ralph. "The Union 76 station there has got a whole wall of what happens when you crack up on Donner Pass. It's enough to make a man sick just seeing that wall of pictures."

"I seen that wall," spoke up a man at the next table. "One time I seen a trucker go over that pass doing at least seventy-five. Driving a Diamond Reo. A real cowboy behind the wheel. Those guys don't check their brakes out and they'll push you clean off the road. He was rolling hot and I saw him again at the foot of the mountain. He was leaning over the side of the cab getting sick. Boy he was scared. Told me he didn't do the brake check and when he went to put his foot on the brakes there was nothing there, the brakes were gone."

"Rolling hot? What's that?" asked a freckled girl sitting at the counter.

"Gawd almighty." Mabel exchanged looks with Lorraine as Little Jimmy, the trucker at the counter, moved in on the girl.

"When you got your hammer down, your pedal to the metal, this is when you're rolling hot," said Little Jimmy. "And strolling down the boulevard, this is when you've got your foot on it all the way, this is moving! Going fifty-five miles an hour, that's the double nickle. A beaver with a kickstand, that's a male hitchhiker, a hippie. A beaver, that's a little thing like you." Jimmy eyed the girl.

"Let's get out of here," Mabel grunted, but not before she heard the girl ask, "Could someone like me learn to drive one of those things?" "Why sure you could." Jimmy patted her shoulder. "One of the best drivers I ever saw was a girl. A fat little Mexican lady. She'd take a load through Donner Pass driving a big Kenworth Conventional doing eighty all the way. Never missed a turn. She was real fine, that little lady."

"Hmmmmph," said Mabel.

As she stood to go a florid wet-eyed man came up to Mabel's table. Lorraine paused in mid-flight. Everyone knew how Mabel felt about Maurice; they had a feud going. The owner of the Truckstop, Maurice Beamus had shared the same stretch of land with Mabel for thirty years, and it galled him that, try as he might to please her, she couldn't tolerate the sight of him. Within his hearing Mabel referred to Maurice as an "Okie" and a squatter.

"Well! Lookee here! If it ain't my lovely little neighbor herself," beamed Maurice. He considered clasping her hand and then changed his mind. "You there, Lorraine," he called out good and loud, "bring these people some of that homemade pie. On the house," he added. There was a snort from Lorraine.

"Stand aside, shorty," said Mabel, brushing past him.

"Now wait a minute, Mabel. No call to be rude," he laughed uncertainly, following her. "Bet you ain't noticed I redecorated a few things around here . . . take a look," he went on, inching ahead of her like a tour guide.

They passed through the front lounge area which was fitted

out with black leather recliner chairs reserved for truckers only. Two rumpled men sat stunned and dreaming before the T.V. set, which was always left on, twenty-four hours a day; the station had gone off the air for the night and a vague grey kinetic blur jiggled and gaped from the blind socket. Two gift shops led off the lounge. One of them specialized in anything a trucker might want, including Saturday-night specials and other pistols packaged in flimsy, dimestore-type toy boxes. The special this week was a red, white and blue Confederate flag overnight case for six dollars.

The other gift shop was set up for tourists and townspeople and specialized in steer-head bollo ties, clear plastic candles with lucky pennies inside, tarantulas and scorpions embedded in plastic paperweights, state souvenir spoons, see-thru baby doll nightgowns and stenciled wallets. Mabel had her eye on a special set of ruby crystal highball glasses edged in gilt that was carefully propped up on display on the top shelf. Each glass was engraved with one of the ten commandments. A cheaper set of glasses embossed simply with the words "Sloth," "Greed," "Envy," "Lust" and so on were for sale on a lower shelf but Mabel couldn't bring herself to buy anything of value from Maurice.

"Here we go," coaxed Maurice leading Mabel, Ralph, Sly Fox and Tommy Buffalo down a long hallway. Rooms for truckers wanting a place to sleep lined the hall. Maurice drew up in front of the Ladies' Lounge and Beauty Parlor. "Well?" he demanded.

"Well, what?" replied Mabel. She noticed a new sign. It said, "No Husbands, Hippies, Hitchhikers."

"I don't see nothin'," complained Tommy Buffalo straining at the door.

"Gawd," said Maurice, disgusted. "I paid eight fifty for that sign in Laredo. You won't see another one like it, least not here in Arizona." Mabel pressed up close to the sign and examined it.

"If I was you," she said at last, turning away, "I'd keep that price a big fat secret . . ." Across the hall another new addition, a large portrait of George Wallace painted on velvet, presided over the barber shop, but Mabel sailed on past it, unmoved.

"Women don't have an eye for these special decorations, anyway," cracked Maurice, nudging Sly Fox. "By the time I get through around here, this place is gonna have real class," he called out at their retreating backs. "It's gonna be the biggest, cleanest, classiest truckstop west of the Mississippi!" He stood a moment in the doorway watching them pick their way across the cool, slick green pools of light at the fuel pumps and out into the darkness. Aroused from fitful slumber, a Peterbilt flashed its lights brazen and unblinking across their path. Mabel's legs shone round and very white. "Bitch," whispered Maurice straining to see the last of them.

The only truck person who had ever been allowed into Mabel's trailer was a woman called Doris Malone. Doris, a big red-faced woman with beefy speckled arms and hennaed hair, was married to a knotty little shrimp of a man, and they pulled into the garage in a white Freightliner with the air lines out. This was ten years ago. Mabel happened to be making one of her rare visits to the garage and was daintily stepping over an oil slick when she noticed Doris climb down from the cab and stick a small grey French poodle she was carrying up on top of the Coke machine where he observed the garage with detached candor.

"You drive this thing?" Mabel asked, curious in spite of herself.

"Sure do." Doris gave the rig an unsentimental glance. Her face was pulpy and tough with hard years and yet there was a sweetness there.

"This old boy has seen his share." She patted the Freightliner. "See them bullet holes?" There was a spray of holes on the passenger door, low down, near the bottom edge.

"Got shot at last week. Near the Alabamba line. Broad daylight too. Lucky they didn't get me in the who-who . . ." Mabel looked at her. Doris winked. "Just a little bit higher and they might've blown my feet off or worse. Never did ketch them . . . never saw who did it. This here is Ron." Doris indicated her husband with a roll of the head. "Ron, he was hauling a load of cars when the air lines went out. We could've jack-knifed but it was raining bad and the brakes was out so's we slid over to the side of the road okay. Seems nothing but trouble following us around this time out.

Been gone three weeks. I've got grankids at home and I'm missing them."

Ron, a hard, compact little man, was a foot shorter than Doris. The sleeves of his T-shirt were rolled up tight and lumpy veins stood out on his biceps. A smudged eagle and the name Sal was tatooed on his arm. He never said much and Mabel thought he was uncouth. He was not asked into the trailer.

Doris was crazy about Ron. It was a side to Doris that Mabel chose to overlook.

"Ole Crab-ass here's the silent type." Doris fingered Ron's chunky midriff with an expert feel. "Silent and mean, ain't you, hon?" A grunt from Ron. Mabel looked away. Doris chuckled with admiration.

"Ole sourpuss and me's been partners for forty-nine years come May. Married him when I was sixteen, God knows why. Ron, he can't hold a candle to his father, though . . . Ron, senior, why he was just about the meanest white man alive. Ate nails for break-fast, the old man did. There was him and the three sons living holed up in a little place called Why, Arizona."

"Cut it out," Ron grunted.

Doris leered lovingly at Ron, who was bending over his tool box searching for a line wrench. "Aw hon," said Doris.

"C'mon into the house for awhile," urged Mabel, who hated to miss out on a good story.

"Why, don't mind if I do!" Doris sensed the honor. The two women picked their way across the back lot.

"Careful of that rubbish heap there." Mabel skirted a pile of fuel pumps abandoned in the dirt. "I always meant to clean this dump out and plant me some more trees, maybe even have a garden here someday," she continued, ashamed to have Doris see the mess.

"Oh, what a beautiful home!" exclaimed Doris. Mabel knew she meant it and, pleased, she removed a section of clear plastic from the best couch so that Doris could sit down in comfort.

The living room in the trailer was filled with knick-knacks and souvenirs. Nothing about Mabel or her home was ordinary, no matter how familiar. It was as if she had a way of turning small everyday things into something of value, something intriguing. She liked to get presents and snatched them away before they had been properly presented. After the paper was shredded off the package she took a close look at the contents. If they were unusually fine or of any value they were left for a time, displayed in their box, on top of the T.V. set. But if the present was mediocre or somehow unsuitable, it was rewrapped with a grunt of disatisfaction and confined to the bathroom closet.

The trailer was filled with an astonishing selection of animals. Wherever Mabel went she had an eye out for brutalized, homeless creatures whom she swooped up from an assortment of dreadful fates. She had been known to wrest the victims directly out of the backyards of the owners themselves. No animal, however bizarre its case history, was beneath Mabel's notice.

Mabel usually sat at one end of the room on serviceable everyday plush. From this vantage point she could gaze across admiringly at an entire ensemble in eggshell velvet. The ensemble reigned in implacable virginity from under an enshrinement of clear plastic, and nearby, terrariums bloomed with an exotic display of sweating, stunted cacti.

Just off the living room and kitchen area there was a hallway leading to the three bedrooms, each bearing clues as to the character of its solitary occupant. Mabel's room was pale pink and lavender and she had a closet full of glamorous clothes—robes edged in bird feathers and fur wraps in unusual colors.

Doris was impressed. Mabel let her try on a violet feather boa, and before long Doris, filled up with the loneliness of the road, felt like telling Mabel her secrets. Mabel liked hearing about peoples' lives; however, she kept her own past wrapped and fading in tissue paper, like ecru satin negligées aging slowly in the trousseau chest. It was only sometimes, late at night, full with sharings, that her memories unfurled. Tiny souvenirs, memories unraveled one by one, fragments from a paper party ball, a rubber knife, a plastic ring, a rocking horse, a silver gun.

Doris began to tell of Ron's family. "One of Ron's brothers was a genius. Least that's what folks said. Have you ever known a real genius, Mabel?"

"I can't say that I have," admitted Mabel, who thought over her family and acquaintances and instantly rejected them as contenders for the obscure honor.

"Well, a genius is a funny thing," continued Doris. "They're not like the rest of us. What I mean to say is, I've heard they don't believe in God and most've them's Communists. But Jud, that was his name, he was one beautiful hunk of a man, not like Ron all wizened up . . . this Jud was real peculiar, just the same. He talked to hisself a lot and wrote funny things on the wall . . . poetry he called it but there was lots of dirty words mixed in with it. The people in Why, they kept an eye on him. You never kin tell about someone like that . . . and nobody knew what to make of him. He was the only genius in town." Doris paused.

Mabel was dying to ask just what it was exactly that distinguished a genius from a crazy person or any of the other weirdies she had heard about but she was reluctuant to show her ignorance.

Doris went on. "Jud got into some kind of trouble with the law so he went on over to Tucson for a few years. He got a job with Fast Eddy and the Rodeo Kings, musicians you know, and he meets this New York girl. I think she was one of them college girls, a real princess. She fell in love with Jud . . . never seen a man like that before, I'll bet. Well, the princess came home to Why with Jud and the ole man took one look at her and said, 'Now Jud, you git that woman outta here afore somethin' happens.' He didn't need to say it twice. The princess took one look at the ole man and the house and that was it." Doris chuckled.

"They were sleeping three to a mattress on some ole rags laid out near the stove in the kitchen. There was a stack of pork and bean cans as high as this trailer and nothing but some greasy ole tar paper on the walls. Nastiest place I ever did see. Jud, he went off to New York City with his lady friend and two months later she sent him off with a one-way bus ticket back to Why."

Mabel and Doris exchanged glances and shook their heads in harmonious earthy wisdom.

"He came to a bad end, that boy. There was some bad business of one kind or the other and the sherriff tracked him and his kid brother Clem down. He got Clem first and then shot Jud dead right out in plain view on the front porch at the house in Why. They found out later he got the wrong man, ole Jeb Mooney, the sheriff up there, but folks in Why, they ain't too particular and nothing ever come of it . . . The ole man, Ron senior, he locked hisself in the house and never came out again. When Ron went to see him he'd open the door just a crack, just enough to let Ron see that long-nosed shotgun he had.

" 'Whadaya want?' he'd say.

" 'It's me, Pa,' said Ron.

" 'Git lost. Did you bring some food? Leave it over there,' he'd say, pointing with the shotgun. He died finally. All alone. The county health department tore the house down. Ron, he's the only one left. It doesn't pay to be a genius. I'd just as soon have Ron the way he is . . ."

"Lord," said Mabel, enjoying herself thoroughly.

There was a scratch at the door. "You in there, Doris?" Ron stooped to peek through the crack between the curtain and the door.

"Well, I'll see you sometime," said Doris. "We git through here now and again."

"You take care now," Mabel replied. Women like that don't have ceremonies for saying goodbye but, as Doris drove off, Mabel sat a long time in her chair and after a while she said to herself, "Now what in hell am I goin' to do today," and she got up to pull the bit of plastic back over the couch.

CHAPTER 2

Mabel was born Mabel McPheeter in a border town partway between Douglas and El Paso. Her sister, Ruby McPheeter, was known to pack a pistol, and between them they carried a little weight around town.

They came from strong southwestern people, the kind of people who were known and had respect. Mabel liked to tell of her southern relations, military folk mostly, but the core of the family was a determined clan of durable women.

Her father, Jim McPheeter, was a mild-mannered man, a miner who died of consumption when the girls were still young. Emma McPheeter, Mabel's mother, ran a still and supported the family throughout Prohibition by driving an old Dodge rum-runner across the desert at night. People came to know of Emma McPheeter and stories went around about moonlight deliveries and her bravery under fire when the chase was hot. Emma never did talk about these things with her girls. She raised them with a heavy hand and they were taught their worth.

Ruby was three years older than Mabel. She had hennaed hair, frowzy and grown out at the roots, a wide open face with plain features and a cast in one eye. There was nothing special about the way she looked. Blue was her color and she tended to wear knits and comfortable shoes.

Ruby once shot a T.V. repairman. He dawdled over her T.V. set and caused her to miss her favorite program, which was "Queen For a Day." They sent the deputy sheriff out to see her and she got him too. Ruby did two years in the state penitentiary, but when she got out no one seemed to hold it against her.

Mabel was the family beauty, though. She looked a little like Mae West only better. In about 1937 Mabel left town on a Greyhound bus. She was then sixteen. Before long, word got back to town that she was seen driving around Hollywood in a baby-blue Cadillac convertible with an older man in a pin-striped suit. Not long after this Mabel's grandmother came to fetch her home.

Granma Watkins was as mean an old lady as anyone ever remembered seeing. Only five feet tall and weighing barely ninety-five pounds, she had awful, compelling eyes which she could hold a certain way for a long time without blinking. This look gave her a terrible power over people.

When she was seventy years old Granma crept up behind Granpa Watkins at the breakfast table and walloped him over the head with a heavy cast iron skillet full of hot drippings. This she did because she had spied him talking with their neighbor, Irma Billings, an old woman Granma had a feud going with. Granpa had over twenty stitches and ever since then some people thought he was queer in the head. Granma did not let him back in the house for over two years. This is the kind of woman she was.

Mabel lived one year with Granma Watkins in El Paso where she got a job selling hosiery at J.C. Penny's. One Saturday night at the Elks Club dance she met Orville Jenks. Brooding, furtive, Orville was almost thirty at the time and he looked like he'd been around some.

No one can be exactly sure why Mabel married Orville. He was a nice man, good-looking, but just not a man given to pleasing the ladies. His younger brother Ralph, on the other hand, wore his hair slicked straight back with pommade and had fine suits. He could tell wonderful stories about big moments in the pool hall and some of the people he met there.

Orville Jenks came from a long line of Texans. Proud people, they were most of them poor and stuck close to one another. They lived separate from other people out at the edge of town in a small house with a trailer and a lean-to.

They lived by the land for the most part, some of them working out as migrant farmers when the crops were good. Alvin Jenks, Orville's father, worked as a mechanic on the railroad. He was crushed between two runaway flatcars and died young. Thelma Jenks, Orville's mother, was a silent woman with soft watering eyes. She smelled of baking-powder biscuits and raised chickens in the back yard.

The family had a plain life and in the evenings they would sit for a long time in silence on the back porch. And then, at about eight-thirty, Thelma would get up and say, "Well, better git on up to bed now."

Thelma kept a diary. She wrote things down along the margins of pages torn out of a Montgomery Ward catalogue. There were no dates, just days and years sliding one into the other in the catalogue.

"Thursday. Alvin's off to the railroad. Got flour today. Jeb's got sick with the plurisy and we put him down with pultice. Hetty don't seem so good today. Sky looks fine. We need rain bad. Next month the boys git shoes. The new hen is layin good."

After Alvin passed on the diary was put aside and Thelma grew silent. She had the three boys to help out but Floyd Jenks, her eldest son, ran off. It was said there was bad blood in Floyd. He didn't like to look you in the eye. Floyd grew up too fast. By the time he was fourteen he had thick hair all over his arms and the neighbor boy said he'd seen it even grew down his back.

The baby of the family was Hetty, who was thought to be retarded. Hetty spent all day poking at the dirt with a stick. She wasn't always that way. As a little girl she followed her brothers around and she liked to play with the chickens. At about twelve years old Hetty took to hiding in the chicken coop spying on people. Then, a few years later when the circus came to town she was found being diddled by one of the sideshow men. Ever since then she stayed home poking the dirt and when strangers came, she ran off and hid.

17

The years went by. Orville and Ralph grew into men and went out on their own. The women stayed home. Besides Thelma and her daughter Hetty, there were cousins who came to live with them; there was Alvin's younger sister, Barbara Rice, a widow, who came bringing her daughter, Barbara Jean Rice. Besides her niece, this Barbara Jean, there was also Thelma's granddaughter, Flo-detta Jenks. When Thelma's eldest son, the awful Floyd Jenks, had gone off years ago, no one had seen him since, but one day, a woman calling herself Billie Jenks had come to the house and asked Thelma to look after her baby who she swore was Floyd's daughter. The child had red hair, same as Floyd, so they took her in and called her Flo-detta after her Pa.

The two girls, Flo-detta and Barbara Jean Rice, were the same age. From the start, there was trouble between them. For one thing, Barbara Jean was actually Flo-detta's aunt and she liked to gloat over this. Also, Barbara Jean liked to taunt Flo-detta about her mother, Billie Jenks, who she said was no good. Billie would blow into town in a big car every so often and take Flo-detta out for a drive. She might buy her a skirt and sweater set or a gold stenciled jewel box from the dimestore and then leave town again. Although Flo-detta was raised by Granma Thelma and loved her, she grew up feeling second best and Barbara Jean knew this. This laid a strain on their relationship.

Barbara Jean grew up feeling pretty and she carried herself in a special way like she was someone who knew secrets. Blonde, with curled hair and a boneless, pallid face, she had plucked her eyebrows until there was nothing left but a few straggling wayward hairs over an arch of swollen pink pores. This gave her a fat-lidded, surprised look. She had bosoms before anyone else did and wore them squeezed together and pointed so you could see a little fat roll under each arm where the brassiere dug into her flesh. All this made Flo-detta feel terrible.

Flo-detta was as angular as Barbara Jean was fleshy. She looked like a cowgirl and wore skin-tight checked pants with things stuffed in the back pockets which gave her strange little bulges. Her hair hung almost to her waist and on Saturday nights she wore it ratted and wavy. Her hands were freckled and the nails short with chipped pink nail polish, all except the little finger. This nail was always long. Flo-detta had a redhead's face with skin that turned pink. Her eyes were sensible and unromantic.

At fifteen Barbara Jean ran off with a peach-picker from Georgia. By the time she was eighteen she was home again, big with child and dragging along a scrawny baby daughter. Nothing much was said between Thelma and Barbara about the peach-picker or Barbara Jean's coming home.

"I see Barbara Jean's come home," said Thelma.

"She got a young un an' one on the way," was Barbara's reply.

"Where's the peach-picker?"

"He's gone off."

This is all that was said. Barbara Jean settled back into her old room and the little one, Sue-Ellen, shared the bed with her mother. All Barbara Jean ever did was sit out on the front step swatting flies and reading movie magazines. If anyone would listen she talked about things she had seen in the big city, meaning El Paso where she and the peach-picker spent a few days.

Flo-detta suspected most of the stories were lies but she listened anyway.

"I seen things in the city," said Barbara Jean to Flo-detta, who was hanging out the wash.

"That so." Flo-detta never asked what, no matter how long it took to find out.

"I seen a nigra out drivin' with a lady in a fur coat."

"That so."

"Had supper in a drugstore. Hot turkey platter. There was mashed potatoes an gravy come with it, coleslaw an' hot apple pie." Tantalizing as this information was, Flo-detta held her ground.

"Seen a picture show," brought out Barbara Jean at last.

"I don't believe it!" This was too much for Flo-detta. "Who'd you git to see? Did you see HER? Did you git to see Betty Grable?"

"Sure I did. Saw her and lots more."

Flo-detta put down the wash and reluctantly sat down to hear more. It was a story she never tired of hearing.

Later, when the time came, it was not easy for Flo-detta to find a good man. Finally she married the man from down the road, Duane Miller. He was a mechanic in the Esso station. They got themselves a little trailer and lived on at the house. Barbara Jean married a hydraulic shovel driver, Larry McCoy, and they moved in closer to town. Nobody liked Larry much but they were glad Barbara Jean found a man.

Mabel was barely eighteen when she married Orville. From the very beginning they looked after Ralph, who was only two years younger than Orville but full of dreams and not so dependable. Ralph had been married once but it hadn't worked out. Mabel was the woman he admired. His feelings for her were innocent; for Ralph, Mabel was a shooting star, shining and full of light.

They tried any number of ways to make a living and eventually found their way to Arizona and the Truckstop where Orville got the idea of working on trucks. They sent for Ralph. The two men found an old cotton mill which they dismembered with a boom truck they built themselves. Piece by piece they carted the mill out to the Truckstop where they put it together again. That was the beginning of Jenks' Diesel.

Mabel was twenty-two and Orville was thirty when they began life at the Truckstop. The closest town of any size was Tucson, a small dusty cattlemen's town. Most of the roads were still dirt in those days, so unless you happened to be going somewhere out on the highway, the Truckstop was a long way from town. It was Maurice Beamus with his grand ideas who built up the shabby wayside cafe and pump into a respectable Truckstop.

Right from the beginning Mabel took Maurice's measure and he sat in his office plotting ways to make her notice him. From his window he could just see the strange new little row of cypress trees and Mabel, round and blonde, in a polka-dot blouse, watering the foreign-looking plants.

He sent her a candied ham wrapped up in red cellophane. There was a card attached. He heard nothing about the ham so the next week he sent a giant heart-shaped box of chocolate creams. Then he kept an eye on the garbage cans to see if the candy wrappers or the hambone would appear. "Bitch," he said to himself when no evidence of his gifts was spotted.

20

"Howja like the ham?" he grinned at Mabel.

"Why, I sent it over to those poor folk across the road," she answered. "Them bon-bons too. We don't need no charity, Maurice," and she fixed him with the evil eye. (Mabel pronounced his name "Mo-reese.")

"Just what is it exactly that you don't like about me anyway?" demanded Maurice, squinting at her.

"You sweat too much, and I never did trust a man whose eyes is too close together. Pig eyes." She looked him over.

He skulked off. "Bitch!" he screamed inside his head. Even so, he wanted her more.

Part of Mabel's character was that she did not mind having a few enemies. She was not mean. It was just that she needed something to keep her going and a good long thirty-year feud fed something inside her. Once and only once, some five years after the candied ham, Maurice laid a hand on Mabel's thigh. "Haha!" she said. "I've been waiting for you to come out of the woodwork," and she prodded his soft underbelly with something hard. Maurice licked his lips and then looked down to see a .44 caliber pistol in his gut. That was the last time he ever bothered her.

They had good years and lean years. The garage prospered. Truckers passed the word around that this was a good place. The work was good, the people were honest. Orville brought his mother along with Hetty and his aunt Barbara over from Texas and pretty soon Flo-detta, Duane and their three boys came. Not long after that, Larry gave up driving the shovel and he and Barbara Jean came over, too. Orville's relations settled down nearby, not far from the Truckstop. Mabel and Orville had a little girl whom they named Loretta and she grew up to be a beauty, like her mother but softer.

At first, in those early years, Mabel's only social acquaintances were Flo-detta and Barbara Jean and her sister Ruby who sometimes exploded into town looking for action. The family stuck close together and Loretta grew up with Flo-detta's kids and Barbara Jean's daughters by the peach-picker, Sue-Ellen and Baby. It came to be that Mabel was the center of the family. The others turned to her; she was the strong one. Mabel's supremacy did not come

21

easy, however, to Barbara Jean, who figured out crafty tricks to make Mabel look foolish, but since this was done on the sly, openly the two appeared to be friends. Flo-detta was in the middle and she scuttled back and forth between the two cousins courting approval.

The days were long and there was not much to do, There were kids to bring up and men to cook for, the laundry to do, the old people to look after, Granma Thelma and Barbara. There was the trailer to clean and other chores, but finally, there was nothing to do out there on the highway. There were no picture shows or dimestores, not even a drugstore of the exciting big-city kind.

The three girls met in the mornings. This was years before Mabel worked the night shift on the books and slept most of the day. Barbara Jean had an old beat-up truck, and she drove over to pick up Flo-detta and then they went over to visit Mabel. Sometimes the three of them and their kids drove up to the junction one mile away to browse through the magazines in Laredo's market or have a rootbeer at the Red Dog Cafe.

Mostly they sat in the trailer and talked. Together they cooked dinner for the men. Duane, Flo-detta's husband, was working in Jenks' Garage and he came in with Orville and Ralph to eat the big noonday meal. The men ate in silence and then, scraping their chairs back, returned to the garage. The women ate later, picking at things from pots on the stove or eating cupcakes and doughnuts from cellophane packages. They had round bellies and loose pouches of flesh under their bosoms. There was no reason to be thin.

Mabel did not discuss Orville beyond an occasional dissatisfied allusion to some of his homely quirks, but Barbara Jean and Flo-detta talked about their husbands day in and day out with droning, disenchanted apathy. These discussions were never held with the idea that rescue from marriage might ever be forthcoming, or that changes even were hoped for. They had married what was available; what else was there to do? These men were necessary to their very existence, and since that existence had already been circum-scribed, even before birth, there was nothing to do but live out the plainness of life as best as one could. It was not a thing a person

22

could feel sorry about or grieve for; this land, the men, the family
—that is all there really was.

Of course they all knew women who had gone bad. Flo-detta's
mother, Billie Jenks, and Ruby McPheeter. But Ruby had ended
up doing time and Billie was looking old. There were no more
presents from the dimestore. Just postcards now and again from
roadside diners in unfamiliar towns.

Barbara Jean and Flo-detta envied Mabel for her trailer. Flo-
detta had pinned up beautiful pictures from magazines on the
walls of her trailer; she had fashioned curtains gay with rosebuds
and a vase of plastic mums adorned her table; but still there was
something so wonderful in Mabel's home, some rare thing in the
air that made all other trailers seem dim and airless. Each time she
came, Flo-detta examined the little figurines, the terrarium, the
velvet ensemble, the spoon collection, the plates, looking for what
it was that Mabel had, looking for the secret.

Barbara Jean only allowed herself to glance around when Mabel
left the room. She was slovenly and the floor of her trailer was
piled up with clothes she'd tried on and then ripped off and
thrown aside in bitter self-disgust. They lay there in heaps, mixed
in with soiled underwear and shoes and Larry's unwashed work
clothes stinking of diesel grease.

She knew every trinket and object in Mabel's trailer, she knew
when a candle was moved two inches on the table, and yet it suited
Barbara Jean best to let on that she didn't care about Mabel's place
or her own. She felt rotten inside when she stepped into Mabel's
home.

There were days when the three girls would laugh and do
makeup jobs on each other and, pouring over magazines, they did
hairdos. Then, all dressed up, they sat and waited for the men to
come in. They looked so different they hardly knew how to hold
themselves and their conversation was grown-up and restrained.
The men came in but no one seemed to notice the change except
Duane. He glanced at his wife and said, "Jesus, Flo-detta, what's
that stuff on your face? You look awful."

Some days they hid behind the curtains in the trailer and spied
on Maurice Beamus. "Look at that ole tub of lard," they cackled,

and then, "Yoo Hoo! Mo-reeeese!" through the window and then they ran and hid, silly with laughter. The children, Loretta, Sue-Ellen, and Flo-detta's boys, playing in the sand, would whisper about their mothers. They thought their mothers were glamorous and wild.

When Ruby came to town things changed. She wanted Mabel to herself and she had a car, so they went into Tucson to the Starlight Cafe and the Flamingo, dancing, drinking, having fun. Barbara Jean and Flo-detta felt left out and they met at Granma Thelma's house and said terrible things about Mabel. After Ruby left town they snubbed Mabel for a day or two, and Mabel was driven to taking up with Minnie the hairdresser from the Poco-hantus, until finally the girls drifted back together. Mabel was the center of the circle; she was the light.

Barbara Jean had a secret. The one thing she wanted most was to marry Maurice Beamus and have power over Mabel in the Truckstop. She was so sick of Larry McCoy she could barely stand the sight of his burnt coarse face, his hairy stained hands. Larry had gone back to driving the shovel when Orville kicked him off the crew at the garage. No one liked him much. He was a braggart, a loud-mouthed bully, and he had taken to calling Barbara Jean "Fatso" and other ugly names.

Her plan was to ravish Maurice with her sex appeal. Slowly but surely she would get him to notice and want her, but there could be no mistakes; he must marry her. Hour after hour was devoted to dreaming of this plan; hours were spent sitting motionless before her mirror staring at what was there. In her high heels, standing with her back to the mirror, naked, she held up a make-up mirror and contorted and angled to see how she looked from the rear. Sick with disgust at what she saw, Barbara Jean crawled into her rumpled bed to dream in the dark, to hide from the merciless bathroom light, the mirror. Her worst gluttony followed these moments of truth and she hid candy bars under the mattress and ate them there in the dark.

Beamus was working in a grease bay behind the Truckstop when he noticed a plump pair of feet in pointed-toe, white patent shoes standing not far off. The shoes were distended and stretched

out at the instep, but all the same they had their allure. He saw
a golden ankle bracelet mashed under the stocking against the leg
and, since there seemed to be some hesitation about where the
feet intended to go next, he slid out from under the belly of the
rig he was inspecting, wiped his hands, and gave Barbara Jean the
once-over.

"Why, Mr. Beamus! Fancy meeting you here under this nasty
ole diesel! I didn't know a gentleman like you worked out here
. . ." she warbled, rolling her eyes playfully towards the offending
rig.

"You're Mabel Jenks' friend, aren't you?" he asked, eyeing her.

"Well . . . sort of . . . ." She hesitated and then, in a whisper, "We
do *know* each other. We're cousins, that's all . . ."

Beamus had seen Flo-detta and Barbara Jean arriving day in and
day out at the trailer. It pleased him to think Barbara Jean might
betray something about Mabel, some forbidden morsel, an intimacy. If nothing else, he thought to himself, eyeing the tight pull
of Barbara Jean's skirt over the bulge of her thighs, I'll get at that
fancy bitch through this fat little number. He offered to show her
around.

Three weeks passed and Barbara Jean began to worry that
Beamus was not going to offer her marriage. No one saw them
together and they had managed to sneak off to Tucson and had
even spent two disagreeable hours grappling in the Big Steer
Motel, to no avail. Barbara Jean had allowed him to press his meaty
palm into her blouse and lower even, down below the wrinkled,
pinched-in waist of her skirt, but never any further. She had wept
and sulked, and in a moment of sordid, outraged virtue, she had
bitten him. Beefy, disgusted, Maurice panted and roared and at
last he stayed away.

One week passed and still Barbara Jean heard nothing from
Beamus. She began to worry. A passionate man like that, she
thought to herself with a shudder, has appetites that won't bear
waiting, that's all. She began in crooked little ways to soothe herself for relenting, for allowing the forbidden image of Beamus,
pink and nude like a side of beef, humping, roaring like a bull, to
dictate her pretty, clean fantasies. Knowing she was going to give

in, Barbara Jean inspected and annointed herself and drove out to the Truckstop to find Beamus.

As it happened, Beamus cared nothing about Barbara Jean, except that she reopened his old wound with Mabel, and the indignity of two such rejections was more than he could bear. When he thought of Barbara Jean's thick breasts and the quivering rolls he'd struggled through, he got a sour taste in his mouth. Even so, he would have her; he was going to do things to this plump cousin that she'd never forget.

Barbara Jean laid in wait for Maurice. She hung around the coffee shop and the grease bay; she sat in her truck doing her fingernails, and the radio was turned up loud, and he saw her but refused to make a move. Two days of agony went by and Barbara Jean almost believed she wanted Beamus. Orville had seen her hanging around the Truckstop and he warned her to go on home, but she didn't care by then.

On the third day it happened. Barbara Jean sat in her truck rereading old movie magazines. The heat was intense and she could smell herself in the cab of the truck. Her legs felt thick and prickled in their stockings. The door opened and without a word Beamus got in. She attempted a flutter of surprise, a word or two, but he leaned over and started the ignition, grunting, "Let's git outta here." Frightened, she grieved over her legs which, by now, had stuck together and were sopping with sweat.

Beamus took a room at the Big Steer for one hour. After pulling the curtains he lay down on the bed fully clothed, with his boots on the spread. Barbara Jean stood helplessly at the foot of the bed watching him.

"Better git them duds off," he said.

"You first," she answered, in a brave sing-song voice.

"Git 'em off." He didn't move.

"Oh, all right." She fumbled with her blouse and then, as the homely image of herself standing nude in all but her girdle flashed upon her, she changed her mind and reached up under her skirt. Tugging, she began to roll the girdle. It made a sucking sound pulling away from the damp flesh and it smelt humid and rubbery. Hot tears came to her eyes as she suffered the ugliness of the moment. She rolled the girdle with the stockings still attached down to her ankles and encountered her shoes. Hobbling to the bed, she sat with her back to Beamus, sweating miserably, and jerked off the apparatus. She pushed it under the bed. Barbara Jean slipped her shoes back on, stood, and said, "You too, Maurice."

He lay there unmoved, lit a cigarette and said, "How'm I supposed to know whether or not you got a deformity or something? Git your clothes off."

Snuffling back the tears of outrage and self-pity, Barbara Jean undressed. Naked, she stood uncertainly. A hog up for auction, Beamus thought. He took her without a word, grunting with the work of it, and when he was through, she heard him washing up in the bathroom. He tossed her clothes on the bed and, half-crouching, she dressed and took him home.

CHAPTER 3

Orville's room was next to Mabel's in the trailer. Lean and sparse, it contained nothing but a cot, a metal table on rollers and a tinted high school graduation picture of Mabel. No one was allowed in this room, not even to clean. Over in the corner behind a curtain there was a set of metal shelves. Secret things were kept here, things Orville found and hid from the others.

Orville never talked much. He did not believe in saying things that did not need to be said. Wonderful-looking, Orville was carved and sepia-colored with straight black lanks of hair. He had the baggy trousers and thin, oval, chiseled face of the miners in early tintypes. Later, in years to come, his mouth and eyes hung sorrowful with the exhaustion of life. Not with pain or self-pity; that was never there. He got tired out looking and you could see the years of work and dust from the land buried in his skin, wearing him down.

No one ever got down inside Orville and knew him. He did good things, he worked hard, he went off on his own. Ralph loved him but it was not something he could show. The two brothers rarely spoke to one another and yet they were together all those years. There were feelings there—this was known—but there was no way to show those feelings beyond going on together year after year.

Ralph's room was neat with homespun cotton bedspreads, several beds, a table and a chair. Next to his bedroom and off to one side of the trailer, Ralph eventually built a poolroom. Everyone took pride in Ralph's talent. People came from all around to challenge him, and late at night relatives and friends sat silent in the false green light of the poolroom watching Ralph shoot pool.

Not many people could beat Ralph. He was good. He loved to talk about the game and, gentle with easy, naive charm, he made friends. Mabel was his friend, his crony. He hovered behind her awaiting some small need, and perhaps it took the two of them, husband and brother, to keep her there in their lives. There was no need to pretend Mabel was good. This wasn't a thing people thought about out there in that land. Mabel wanted to get filled up and she saw no reason not to.

It's hard to say how Orville and Mabel got along, since neither of them condescended to talk about it. It may be that as the years went on, as Mabel's rancor and independence increased, she ceased to need Orville in any of the subtle ways a woman needs a man. She knew that if a woman were going to get satisfied she had to do it on her own. She kept to the old ways of honor in marriage without any of the sentimental trappings or sullen hysteria, the betrayals that the other women she knew eventually resorted to as the ineffable disappointment of marriage finally closed in on them.

The years went by and somehow Mabel, Orville and Ralph survived them with more tenacity than most people. The old trailer gave way to new trailers, but the cypress trees stood loyal in tall and slender guard around their home. Outwardly, life was as it had been.

Orville was silent still. To his silence had been added the silence of all the years. Timeless in his mute destiny, worn and veined, he was the rock rubbed smooth by wind and sand. When things were going well at the garage he'd go off alone in his truck with Toots, his dog, sometimes for days or weeks. He said he went fishing. No one asked much about it or knew what he did.

Granma Thelma was still alive and she lived with Hetty, who was a large gangling woman of forty now. Hetty had been collect-

29

ing cats and she had some thirty of them on the place. She loved these animals and the only time she ever cried was when one of them died. The rest of the time she went around smiling to herself and sometimes she whistled.

Flo-detta and Duane had seven kids. Matt, their oldest boy, hung around Loretta, mooning and wasted. The boys were sallow like their father, and Burt, who was sixteen, was cross-eyed. Flo-detta let them run wild and they came to no good. Duane worked on in the garage, but he had never asked to be made a partner and no one had ever thought of it, so he was still a mechanic.

Barbara Jean looked pretty good. She had drifted away from Larry McCoy and she, Sue-Ellen and Baby had moved up to Tucson where they had a house with a yard and a fence. This all happened because Barbara Jean had been Maurice Beamus's mistress for close to twenty years. He'd bought her a Cadillac and a fur coat and set her up in style in the house. She had stuck with him because he had never married her. Until she got that, she would never let go.

Beamus never did love Barbara Jean. He stuck to her, though. He wanted to get something out of her that she didn't have to give. Some people thought he was still in love with Mabel and that's why he hung on to Barbara Jean, but nobody knew for sure. He had married three times. Each time Barbara Jean had threatened to kill him, and on his third wedding night she drove her car right into the side of his trailer, honking and screaming dirty names.

He married three women who took him for what they could get. Two of them ran off with truckers and the third one just disappeared one night. He drove up to town two or three times a week to see Barbara Jean and she looked after him in her own way. Barbara Jean had lost weight and dyed her hair, and she had capped her teeth, but still she couldn't get Beamus to marry her.

The center of life in the trailer was Mabel but the person upon whom all their pride revolved was Loretta. It can be said that for each of them this girl was the dearest treasure of life. They shared her with triumphant joy in their creation, and there, in that trailer, out at the Truckstop, she grew up fine and clean among them all.

From the very beginning, isolated as she was from the coarseness of the Truckstop, Loretta had a fineness about her that did not seem to have come from the land. She was different from other people. She saw the difference as a responsibility and bore the weight of it without giving herself airs. If she had a particular problem it was that she had not laid claim to her own life; she knew the importance of continuing her mother's line but in spite of everything Loretta was the end of the breed. Her restraint, her refined way of being foreclosed on the smell of the earth and the vigor of the land, on the coarse vitality which had determined the essence of her ancestors.

If ladies are born, if they spring up mysteriously from nowhere, then Loretta was a lady. She had about her an implacable ordinariness that, in those environs, was as disturbing as a cornflower growing up out of the beet crop. Nothing about her caused that earthy sprawling clan to feel clumsy or misbegotten and yet, she stood apart.

Her room in the trailer stood slightly apart from the others in that it had been added on when the poolroom was built. She kept it clean, and her pride and joy was a little glass case filled with china figurines and perfume bottles, most of them empty and given to her by her mother. When she was nine she was taken down to the department store in town and allowed to choose a suite of bedroom furniture. Loretta chose a headboard, two bureaus, a night table and one chair called the "Waldorf Royale." They were cream-colored carved wood pieces, banded in gold. There was nothing mysterious about her room; she didn't hide things under the mattress or in the closets; nor was there anything about the room that betrayed who she was.

Like many another only child who grows up weighted with the heavy promise of a special destiny, who grows up alone, pinpointed and watched over under the doting parental eye, Loretta knew she was meant to be the solution for disappointments unspecified, unresolved in her parents' lives. She grew inward, and it was as if her own life were held in abeyance, suspended, in the shadow of the larger duty of fulfilling the family dream. She hid

31

her own vitality, her own needs so well that they were never missed. Far from being deprived or feeling regrets, she had all the gratification of being so great a source of joy, of filling a need, of being loved.

At twenty-three Loretta was living at home with her family. By now the trailer was enormous, bigger than many houses. Loretta had grown up in the din of pneumatic drills and diesel roar. Each time a truck pulled in or out, it expunged a fragment of its grime on the house and land she grew out of. A wall of rough, slouching men circumscribed her world, and her mother, full of the fever of living, was off somewhere, night after night, drinking, driving around.

Loretta had two years of college at the University of Arizona. No one in the family had been to college until now. She had traveled to Mexico and even to Europe, where she spent a summer in Barcelona as a Spanish transfer student, and yet there was no arrogance upon her return. If Loretta was spared the disturbances of a more passionate nature, she shone forth with virginal complacency.

Where Mabel's flamboyant looks were seductive, her daughter was distinguished by a pleasant blonde tranquility and regular features. There was nothing about her that demanded recognition or haunted the senses. Just as Mabel's presence, voluptuous and quixotic, defied convention, Loretta's looks were veiled, impassive. She had the kind of discreet beauty that made people feel comfortable.

Loretta loved her family. She continued to identify with them even while there were other possibilities open to her. She stayed one of them; that was what she chose to do.

Mabel could not drive a car, but Orville gave her a big white Cadillac with flame-colored seats in which Ralph drove her around. Ruby, Ralph and Mabel were drinkers, and when they got together there was always trouble. Then late one night during a four-day binge, Ruby called up Alcoholics Anonymous. They sent a woman named Alma Copechne out on a twelve-step call to deal with Ruby, who was lying drunk and mean on the floor of her trailer. When Alma stepped into the trailer she saw that Ruby was toting a loaded pistol.

"What are you doing with a little ole thing like that, honey?" asked Alma. "Why, if you're gonna pack a pistol, git yourself something that'll do you some good . . . I always carried a .44 myself."

This got Ruby interested and she called up Mabel and Ralph. "Sister," she said. "Come on over here. These people are talking some sense."

Mabel and Ralph joined up right away but Ruby never did take to A.A. on any permanent basis. Mabel loved those meetings. They were the turning point in her life. She came back from the meetings, if not quite reformed in her soul, sober at least for the first time in years. Full of tenderness and hot-eyed admiration for some of the people she met there, pretty soon all her friends were A.A. regulars.

Ralph went along to please Mabel, but he never felt comfortable there. Mabel could go anywhere. She got to know important people but never rearranged her character to oblige anyone. Although Mabel was not above provoking trouble, her kind of bravery defied ridicule and more often than not she inspired admiration.

Besides Mabel's regular A.A. meetings, she joined a group who called themselves the Club and met on Wednesday nights in a room in Odd Fellows' Hall. This place became the setting for many an intrigue. The group consisted of the regulars, about ten people, and a variable band of newcomers and fringe people. Mabel liked to tell stories about these people, and late one night out at the Truckstop she sat talking with Doris, who was passing through town.

"I wonder if I ever told you about that woman in the Club who calls herself Sweetie Pie Raymond? No . . . well, Sweetie Pie Raymond is a girl who moved to town from Abilene. Her real name is Dorothy Brown. We all knew her in the Club as Dorothy. She'd been coming in for years. She was a mousy little thing, plain as all get out. Then one day, it was a Wednesday night meeting, in she walks bold as brass calling herself Sweetie Pie Raymond and rigged out fit to kill. She'd done her hair over . . . it was orange, an orange you would never believe unless you saw it with your own eyes, and there must've been three feet of it all done up in a hairdo. I don't know what all she'd done to her head. There were braids and ringlets, long sausage curls hanging down her back and spit curls going every which way. Told me it'd taken two hairdressers all day to get it up there like that . . ." Here Mabel gave a snort of voluptuous enjoyment and allowed one plump hand to dip into an open box of Russell Stover chocolate-covered cherries.

"Anyway," she went on, smacking with pleasure, "she was wearing chartreuse chiffon all swooped and swirled with bows and tassles and God knows what all. Her own mother wouldn't have known her. Well, this particular night, when she came sashaying into the Club, all gussied up, she said to some of us who were standing around, 'Hello, you all.'

" 'Evening, Dorothy.'

" 'I'm not going to be Dorothy Brown anymore. I'm now Miss Sweetie Pie Raymond.'

" 'Oh, sure you are,' I sez. 'And if I may be so bold as to inquire, what have you done with plain ole Dorothy Brown?'

" 'I don't even know her anymore, that's what,' said Sweetie Pie, real haughty and grand. 'I've turned myself into someone else. I'm a lady now, see if I'm not!'

" 'Hmmmmmmmmmm,' I sez. 'You sure don't *seem* to be that other person, that Dorothy Brown we all thought we knew, but just what is it makes you sure you're really someone else?' "

At this point Mabel cackled with pleasure over her story. "Well," she continued, dragging it out some, "Now we all of us knew Dorothy Brown was forty if she was a day. She'd been around some, there's no doubt about that. She'd had her share, if you know what I mean. She was no angel. Well, right there, she says to us all, 'I went out today and did something. I bought me some brand new underwear. And this new underwear is white. Fresh and clean and *white.*' Everyone just gawked at the poor girl.

" 'This new clean underwear, this means one thing,' Sweetie Pie went on. 'It means I am a virgin.'

" 'Oh it does, does it!' I said. 'Well now, isn't that just fine!'

" 'Here!' cried Sweetie Pie, and she whipped out a piece of paper, something legal-looking. 'It says here that I am now Miss Sweetie Pie Raymond of 1422 North Seventh Avenue. It's all legal.'

" 'Lemme see,' I sez. And there it was, only when you looked real hard at that piece of paper you could see there was one thing wrong. Instead of Raymond, it said Raymon."

"Ramón?" breathed Doris.

"That's right. Ramón. So I sez, 'Why'd you pick yourself a Mexican name, Sweetie Pie?' "

" 'Mexican!' she screams. 'Can't you read! What on earth are you talkin' about? There's nothin' Mexican about a fine ole American name like Raymond!' She got all puffed up and condescending," Mabel chortled.

" 'Well, just take a look here,' I sez, 'cause you've gone and legally called yourself Ramón . . .'

"Sure enough, Sweetie Pie, who never could spell worth a darn, had gone to all that trouble to end up with the plainest name in the world when all along she had a perfectly good name like Dorothy Brown to begin with."

"Hah!" enthused Doris. "Whatever happened to her?"

"She's around. Them kind never sink. She found herself one of them sugar daddies from Arkansas. He gave her a Cadillac, a fur piece, a wristwatch with diamond chips. Little bitty ole things. You could hardly see them. And every New Year's Eve he takes her to Las Vegas. The thing is," continued Mabel, beginning to show she had a grievance, "he even took her to Hawaii . . . when she got back she was sportin' the prettiest pair of sea-shell earrings I ever saw. Dangling ones. You never saw such a color. Lavender." Mabel shook her head regretfully. The earrings had become a terrible sore spot for her and she had tried every way humanly possible to get them for herself.

"Maybe she'd trade you for the earrings," suggested Doris.

"Hmmph," grunted Mabel. "I tried all that. Nope. She's holdin' a grudge because I found out about her new name really being Ramón . . . but I'll tell you something, Doris." Mabel leaned forward, eyes glinting. "If there's a way to get them lavender earrings, I'll find it!"

"Sure you will," sympathized Doris, and they sat a moment in silence.

"Well now, who would have believed a thing like that!" began Doris, who was delighted with the story. "You meet some pretty weird types out on the road . . ."

"Don't I know it!" Mabel shook her head in disdain.

"That Sweetie Pie Ramón makes me think of this woman I used to know. Maureen Laverne she called herself . . . She came from a little bitty ole town, Rodeo, Arizona . . ."

"I've been through Rodeo."

"This Maureen grew up tough and mean. She could fight with her bare fists. Just like a man. Nobody messed with Maureen once they knew how tough she was." This was impressive coming from Doris Malone, who looked like she could wring a man's neck with her bare hands, given the chance. But Doris was a big leathery woman whose toughness came not from intention but from the earth, beating the road with her face to the wind, getting the good hauls, living day by day from one truckstop to the next, fighting the odds.

"She was a pretty thing, all the same," continued Doris wistfully. "She was blonde like Jean Harlow. She stopped the men cold, right in their tracks. When she was sixteen she married an old man; he was sixty if he was a day. Called himself a rancher, but he was a dirt farmer, that's all. They lived out in a one-room shack, out there on the land. God it was ugly." For a woman like Doris, a trucker, the confinement of standing still on one small piece of land was unbearable, but Mabel understood it. It was in her blood.

"Why'd she marry an ole man like that anyway?" Mabel asked.

"She had no choice. There were eleven of them at home, brothers and sisters. Her ma was dead and her Pa raped her when she was twelve. This ole man was a friend of her Pa's and he sold Maureen off."

"God almighty," said Mabel. Even so, she knew people like this; they were part of the land she came from.

"Maureen stuck it out four years. She had four kids in four years, dirty little things. Then one night when the ole man was gone to town, she took them four kids an' killed them off one by one. Stuck bags over their heads. Then she lay in wait for the ole man to come home. When he came he saw them four little bodies all lined up stiff and blue on the bed and he started to cry. That's when she got him. She chopped him down with the axe. He never knew what happened. Then she set fire to the house and got in his truck and drove off and she drove until the gas gave out. She left the truck on the side of the road and that's how she started hitchhiking on the diesels.

"Pretty soon she got good at it and she'd get picked up by some guy who couldn't believe a dish like that'd be out there on the road. She rolled them for all they had. Picked them clean. At first nobody was going to talk about it. Who was goin' to admit he'd been had by a pretty little thing like that? But the news leaked out and all of a sudden it seemed like that was all the guys was talking about, this mysterious blonde who'd taken them all, and they set up plots to ketch her. One night a trucker named Shorty Grogg out of Laramie, Wyoming picked her up on 101. They had a trap set, so he took her to a motel where six of the guys she'd rolled were waiting for her. Well, they beat her up pretty bad and they raped her and they stole all her money an left town."

"I guess she got what she gave," Mabel put in.

"The funny thing is that no one knew what happened to her after that for almost ten years. My guess is she went to work in a cat house somewheres. But I know where she is today," claimed Doris with a gloat of self satisfaction.

"Where?" Mabel demanded greedily.

"Well, you're not goin' to believe this but it's true, so help me God! She's married to Huey Durango, the mayor of El Paso!"

"No!" Mabel was thrilled but not convinced. She had only just begun to meet politicians through some of her A.A. friends and for her they were still important people. It wasn't that she believed they were better than anyone else, but that anyone "privileged," educated, should mess with the scum of the earth, poor white trash, was inconceivable.

"Mabel, I kin prove it. Me an' Ron, we had a layover in El Paso not too long ago. It was on our thirty-fifth wedding anniversary and Ron took me to Scordato's. You know, that fancy place on Meyer Avenue? We was sittin' there celebrating when in she walks. There was no mistakin' her, not for a minute. Ron knew her plain as the nose on his face. You see that night they got her in the motel, one of the guys took her picture and all the truckers saw it. They put it up in the truckstops. I saw it too. So Ron, he asks the waiter who that blonde was. She was sitting with a big, impor- tant-looking man and everyone was fussin' over them. 'That's Mrs.

Durango, the mayor's wife,' he sez, 'an' that there's the mayor himself.' That waiter looked at us like we was from outer space. Well, Ron, he didn't believe it, so the next day he looks up Huey Durango's address and he went to the house and hid by the bushes until he saw Durango leave. Then he rang the doorbell and a maid answered; she was a colored woman in a uniform. He asked to see Mrs. Durango but the maid was some kind of a snot an' wouldn't let him in. So Ron hid out on the street and sure enough she came out later all dressed to the teeth. She had on jewels and a fur coat and real alligator shoes, Ron said. He steps out from behind the bush and sez, 'Mrs. Durango?'

" 'Yes,' she sez, 'who are you?' looking like he was some kind of worm or something.

"He looks her right in the eye and sez, 'Do you remember anyone called Maureen Laverne?'

" 'No, I don't,' she sez. 'Now beat it, buster, or I'll call a cop.' But he knew it was her. We asked around some and she'd come to El Paso as Madelaine Fresno and she sang in the Flame Room. That's where he met her, Durango. She was a singer."

"Can you beat that!" exclaimed Mabel, convinced. "But where'd you find out she was from Rodeo and murdered all those babies?"

"Well, that's the funny part," said Doris. "I'm from Rodeo and my folks live there still. My sister went to school with a girl called Betty Oman. That was her. Everybody knew Betty and we all knew her pa was screwin' her. She used to come to school an' tell folks her pa had a poker on him the size of a bull moose in rooting season." Doris slapped her thigh and cackled.

"Hmmm," said Mabel. For all her earthiness she didn't cater raunchy talk. It just wasn't something decent ladies did. But she had her exceptions (it was Mabel's exceptions that made her so thrilling), and Doris was one of them so she let it pass.

"It just goes to show. You never do know who a person is . . ." Thoughtful as she was about all she had heard, nothing surprised Mabel much, not after the revelation wore off.

"Yup," said Doris after a long moment. "That's right. No one knows who a person really is. We all got something to hide."

CHAPTER 4

On her first visit to Alcoholics Anonymous Mabel surprised herself by feeling shy. She wasn't used to the idea that perfect strangers, people with no apparent connecting links, no known histories, no addresses or even last names, could stand up in public and show their troubles and not be taken for fools. The idea that strength could come from admitting a weakness, from seeking help from strangers and showing your faults, amazed her. Ruby covered up her own embarrassment by making snide cracks about the place, about their being there to talk out loud about all the nastiness in a person's life. Getting help was altogether alien to a member of the Jenks-McPheeter clan.

It did not take Mabel long however to see that A.A. people were her kind of people. Their amazing courage thrilled her. For Mabel, they were sinners, the only kind of people she could trust or understand and their will to fight for survival without hypocracy or an oppressive false innocence was something she could endorse whole-heartedly. A.A. was the community, the arena her energy had always needed for, if nothing else, people in all their preposterous disguises were what she fed on. With all the stored-up hopes of a farmer come to market to sell crops and buy feed, Mabel, in an old unresolved hunger, gave herself to A.A.

She was quick to find her best element. Much as she enjoyed the boundless inspirations and sharings found each week at the large A.A. meetings, her true energy came to focus on the small group of A.A. regulars who began to meet on other nights. There were a number of smaller groups within the Program and they met on pre-arranged occasions in one another's homes or, as in the case of Mabel's group, the Club, in a spare room in Odd Fellows Hall. It was at her third A.A. meeting that Mabel was discovered and brought into the Club by a man named Alexander Dautremont.

Prismatic and rare, Mabel had stood out as separate from the grey-brown crowd as a diamond glittering among zircons when Alexander, who had an eye for the real thing, spotted her at that A.A. meeting. Absurdly out of context and sitting alone, Mabel appeared so singular and grand to Alexander that he was unable to take his eyes off her. She turned at last and saw him watching her. Captivated by her droll sapient eye, which seemed almost to say, "Now what on earth is an old fool like me doing looking for salvation in a dump like this," he was drawn from the disguise of his customary reserve into her comfortable clarity. He came to stand by her chair, and although he did not bow there was something in his manner that conveyed a shy homage, and she felt it immediately.

"Hello," he began, smiling with a sweet candor that took her breath away. "I am Alexander." She looked him over thoroughly and, cocking an eye, said, "Well! Take a seat." From that moment on Mabel was his friend. She had found her place and was restored to her own beauty.

While there was nothing compelling in Alexander's appearance, his reserve and bearing were such that, for Mabel, the elegance of the man was unique. Without ever having been schooled, Mabel knew about fine things. She saw that Alexander's shoes shone with the kind of patina no amount of polishing could bring to ordinary leather. He wore pleated grey flannels that hung, with an easy disregard for fashion, from his thin waist; these trousers and his soft chambray shirts were worn without affectation but fuller than most people continued to wear their clothes, and they gave the man a striking grace and thinness. He wore limp tweed jackets of a kind Mabel had never seen before.

Although Alexander's appearance was utterly simple, his quiet elegance hurt Mabel's eyes, and for the first time in her life, feeling like a raw-knuckled farm girl, she sensed the awkward pinch of her own tight shoes in the proximity of so graceful and worldly a presence.

The effortless part of Alexander's charm was that he knew how to appreciate Mabel for some of the very things she was least disposed to appreciate in herself. Any awkwardness she may have felt was quickly dispeled by the thorough admiration in his eye.

"He's the most distinguished man I ever saw," Mabel said to Loretta after that first meeting.

"What makes him so special, Mama?" Loretta wasn't used to seeing her mother dazzled.

"I can't explain. He's a real gentleman, an aristocrat, not just one of those 'two-bit gentlemen' . . . maybe you seen someone like that when you were over there in Spain . . ."

"I don't know," Loretta said, thinking. "You mean like royalty?"

"No," answered her mother. "Not grand like royalty and not fancy either. He's not one bit stuck-up or hard to talk to; he's a real gentleman, that's all." Intrigued, Loretta asked Ralph about him later, but all Ralph had to say was, "He's not like one of us. He's different."

At the next meeting Alexander sought Mabel out and they sat together with Ralph. Ralph felt shy with him. He couldn't talk about pool with a man like that, although Alexander would have listened. His amazing courtesy made Ralph feel tight under the collar, loud. So he sat and took pleasure in Mabel's sparkling eyes, in the shine of the diamonds he had won for her.

When Alexander asked Mabel if she wanted to come to the Club meetings with him she was thrilled. Beyond the cultural differences that proved so fascinating, the thing that delighted each of them about the other was a thorough appreciation for best of breed; they recognized, each in the other, a rare species, now almost extinct. And then, no two people took a greater pleasure in the foibles of others. With a particularly benign connoisseur's eye, they watched people and saw things with the quality of appreciation that somehow inspired the best in most people. Even so, neither one of them, with all their humor and appreciation, was ever able to rub up next to a naked soul.

Alexander was thirty-eight years old, eight years younger than Mabel, when they met. He had yet to be married, although, as Mabel was quick to find out, rumor had him deeply in love with his cousin. He was just of average height and somehow inclined to appear even smaller and more slender than perhaps he actually was. There was something in his graceful slouch that distinguished him with a comfortable elegance and an absolutely natural dignity that few men carried off with such disarming charm. His fingers were especially beautiful, long and fine with pale clean nails of a healthy pink color, and for Mabel, unused as she was to the sight of a gentleman's hands, they were grand beyond belief.

If Alexander was, among the Club members, that rarest of all things, a complete gentleman, then the other members were what Mabel termed just plain folks.

"Now, I'm not saying I'd ever hold a man's humble origins against him," Mabel was fond of saying, having no illusions whatsoever about "plain folks," "but there's no way around the truth. A humble man's got to work a helluva lot harder than a gentleman if he's going to get any respect out of me!"

Besides Alexander, there was not one member of the Club whom Mabel could bring herself to flat out accept until many months had passed; she enjoyed them, she cared about them, she went out of her way to help them if she could, but her respect was a thing that had to be earned.

There was a couple in the Club called Arlene and Ed Cook. Ed Cook had suffered a heart attack so he was quiet and didn't say much. Arlene gave herself airs and always went first in line for coffee and grabbed the best chairs, saying, "I guess I'll just sit over here with poor Ed . . ." and then, with a meaningful roll of her eyes, she dropped her voice to a tragic whisper. "He's got a little heart problem, you know."

No matter how early Mabel and Ralph left for the Club, Arlene was there first, sitting in the best chair. Arlene let it be known around the Club that while she personally had nothing against people of good, plain stock—ordinary folk—her own family were genteel and could be traced back through endless generations of impeccable ancestry.

Now Mabel, whose own family was a source of distinction and pride, was not going to allow any such dubious claim to gentility crowd her own claims. Mabel bided her time and lay in wait for Arlene.

"You don't have to move one step out of your way to catch up a blabber-mouth hoity-toity like Arlene," grumbled Mabel one night as she was preparing herself with fastidious determination and no small amount of pleasure for a meeting at the Club. "A woman like that will trip herself up without no help from me. You'll see."

And shimmering from head to toe, done up to the hilt in her most brilliant plumage, Mabel sailed out the door.

On ordinary A.A. nights Mabel wore pantsuits. She tended to favor lavender knits and overblouses with emphatic flower patterns bravely splashed across shiny, newly invented fabrics. On Club nights, however, Mabel's entrance inspired a murmur of admiration from the group.

Her arrival, calculated and yet somehow without apparent artifice, was made in portentous slow motion up the staircase and was heralded by the important swishing of silks. Petticoats and pantyhose, silky skirts and silky coats rubbed and slid together in a thrilling ritual of female rustlings as Mabel crossed the room. On special nights her dress was an electrifying royal blue with dazzling sleeves all encrusted in an armor of sequins of this same powerful color. Beside Mabel, other women looked puny and underfed.

Arlene Cook always made a point of rising to welcome Mabel with a gracious nod how-do, as if this were her own parlor and she had granted an interview. This courtesy did not fool Mabel. With a menacing tilt of the head, her favorite diamond earrings ponderous and swaying, Mabel allowed her eyes to slither over Arlene in humorous condescension.

Arlene, who had spent an equal amount of time outfitting herself for battle, had chosen as her particular style that of the virtuous heroine. She radiated a sweet, pained tolerance for the flamboyant lapses in her good friend Mabel's taste.

Arlene carried herself with the physical discomfort peculiar to women burdened with the duty of appearing refined. Although she was thin and devoid of the sort of compromising flesh that betrays the dignity of a lady by jiggling, her body was always entrusted to the integrity of a strong girdle. It was no doubt the girdle that lent her face a distracted, pinched look as if down there, under her dress, some dreadful affliction held her captive and estranged from the rest of her body.

Her hair was an undecided yellow worn in finger waves that sloped upwards into a crown of sausage curls. These curls were fastened with a velvet bow and sometimes encircled by a ring of daisies or violets. Glasses hung from her neck on a long elastic string. The back of her neck was always slightly red as though she had just come out from under a hair dryer.

Demure organdie blouses with enormous puffed sleeves and full taffeta skirts, tightly waisted and showing a peek of fluffy petticoats at the knee, an innocent bouquet of violets at her waist, T-strap shoes—this was Arlene's outfit. She wore a lace hankie tucked in at her wrist and had the thin nervous hands of a piano teacher. Veined, they were speckled with liver spots.

Arlene carried a small brown paper bag which was worn and wrinkled from reuse. Coffee was passed out during the meetings and it was served in paper cups. Smiling with pleasant forebearance as her friends drank their coffee, Arlene reached into the paper bag and brought out a special china cup. It was pink and white with a shepherdess and sheep. Then, with every eye in the room riveted to her bag, she took out a tiny enameled pill box. One minute pill was carefully selected, broken and dropped into the cup.

Next, a silver spoon, lumpy with vines and flowers, was produced. Slowly, with infinite care and many dainty clinkings, the pill was stirred into the coffee. It was this last gesture, the torturous stirring and clinking, that almost drove Mabel mad with disgust.

"Get a load of that!" Mabel whispered to Alexander, who was as amused by Mabel's disdain for Arlene as by anything else. His own humorous appreciation of people was seldom perturbed by a condemnation of them.

Of course it was no small thing for Mabel to have the protection of Alexander's friendship and support. It didn't take her long to find out he was held in great respect by every person in the Club. Beyond having that indefineable thing in his bearing that presumed great wealth and great ease with wealth, which in itself was awesome, he was chivalrous with the sort of delicacy that forbade others to feel clumsy. He had a way of making even the simplest person in the Club feel useful, appreciated.

Fred Rudd was just such a man. He had a sad story, and piece by piece Alexander had come to know it and feel for the man.

Fred and Betty Rudd were two of the regulars at the Club. A rancher all his life, Fred had started out with a small piece of land that over the years he worked up into a sizeable holding. All Fred cared about was the land. No man worked harder to make a decent life for himself. In the early days, back in the thirties, he was married to a tall spare woman, Amanda Rudd.

Amanda was lonely living on the ranch and the only thing she liked to do was walk five miles down the road to the mail box every day to see if she had a letter from home. If there was no letter she stood for a long time in the road near the mail box and then turned and walked back to the house. On the days when a letter came, Amanda put the envelope inside the front of her dress and slowly walked home.

All this took a long time because the sun was hot and the road was long. Once home, Amanda did the wash and fixed supper for the men and cleaned up. Later on she sat out on the porch in the shade. After a while Amanda took the letter out and, holding the envelope up to the light, she tried to see what was inside. Finally, perhaps that day or the next, she opened and read the letter. Then it was folded back up and put away in a shoe box.

After some years Amanda had a daughter. Not long after that Amanda began to hear voices and gave up walking to the mailbox. She told Fred the devil was coming to get her, and she couldn't sleep at night unless he put a clove of garlic in front of each window and near the door. This was to keep the devil out. Then, when even this didn't work, she sat up all night with a meat cleaver, waiting for the devil to come.

The neighbors never did know what happened to Amanda. She just disappeared quietly one day and Fred said she'd gone off to visit her folks. Every Sunday Fred got out the car and drove seventy miles to visit her on the loony-farm where they'd taken her.

Fred's daughter, Edna Rudd, grew up wild. When she was sixteen she married a man from Texas and moved away. She was a mean-eyed, sullen girl, and the only time she wrote home was when she needed money. Fred loved her. She was all he had.

Not long after Edna moved away, Fred met Betty. By this time Fred had a nice piece of land for himself. The house had been fixed up and there was a Papago woman to see after things. Betty didn't have two cents to her name. She liked fast cars and fine clothes and she saw that Fred was lonely. Betty came over to see Fred one day and said, "Fred Rudd, I see you're here all alone with nothing but that Indian to keep company with and I sez to myself, 'Betty, why not go on over and tell Fred I'm available just in case he should want a wife.' Now I'm not goin' to beat around the bush. There's no need to court me. I'm not exactly young but then I'm not bad-lookin' and I've got good years ahead of me yet."

Once they were married Betty showed her true self. She liked having her own way and buying things and she wasn't too particular about where the money came from. She tried teaching Fred to have fine ways, and he wanted love so he worked to please her. One Christmas he went into town and bought her a pin. It was a dainty gold-plated leaping deer with a diamond chip for an eye.

"What's this?" she said, looking into the box where the deer lay posed on cotton. "Why, this thing isn't even real gold." She looked at it carefully.

"It's only got a bitty little chip of a diamond as well . . ." and the pin was put back in the box. The next day Betty drove into town and turned the pin in as down-payment on a big chunky purple-colored filigree ring.

For a time they lived high off the hog. Fred took Betty to the

Greyhound racetrack and out dancing on Saturday nights. They went to fast places like the Crystal Palace and the Buckskin, places that made Fred feel uncomfortable. He sat alone at a table and watched Betty dance with cowboys and drifters. Betty said he didn't dance right and that he embarrassed her in front of her friends. The other men all danced with bent knees and they held their elbows crook'd while doing a side-arm pump. They wore black hats rolled up at the brim and kept their heads forward and down for the fast dances and the polkas. The women danced with their chests stuck out, straight spines, crook'd elbows and their heads held up very straight. Their eyes were off somewhere, wandering. Fred sat at the table feeling plain as Betty twirled by in her red toreador pants, pleased and glassy-eyed. Before long he started to drink.

Betty liked Fred to think she was having affairs. After the noonday meal she took a long bath. She kept two pairs of nylon stockings folded up with an empty perfume bottle in a piece of tissue paper in her top drawer. On ordinary days Betty slid into a washed-out wrapper after her bath and lay down in the dark, listening to the radio.

Other times, when she had an outing planned, she'd take out a pair of the stockings and with fingers spread, the nails hooked and red, slither first one bird leg and then the other into each dangling, fragile skin. "Watch out for my nylons," she'd say, smoothing a leg. The small blue bones in her hands and feet were so puny Fred was afraid to touch them. Eyeing herself in the mirror, Betty reached down into her panties to dust herself with a special sweetish powder and Fred, fascinated, watched the tiny movement of flesh on the backs of her wrinkled, pinkish thighs in the gap between her stockings and the panties. Reaching into the closet for the outfit wrapped in cleaners' bags, Betty whispered seductively to herself.

Iridescent, dressed, Betty moved about the room pulling glittery little trinkets from boxes, trying on bits of ribbon and scarves, and Fred listened for the tight dry rub of her stockings sliding one against the other. Then he went back to work. From far off in a withered field, Fred, bent to his hoe in a dried out tangle of snakeweed, heard the roar of Betty's beat-up Buick heading for town trailing a weary parachute of yellow dust and a throbbing garbled lament from Lefty Frizzell, singing "If you've got the money, honey, I've got the time."

Fred had the red neck and thick hands of a man who works outside. His belly was large and worn over his pants, which hung as low as possible and were supported by a tooled brown leather belt with a silver buckle and "FRED" burnt in the leather in back. He had one pair of work boots, cowboy, and one pair of dress boots of the same plain brown color. His was a gentle, bewildered face, smooth-skinned and very white in the forehead. There was a ridge around his skull with flattened, indented hair where his hat had left its mark. He had strong yellow horse teeth. Fred was well liked, but after a while people tended to forget he was there.

By the time Mabel met Fred and Betty in A.A., they had been together thirty years and settled down into a relationship of pained tolerance on Fred's part and bare hatred on Betty's. She used to refer to her husband as "that dirty ole coot" and "killjoy." Several things had happened that released Betty from even a pretence of having respect for Fred. His daughter Edna had bled him dry. And Fred had fallen in with the wrong people and lost his ranch.

Over the years Edna had written home for more and more money. Fred gave her whatever he could. Then one day he had nothing to give her but a share of the ranch. He fell on hard times and took in a partner, a low character called Larry Slade. Slade and Edna squeezed Fred out of the ranch and then Edna sold out for cash. In this way Fred, when he was sixty-seven, was left without anything but a few saddles, a little cash and a small, unfamiliar house up in town. It almost broke his heart but Fred and Betty moved to town. Betty liked living there, but Fred had nothing to do but watch television and go along with Betty to the Club.

Mabel, one of the few people who refused to be scared off by the asperity of Betty's tongue, became their friend, and it wasn't long before she was familiar with the intimate particulars of their lives. One night as she sat talking about A.A. with Doris, she began to describe the Rudds.

"I never knew two people who hated each other more," she began.

"Marriage kin do that to a person," affirmed Doris.

"As far back as anyone kin remember, Betty had a little ole dog, one of them dachshunds. It was brown. She called it Peachie and it was a terrible little thing, always yappin' and showin' its teeth. Betty loved that dog, and when it died she got another one just like it, brown, with a horrible face, and she called it Peachie too. Now Fred, he had a dog also. The funny thing is, Betty's dog had a pointed face and skinny legs just like she did and Fred's dog was black and tan, a dachshund also, and it had a nice round face like Fred. Fred's dog was called Bitsy.

"Every night Fred and Bitsy sat in Fred's special chair by the T.V. set and Betty and Peachie sat across the way on the couch. They fought over the programs. If Fred got up to switch the station, Peachie growled and snapped at him and when Betty got up to change the channel, Bitsy growled at her. Finally it got so bad that when Fred went to his room he'd have to walk way around Betty and Peachie, in a wide circle, all around the edge of the room. And when Betty wanted to pass near Fred and Bitsy she'd run by real fast before Bitsy could git her. 'Now, now, Bitsy,' Fred would say, 'there's a girl,' and he'd stroke and pat her while Betty would say, 'That vicious mutt's gonna turn on you one of these days, serve you right; see if it don't!' and then she'd threaten to call the dog catcher and turn Bitsy in. Fred, he didn't say much but he never let that little dog of his out of his sight." Mabel laughed and shook her head. "That Betty, she could be real mean. She used to tell me how she'd follow Fred around with a can of Lysol spray. Said he was so nasty she couldn't use the bathroom or even sit down in the living room till she'd given things a good spraying after Fred had been there. Why he put up with her, no one knows. He was a lonely man and too tired out to care much . . ."

Mabel shook her head in disgust and went on to tell about how Fred died. "Fred stuck with the program but Betty, who got him into it, used to say, 'Now that the old geezer's stopped drinking he's so boring I can't stand him.' She tried everything to lure him back into his old drinking ways, but Fred just let her talk. Then he got sick; he got some kidney thing. After the hospital she stuck him in a home . . . one of those awful places for poor people.

Imagine, a man like that. All alone. The daughter, she never did get herself over here to see her father . . . he just ended his days in the home and then he died.

"The daughter came for the funeral though. She was wearing a big ole fur coat way down to her ankles on one of the hottest days of the year. She was all done up in white leather like some fat ole rodeo queen. What a sight. You kin imagine what happened when Betty laid eyes on her. It was something. I was standing right next to Betty at the time . . . She went up to the daughter and said, 'You got some nerve, showing your face in these parts, you two-bit hussy!' and the daughter, she just laughed in Betty's face and said, 'An ole bag like you deserves what she gits.' That was the only time they ever met."

"Lord," remarked Doris at last, "wouldn't you know a sweet ole man like that would go and die and that Betty would git to live . . . too mean to die, I suppose."

Mabel laughed. "Oh, I don't know . . . we all miss Fred, particularly Alexander. He liked him a lot. Seems like he was a man people miss more now that he's gone than when he was here, if you know what I mean. But Betty, she's got a right to live, same as anyone else . . ."

"What happened to Bitsy?" Doris asked. Mabel gave her a wink and said, "Why, I just thought I'd bring Bitsy home with me . . . that's her over there." And sure enough, over in the corner there was a wizened-up dachshund sleeping on a bit of shag carpet.

CHAPTER 5

After the Club meetings each week certain of the members went off to have coffee together at either the Flamingo or the Starlight Cafe in Tucson. Most often, Alexander joined Mabel and Ralph and another regular in the Club, Viola.

Viola was Mabel's protegée. Just as Mabel was captivated by everything graceful and elegant in Alexander, so was she appreciative of the innate clumsiness, the helpless indiscretions that characterized Viola. She devoted hours and months to Viola, nourishing and pecking at her with all the improbable tenderness of a mother swan for a baby goose.

Viola was a large, soft-skinned, juicy woman. Thirty when Mabel first met her, with an overripe body like a canteloupe the day after its prime, Viola had caved in slightly from the bulk of her own fullness. Heavy, sagging now with the weight of her juiciness, she was no longer fresh. Her face was pulpy and undecided, yet there was about her a certain soft brown animal glow. Indolent, sensual, she was the inevitable prey for hungry men.

A lusty violent drinker, Viola was for the moment precariously balanced in A.A. Her weaknesses were those of the flesh, and blindly, like an animal sniffing out trails, she followed her nose wherever it led, from smell to smell. Unable to distinguish aroma from stench, she floundered and went astray.

Mabel was not in the habit of encouraging Viola to visit the Truckstop. The dangers there for a woman so indiscriminately admirous of all men were more than Mabel could bear thinking about.

However, one night after the meeting, Alexander suggested they go out to the Truckstop. He had never been there, although he had lived in town most of his life. So a small group consisting of Mabel and Ralph, Alexander, Viola and Alma Copechne went out to the Truckstop Cafe. Loretta joined them. It was the first time she had met Alexander.

"You know," began Alexander, turning to Loretta, "I've been told so much about you, by your mother here, that it's almost unfair. I have no right to feel I know you, but it seems like I do."

"Yes," she smiled, comfortable with him immediately. "Mama's told me a thing or two about you . . ." They began to talk about Tucson, about how their lives there went on year in and year out without much change. This was something they both felt strongly about and while there was nothing deep or revealing in the conversation, they each began to penetrate a hidden pain in the other. They were both prisoners of the very thing they loved most—their families, the land, a way of life. Without complaint they were each living out destinies chosen for them by others, and so, even as their talk was of small things, it circled around an affinity, an awareness of how things really were for one another.

As they sat in the Cafe talking, a tiny seed took possession of Mabel. There was something, to Mabel's eye, so singular and agreeable about Loretta and Alexander, sitting there wedged into the booth amongst them, talking in low voices in their own genteel ways, so unlike their earthy raucous friends, that Mabel saw in Alexander the solution for Loretta.

With thrilling clarity she saw what she had never been able to define for Loretta. She had pushed her brooding for the girl to one side of her brain; the dreadful fear that out here, in this God-forsaken hole, there never would come a man clean enough to take her girl away. Each time some soil-stained low-looking man had dared to come near, Mabel had clubbed him back into place. Out here, in this truckstop, her daughter remained rare and pure.

After a while Alexander said he wanted to look around the Truckstop and see the garage. Mabel and Loretta went home to the trailer. Having sealed Loretta's fate with the wish in her mind, Mabel was far too sly to rush things. Leaving Viola to Alma and Alexander's care, she went to bed, peaceful.

* * *

Ralph showed them around. They were sitting in the garage talking when two truckers calling themselves Flim-Flam and Daddy Dirt pulled up in a flashy orange and green Kenworth with "Move Over Baby" and "Slidin' Easy" written on the doors. A hitchhiker named Bonnie sat up in the cab. Alexander saw her feet on the dashboard; she was wearing high-heeled white wedgies, the small town kind with thick vinyl straps, and listening to dirty jokes on the tape deck with the volume turned up good and loud.

Given the chance, Alexander had a way of putting people at their ease and talking to them about almost anything. It was not long before Daddy Dirt—with one eye on Viola, who was slurping down a bottle of Dr. Pepper close by—began confiding in Alexander. The men got to talking about rigs and the cost of running one.

Daddy Dirt said he bought his rig, a Kenworth Cab Over Engine, for $41,000 dollars the year before. He'd gotten a deal on it so it was sold below list price, which was $57,000, and he said it would take him four years to pay off the bank. By then, he continued, if you're doing 100,000 miles a year or more, you either need a new truck or the engine gets rebuilt.

"These things only make it about 400,000 miles if they're lucky," said Daddy Dirt to Alexander.

"Aw, hell," Flim-Flam spoke up, "I've seen 'em git 18,000 miles on 'em and blow all over the road, literally come apart."

Daddy Dirt saw Alexander was interested so he began to tell him more. "It's not easy, havin' your own rig. I pay $857 a month in truck payments to the bank, $255 a month insurance, my telephone bill is $200, the Michigan license bureau gets $250 every three months and the cost of fuel and eats on a one-way trip from Pennsylvania to California is $700; that's feedin' two plus a hitch-hiker. Your average rig burns about 600 gallons of fuel in a twenty-four hour day, that's eighty cents a gallon at about five miles to the gallon if you're not doggin' it too bad."

Alma asked Daddy Dirt why he paid for the hitchhiker's food. Looking sheepish, he said, "Aw, well, you know how it is . . . none of them's got a nickel, and after a few stops when they've watched you and your buddy eatin', you just can't stand it any longer. So you give them food. There's a lot of beavers out there hitchhiking. They just go along for the ride until the trucker gets tired of them or they want to get off. Then they get on the next truck. Back and forth, drivin' around. They see the country that way, they got no place to go."

"Gol-ly!" said Viola, caught up between the adventure of it and the uncertainty of the road.

Two trucks pulled in, a gleaming Peterbilt, long, thrusting with power, and a clumsy, hulking Diamond Reo. The truckers came around to talk. They were most of them young, in their late twenties or so and full of play and humor, proud of being truckers even though they knocked it. They talked about the hardships but there was an excitement, a real love for the road that made Alexander ache.

Most of them agreed it's in the blood. You can't stop truckin' even when you want to, it just gets you like dope and you've got to go on. One trucker came up to Alexander and said, "If you want to know the story about truckers, well, here it is." Out came an absolutely empty stenciled cowhide wallet. "There it is, all right there in that empty wallet. That's our story."

Alexander was not sure he liked the man's tone. He felt acutely aware of his own full wallet, and his eye fell on the trucker's boots, which were beginning to come sprung from their soles. At this moment he felt overfed, sleek.

Flim-Flam told them he had started out driving a milk truck in Nashville when he was twelve, "Twenty years ago, an' I've been doin' it ever since . . . hell," he drawled, leaning against the Kenworth, "I kin remember when the most powerful thing goin' was a 228 Detroit. Oh, I stopped for a while and drove busses for people like Mel Tillis and Loretta Lynn. I've known Elvis all my life." Viola jerked to life. "Elvis used to drive diesels before he got big. He's got a big ole Kenworth all done up, parked out back of his house . . . He drives it late at night, takes it out for a run. But even though I hate it, hate the addiction, I came back and I'm savin' to buy my own rig. Shoot, man, you gotta drive one of these rigs to know about trucks, you gotta feel that road movin' out. Road fever. There's a guy in last month's *Overdrive*, he's been drivin' for fifty-nine years. Started out drivin' a horse and buggy. That's a trucker."

There was nothing good-looking about Flim-Flam, but he oozed a cocky, cheap-thrills, king-of-the-road sex appeal. He wore his pants low and walked like a man who has known his way with women. With slow tricky eyes, a mismatched face and oily black hair, he looked like a million other roadside guys except that he had a power and that made him special. He had the arms of a man who has not done much; they were round and curiously white, naked at the top and tapering down into a delicate almost hairless forearm and small hands. He wore a red T-shirt stretched thin over a meaty soft torso. His skin and belly were those of a man living on Fritos, Corn Curls and beer. In some way, however, he was the kind of man whom most people liked in spite of themselves.

Daddy Dirt was young-looking, undecided. His hair was pale brown and caused him trouble. He looked like he needed to daydream a lot. He talked about finding a good woman, about needing someone to love and keeping it good.

Flim-Flam went over to the rig and motioned to Bonnie, the hitchhiker. She appeared feet first, giggling. Slow as a snake, she slid down from the cab onto Flim-Flam, who nuzzled her a bit and then brought her over to the group. Bonnie couldn't have been more than eighteen. She looked like one of those high school girls from a small, dusty southwestern town—Enid, Oklahoma or Globe, Arizona—the kind of place that still looks like 1958, where the girls cut pictures of Debra Paget and Natalie Wood out of back issues of *Silver Screen* to pin on the wall and study for beauty hints. This is what Bonnie was like. She had gotten everything about herself from picture magazines in Walgreen's. She had drugstore eyes, bangs and lanky dark brown hair still indented from the pin curls.

After a cursory peek at the group she said, "Come on, Flim-Flam, honey. Let's git on over to the rest area and have us a look around . . ." and with a playful, self-conscious pat on his rump, she got him to follow along.

Most of the truckers would hang around the garage all night, telling stories, joking, taking naps, getting haircuts, eating, making friends, working on their trucks. Most of them never seemed hassled about leaving. A lot of them ran out of money and had to wait for it to get wired in, and a number of truckers were wildcat, independents running hot freight, and they would wait in the truckstops by day, hiding from the "Arizona Coon Catchers" (the A.C.C. or Arizona Commerce Commission). Usually the A.C.C. quit for the day at five.

One guy, a Texan, looked at Alexander and said, "Hell, I wouldn't haul no hot freight. They kin git you for $1000 or more. In some states they'll take your rig—Missouri'll do it—or throw you in jail." Another trucker said, "Aw, man, yore haulin' hot freight and you don't even know it. Most of us are. They don't even tell us what's hot an' what's not. It's the trucker that gits the rap for that, not the supplier, even if the trucker don't know the haul is hot.'

A trucker called Henry told Alexander some things about the independents being squeezed out by the unions. Henry and other independents like him were pretty much left to haul "garbage" (produce) and stuff like that, but the good money was in hauling toys and candy—union jobs. The union guys got big money: eighteen dollars an hour to sit out a layover; they didn't get deadheaded (being made to run empty from one place to another); and they could take a lot longer to deliver. That was mostly because they make a lot of truck changes.

"There's bad feelings coming from the union guys. No one knows why," said Henry. "They're hard on us. Even though an independent doesn't make much money, he's his own guy, he's free. When you're runnin' empty, that's the worst. You say you're haulin sailboat fuel or Volkswagon radiators. And of course Volkswagons don't have radiators. And bobtailin' it across the country, that's when you're pullin' nothing, not even a trailor or a flatbed. The funny thing is, you can spot a union man. They look different. In a way, it's like those guys you see ridin' in the rodeo parade. They look great sitting up there. Big horse, big saddle. New pants. Big new hat. Real clean. That's your union man. Then take a look at the independent trucker. He's the guy down there ridin' in that rodeo. Same hat, same horse, but this guy's got mud on his boots."

One of the truckers spoke up, "You wouldn't believe some of the people driving trucks. I know a doctor, two retired full colonels, a guy with a Ph.D. in psychology or something like that. There are all kinds of people driving trucks!"

Henry added, "Well, they do it because it's exciting, because there is nothing else like it. It's free. And the money's good. You make what you want."

Daddy Dirt thought about this and then remarked, "I wouldn't know what to do if I was rich. I couldn't live without working . . ."

"There's rich people that work," said Henry. "Hell. You wouldn't have to stop."

"Well," replied Daddy Dirt, thinking about it, "truckin' . . . hell. It's all I know. It's all I kin do . . ."

There was silence for a moment, and one of the truckers asked Viola, half-asleep and propped up next to the Peterbilt, "You want to come on over to the cafe and have a drink or something?"

"Oh!" she began, looking pleased, but before she could get the words out, Alma said, "Not tonight, sonny. We're goin' home." Leaving Alexander to say goodbye, she steered Viola to his car and saw her safely into the back seat.

Alexander took the ladies home and then, returning to the highway, he raced against the road filling up on engine roar and the black desert air. A sudden gust of rain air blew up from the earth, a cool caress, and he smelled the bitter creosote and knew that somewhere nearby it had rained for a moment. Alexander knew the moods of the desert by smell. Even in the dark he knew when the promise of rain would yield only dust and angry tufts of wind. He knew the land and was at peace with it.

* * *

On arriving home the first thing Alexander did was check the hall table for messages. His housekeeper, Ruth, left him notes, torn off the kitchen pad, on a silver tray. Even while he resented the tyranny of the notes, he was unable to resist reading them.

Taking up the little pile of notes, he proceeded through the dining room without turning the lights on, past the dark shapes, silent mahogany specters, reassuring in their familiar bulk, solid, ancestral, rubbed smooth with family dinners, memories. A sliver of moonlight trespassed along the seam of the fine old table waiting, arms spread, to bear the weight of breakfast. Alexander imagined he saw his father there, at the head of the table in the dark, and Lily, his mother, layered and gauzy, float past.

He went into the kitchen and turned on the light. Ruth had left him a slice of blueberry pie and a glass of milk sealed in plastic wrap on a shelf in the refrigerator. He took these up to bed with him on a tray and read the notes while he ate the pie. Three of the notes said, "Miss Eunice called" and gave the times. One note said his man of business wanted to see him in the morning, and the last note said, "Goodnight Mr. Dautremont—sleep well." It was signed, "Ruth."

His room was white and peaceful. Two Hudson River paintings hung alongside a Thomas Eakins of two men sculling; there were several Audubon prints and a sepia rendering of his great-great uncle, Gilbert Hawes Dautremont, charging into battle at Richmond. One corner was graced by a stately Chippendale highboy, and on the only other chest in the room there was a fresh, white linen bureau cloth laid out with a set of his father's military brushes, a yellowed bone mirror and a silver bowl for the loose change in his pockets. There was a serviceable and enduring grey-blue hooked rug, a leather wastebasket, a double bed with a white chenille coverlet, a Pennsylvania blanket chest piled high with books and a night table also covered entirely in books. One entire wall was filled with record albums, and the first thing he did upon entering the room was to reach for a record, almost without noticing what it was, and, placing it on the old record player, turn it on. He seldom heard the music but having it on comforted him, and there were moments when, glancing up from his book, he paused over the dim but pleasant recollection of a particularly lovely sound.

Next door to Alexander's bedroom, in what had once been his schoolroom, there was a large airy study filled with papers and books, maps, charts and an enormous oak desk. Under a large colonial map of Africa there was a globe, a set of encyclopedias and a small boy's desk on which was laid out the Wildlife Society calender and a small old-fashioned model of an airplane. Propped up next to Plutarch's *Lives* and a volume of Horace Greeley there was a woven Seri Indian bowl filled with rubber bands.

These two rooms had always belonged to Alexander. As far back as he could remember they had looked exactly the same. He had meant, years ago, to move down the hall into the larger set of rooms, that awesome and forbidding master suite, his father's shuttered and deathly still domain. Somehow the prospect of violating those rooms, of sharing closets and bed and bureau with that terrible solemn presence, exhausted Alexander; except for a new and sturdier desk chair, the accumulation of books and records and a large photograph of his cousin Eunice in a silver frame, nothing within the comforting hospitality of Alexander's two rooms had changed in the last thirty years.

Crumpling the notes, he threw them away and settled down in his bed with a pile of books. After flipping through *One Hundred Years of Solitude* and Isak Dinesen's *Seven Gothic Tales,* old favorites he had read over and over again, he reread the last pages of Conrad's *Victory,* searching for something he could not find. He read for three hours, long into the night, and then turned off the light.

He was deep in his first sleep when the phone frightened him awake. It was his cousin Eunice, whom he called Lolly.

"Why haven't you called me?" He heard the high crackle of her voice over the wire and then a petulant jabbering. There were times when he hated her. He made some excuse.

"Oh, Alexei!" She called him "Alex-ee." It was a little pretension of hers. "Goddammit. You can be so mean. Drew is in London. Our divorce is final . . . a horrid little creature came slithering up to me with the papers today. Too awful . . . and you are never here, you never call when I really do need you. I'm so bored, New York is boring . . . are you coming to see me?" He heard her scratching to light a cigarette. Making up a lie, he told her he couldn't come. Alexander was able to lie beautifully without using the same excuses too often. Frustrated, Eunice hung up at last, and Alexander thought, she needs me too much, I can't bear it, and then he went to sleep.

It had not always been that way. A solitary child, Alexander had grown up close to the land. His father, Eugene Hawes Dautremont, a scholar of sorts, had been a Southerner from Virginia. He had moved out west for the air when it was discovered he had bad lungs. Alexander was born in Bisbee, Arizona in a large white frame house looking down on the town. Agnes, Alexander's aunt, lived there with them.

When Alexander was very young, Inez Hoover, his old black mammy, allowed him to play in the dirt out back by the pump. He amused himself by throwing pebbles at the chickens or making things out of bits of string and chips from the woodpile. Lying in the dirt, motionless, he looked at ants as they filed past, and once he watched a long time as an ant belabored a cumbersome tidbit up a particularly steep hill. When it finally reached the summit, Alexander squashed the ant.

Afterwards, feeling scared for at least a week, Alexander waited for God to strike him down. There was nothing to do most of the time so Alexander whispered to himself, taking on different voices for different moods and hiding out in places no one knew about. Sometimes he heard Inez call out, "Alexander! Alexaaaaaaa- aander! Now where'd that nasty boy get to . . . he's going to make an ole woman outta me yet . . ."

Only a few feet away Alexander waited, watching Inez until sooner or later he'd catch her doing something not nice. Like the time she looked around and then lifted her skirt and took a long satisfying scratch. At times like this, delighted as he was to catch her, Alexander felt disgusted with himself.

He had several different characters he could pull out of himself to suit the occasion. With Inez, he was sly and fractious unless he wanted something from her that demanded a display of respect. He also knew how to slump over on the back porch with his head buried in his arms and wait until, spying him there, a tragic heap, she was unable to withstand the sight and would give him anything.

Agnes, his maiden aunt, was best appealed to after a fright. Sometimes he crawled out on the steepest slope of the roof and blubbered for help. Disappearing for a number of hours was another sure way to get things. Agnes was prey to terrible imagery. She saw Alexander being gnashed to death and slowly pulverized in the cold iron jaws of the machinery over in the mine. There was no dismembering, mutilation or other bloody atrocity she had not foreseen and endured on Alexander's behalf, and he knew this.

After such a cruel disappearance, when Alexander finally came meandering home, he found Agnes stretched out on her bed on top of the white coverlet, in the cool dark upstairs room. Two crumpled lawn handkerchiefs, dampened with lavender water, were pressed to her throbbing eye sockets, and a tiny mustache of perspiration glistened on the fur of her upper lip.

He waited a while until Agnes, hovering in an uncertain twilight near sleep, her blue-veined hand twitching in the forbidden hollow of her tweed lap, at last opened a frightened eye.

"Alexander! My dear, where have you been? You gave me such a turn!" and with a maidenly droop of self-pity, Agnes turned her face to the wall. Alexander stroked the thin hand and his aunt, aflutter with the little attention, granted him almost anything.

The person who mattered most in Alexander's world was his mother, Lily. He adored her. Most of the time she was away somewhere far off, traveling. And then one day, hearing a commotion in the downstairs hall, he would catch the sound of her beautiful clear voice calling, "Alexander! My darling!" And then at last, once again he would feel the nap of her brown suede gloves, as wonderful and soft as the nose of a horse rubbing his cheek, and find as always the reassuring warmth of her pale neck lost in the fur of her coat, furtive comforts to exult and suffer over, his mother was home at last.

Moments with Lily were shimmering; little splinters of broken glass, fragments taken up and lost again in the long stretches of days and years. Alexander treasured these moments all the more because he was continually aware of the others whispering about how long she would stay this time. He was never quite sure Lily would be there when he woke up the next day.

People felt that way about Lily. They never seemed to have enough of her. She slipped through their grasp quick as summer rain coming from nowhere, drawing up earth smells and seducing from even the palest field all the deepest colors for one fleeting moment. There was no way to hold or contain her. You might just as well fence in the moon or bottle up the summer rain. It was hard on Eugene and Alexander. They needed to know she would be there for them. Life without Lily was the field without rain, pale brown and dried up.

Early in the morning Alexander crept into Lily's bedroom to wait a shy moment at the edge of her bed. At last, from deep within her silken cocoon, the enshrouded figure rustled a tiny encouragement. Groping for her as she lay there dismembered somehow by the silken web of covers, he brushed her cool, creamed cheek. The smallest movement of the sheet stirred up the thick night smells, and Alexander wanted to rub himself deep into the sheets and curl in the dark against Lily's moist back.

He had tried it once. She had been too sleepy to know he was there, or perhaps in her dream she had felt as he had and curled around him like a round-bellied possum hidden deep in the forest on a bed of wet leaves. Eugene came in and, finding them there asleep, cried out, "Oh my God!" in such an awful voice that Alexander had never again dared to creep into his mother's bed.

He searched for his lunch money in the dark. There on the floor, fat and secret, tangled in a vine of trailing lingerie, was Lily's pocketbook. Taking the money from its shadowy, intimate hiding place, Alexander felt like a thief. He thought about his mother on his way down the hill to school.

Sometimes after school he found Lily all alone, and when she was happy, Alexander sat on the floor and watched her dance and play with Morton, her bulldog. She tried to teach the great lumbering animal to rhumba and they laughed with gleeful, secret pleasure. Alexander was pleased because he was seeing a side of Lily she kept only for him. Then his father came in, and Lily, drooping in the corner of the big red damask couch, poured tea.

In the evening as Lily dressed to go out, Alexander hovered near her dressing table, in awe of her elusive fragrance of faraway places and forbidden flowers, watching her ritual pattings and delicate facial maneuvers, all of which conspired to hold him there swaying, entranced, at the outermost edge of her magic radius. Wrapped in rosy silks, her long fingers glittering with glassy red and green-eyed stones, amazing rings and curving nails, Lily cast smoky magic spells with even the simplest gestures. She carried a slender tortoise shell and ruby cigarette holder which trailed thin curling vapors long after the cigarette was gone.

Eugene died when Alexander was eight. The thing he remembered most about his father was the tiny porcelain clatter of spoon against plate as Eugene ate his morning egg. Except for the spasmodic twitching of his own foot against the chair, there was no other sound in the dining room. The privilege of having breakfast alone with his father in the dining room each morning at seven o'clock had been granted Alexander on his sixth birthday. Eugene was not inclined to talk in the morning. Once Alexander had finished his oatmeal, he gave himself up to the solemn perusal of familiar objects on the table, with an occasional timorous peek at his father, who was entirely given to the methodical ingestion of one four-minute egg and a piece of toast. On Sundays this regime was varied by the addition of kippered herring to the usual fare. Alexander was not encouraged to leave the table until his father was through.

The other memory Alexander had of his father was from his seventh birthday. "Now, Alexander," Eugene had said, "Come here. I have something for you," and he held up a silver dollar. "I don't expect in your circumstances you will need to spend this, so I will keep it for you in my desk."

When Lily was away, the center of Alexander's world was the riverbed. In the heat of the long summer days he would slip through the sagging rhubarb patch and, unseen, make his way down the hill and out to the edge of town. It was not far, but for Alexander it was his own place, secret and far away.

The riverbed was dried out and had been that way for as long as anyone could remember. Strange squat trees peopled the forsaken banks, their scraggly arms grown askew and interlaced, locked forever in grotesque embrace, pygmies gyrating in a macabre river dance, forgotten in a place where rain no longer fell.

Humpbacked roots marked the gloomy corridors below, and it was here, where the light never came, that Alexander whiled away his hours, cradled in the dried-out carcass of a river tree. In the gothic grey light he dreamed and watched over his shrunken cathedral. The only visitors to the twisted, vaulted catacombs below his perch were the wild pigs who came to wallow in the cool gloom. Sometimes the rhythmic rubbing of a stray cow scratching along the spine of a tree would loom large in his ear, and in his fright the crooked forest grew ominous with trolls.

On the days when there was wind or a chance of rain, Alexander sought the meadows beyond the hill and lay in the grass with his ear pressed and waiting, in hopes of hearing the earth move. When the rains came, he felt at one with the earth, and he lay there matted and joyous, drinking up the rain along with the land.

The wind was his particular ally; he could fly in the wind, and this power belonged to him alone—of that he was sure. He grew up thinking the wind was a presence, perhaps a god, and that it could lift him bodily away from the earth, that it could free and empower him.

He had no friends. The other children wore thick shoes and they played ball and clung in tight little groups. Alexander found them noisy and loud. The wind and the rain, the green meadow and the riverbed were his friends. He had names for them: the meadow was Green Song, the rain was Yellow Sky, the wind was Wind Song and the riverbed was Grey Halls.

Exhausted by a night of dreams, the ghosts of his childhood, Alexander awoke the next day feeling guilty about his distrait behavior to Eunice on the phone. He wired a dozen yellow roses to her in New York and felt absolved. A part of his childhood, she remained rooted, the last link to that part of himself that, unresolved, hung like a taunt over his life. He could not let her go.

He sent for his man of business, John Hatch, who was there to remove the burdens of the day from Alexander's life; relaying messages to Alexander's stockbroker in New York, paying the bills, handling complaints from the staff, writing letters, calling the plumber, he also opened the mail, weeding out circulars and letters he knew Alexander couldn't face.

Alexander's money, which had been left to him by his father, had enabled him not to work. He had set up his life in such a way that the only thing he had to do was take care of his own person, and Ruth bore the weight of this since she was even more particular than he about what he ate and how his shirts were ironed. She inspected each morsel the cook prepared, each shirt the laundress washed. Nothing slipped by Ruth.

And yet, Alexander was not an idle, wasted man. He filled his time with a graceful expenditure of energy and served the day with a gracious homage to detail.

If an elderly friend were ill, he sent John Hatch over with a basket of cherries and a new novel. If a trailer on the south side of town caught fire or blew over in a twister, he had John take the victims a check, a box of food and his old clothes. With his ear to the pulse of the earth, he knew what was happening and he was there for all who needed him.

Alexander served on the vestry in the Episcopalian church; he sent anonymous funds to Boy Scouts, Big Brothers and other causes; he supported the Southern Poverty Law Center and was active in Planned Parenthood, Crime Prevention, the Black Mesa Defense League and various conservation and wildlife preservation societies. Without any false pride, he was a man who was available and willing to help people.

Orderly in his approach to the day, Alexander had his boiled egg in the dining room, as his father had before him. He then telephoned New York on business. John brought him the mail and, sitting at his desk, he stamped the incoming journals and magazines "Received" with the date and his name in black ink. Sometimes it would be months before he was able to read them, and in some instances they were donated to his dentist or thrown away unread.

Long notations and various thoughts, observations and information were then carefully written in a journal. Alexander wrote down things he had learned, words he had looked up in the dictionary and did not want to lose. His favorite quote was this from Chazal: "Monkeys are superior to men in this. When a monkey looks in the mirror, he sees a monkey."

On days when he was alone for lunch, Alexander preferred a peanut butter sandwich on white bread, and for dessert, a pear with the skin cut off and two chocolate chip cookies. It grieved Marie, his cook, to serve him so paltry a luncheon, and she attempted to embellish the plate with wedges of cheese, parsley or fresh radishes, but he left these offerings untouched. When guests were there for luncheon, they were served pork chops, fowl, roasts with gravies, potatoes and rich puddings and jelly roll for dessert. Alexander invariably ate in the dining room, even when alone, and he rang the silver bell for service.

After lunch, when there were no board or vestry meetings to attend, he told John Hatch he was going off to work in his study. In fifteen years, John had never inquired as to the nature of this work and he could only imagine that Alexander, who had a degree in archaeology, was bent in deep perusal over scholarly papers. In fact, Alexander shut himself into his room, pulled the shutters, took off all his clothes and lay down to read a novel and sleep.

The two things Alexander enjoyed doing most were slipping off to his machine shop behind the house to work on a model airplane, and taking his Labrador Rex (all his dogs had been called Rex since he was a child) into the mountains to romp and play in the blue of the late afternoons. These were pleasures nobody knew about, for he had never shared them.

He was hardly ever alone in the evenings. An immensely popular man, sought after by hostesses and matchmakers, Alexander was asked to dinner or cocktails every night. He was agreeable to everybody, and the women hoped they would be seated next to

66

him at dinner. The men talked to him about their work, about ideas, and he could talk with as much savvy about fishing the Colorado as about Kant, Descartes or the latest styles in ladies' shoes.

The thing is, he didn't have one real friend. Of all the people he knew, there was no one he could talk to about the things that really mattered, about being alone in the dead of the night, about growing old, about Green Song and Grey Halls and the wind, about days gone by and Lily. There was no man he could talk to about being a man, about women, about money. There was no woman he could talk to about God, the land, the tall grasses, the wind on his skin.

In her silent endurance of the fact of life, in her tie to the land, Mabel came closest to being the person he could trust as real. But the land she knew was a harsh land, and her life was without the fine old embroidery that wove into the fabric of his past. She couldn't know him, she couldn't imagine the layers upon layers in his mind, she who—however opaque—was as clear and direct as a field in the sun.

CHAPTER 6

Loretta's cousin, Matt Jenks Miller, followed Loretta around with the heady love of a mongrel for a thoroughbred. He was a year older than Loretta and, even when he was only ten, he knew he would lie down and die for her, should the need ever come. He found ways to bring her little delicacies, unusual marbles, a locket on a chain, an empty blue carved perfume bottle. Some of these things he stole.

Loretta hid the things from her mother, but all the same Mabel knew they were there. So, against the ways of her people, Mabel took Loretta out of the Junction School and had her driven in to St. Joseph's Academy, the best school in town.

In the early years it was one of the things that made Loretta special. Until the fifth grade she had been bussed to the Junction Valley School along with the other highway kids. Mabel noticed she was falling in with a rowdy group—her cousins, Flo-detta's children and others. It wasn't that Loretta was meant to snub her cousins or have airs, but she was expected to grow up different. Even though family went on being family and they would never be cast off like worn-out shoes, all the same, there were differences to be respected and maintained.

At first Loretta yearned for the highway, for her cousins and the children she had known all her life. She saw them on weekends but things were different now. The other children sensed she was changed long before the changes came, and they were quiet with her and made furtive faces behind her back. They imagined she considered herself too good for them, and after a time, because she was isolated from her own tribe, it became true.

As the distance grew greater between them, Matt loved her more and brooded to see the pull of their lives sever them. He had no way of knowing how hard it was for her there in town, how separate she felt from the pale city children with their stucco houses, their lawns, their sidewalks.

The Academy children had never met anyone who lived in a trailer, and before long Loretta saw that, for them, trailer people were poor folk, gypsies, poor white trash living huddled and outcast at the edges of town. It took all her dignity, all the McPheeter pride and the fierceness of her claim to the land, to outweigh the arrogance of these city people.

Her power was strong, but it took time, more than a year, to overcome the resistance of the clean little girls, not unlike herself in all but the circumstance of home. They asked her questions like, where do trailer people go to the bathroom, and did they all sleep together in one room. One child asked Loretta if trailer people, when they died, got buried in the cemetery, same as other folks. One of her classmates was Arletta Cook, who was not allowed to come to her birthday party because her mother, Arlene, didn't want her associating with the trailer people. Loretta did not tell her mother about this incident until Mabel joined the Club at A.A. and she heard about Arlene Cook's being one of the members. It rushed over Mabel like a cold wind, the humiliation, and she swore she'd get Arlene.

It didn't take Mabel long to figure out that the thing dearest to Arlene's heart was her daughter Arletta, who was her one major accomplishment. She was the culmination, or so Arlene thought, of years of selfless, disinterested labor, the by-product of selective, cautious design. The configuration of Arletta's life had been as daintily and carefully worked out as the petit point in a lace doily.

Nobody could deny that Arletta was a beauty. Her skin was so clean and white she looked like a glass figurine. You could almost see through her, even on a hot day when everyone else turned thick-colored and sweaty. Arletta never perspired. Her eyes were a strange blue, the faraway color of oceans on foreign picture postcards. Her hair was very black and she wore a big hibiscus bloom behind one ear. She was so perfect that even when she laughed you never saw her molars.

However, once, when Arletta was nine, Arlene had surprised her in the act of sticking two cautious fingers up under her long flannel nightgown. There was a terrible moment when Arletta was allowed to think the end of the world had come and, after that, she was made to sleep in wool gloves.

Loretta and the other girls arrived at school in skirts and cotton blouses, but Arletta was sent to school in rosebud-pink tulle dresses. She was so afraid of dirtying these dresses that she sat at her desk all through recess. Everyone else brought a paper bag to school with one apple and a bologna sandwich, but Arletta carried a lunch pail with flower cutouts tacked on. Inside the lunch pail was a thermos of lemonade, a Hostess cupcake with a cream center and one small jelly sandwich with the crust cut off.

The first year at St. Joseph's Academy was a lonely time for Loretta. The only friend she had was Geraldine Faldutto. Nobody else would play with Geraldine because she was the richest kid in school and her father was Vito "the Weasel" Faldutto, a gangster.

That year the Sisters of Divine Charity decided to raffle off a wonderful doll. The nuns made it themselves and it looked like St. Teresa, with a miniature rosary and clothes made of special bits of holy cloth extracted from the habit of a particularly virtuous, recently departed nun. There were those who believed a tiny fragment of hair, possibly even a sliver of fingernail, taken from St. Teresa herself had been sewn into the hem of the doll's costume. Everyone believed this doll would bring the new owner powerful luck.

On the day of the raffle there was so much excitement that the parents, including Mabel, came to school to see what would happen. There were five hundred raffle tickets for sale. Those children who had a dime each bought a ticket. Mabel bought Loretta five tickets on the sly and gave her one to hold. There were about three hundred tickets left when Vito Faldutto pulled up in a long black car and bought up all the rest of the raffle tickets. Geraldine won the doll.

After that, Loretta was not allowed to play with Geraldine anymore and so she had no friends. After school, she walked over to Barbara Jean's house to play with Sue-Ellen and Baby Jenks, the peach-picker's kids. School boys followed her calling out dirty names, like "Fatso, Fatso, ya ya!" and, afraid of them, she ran all the way to her aunt's house. Shorty, one of the mechanics from the garage, or Ralph drove into town to pick her up there and it wasn't until she got home to the trailer that she felt right about things again. But she never told Mabel this; she kept it to herself.

Eventually Loretta made friends, and the other girls liked her —except Arletta who held off and kept to herself. When Loretta and Arletta were seventeen, Arletta became the most popular girl in class because it was known that she was going to Hollywood to become a movie star. And then, even before the school year was over, Arlene took her daughter to California and they were gone almost a year. Arlene came home alone and when anyone asked what had happened to Arletta, she looked important and began to hum a catchy tune under her breath. Not long after that, the town was thrilled to recognize Arletta on television in a Vick's Vapo-Rub commercial.

Word spread that Arletta Cook had come home sporting a new fox chubby and was seen carrying a lizard-skin vanity case with a gold handle and her initials stamped on top. Arlene had friends in for coffee and cake after dinner and they talked about Arletta's career.

"Career!" hissed Mabel. "Now let me see . . . that must've been your wonderful girl Arletta I saw just the other night starring in a rerun of 'Dragnet' . . . no? Well, maybe that was her I saw on 'Perry Mason' . . . the one where that pretty secretary gets hacked to bits and thrown in the swamp . . . no? Maybe it was one of them science fiction thrillers, 'Ant People Take Over the Earth,' or something like that . . ."

"At the present time I am not at liberty," said Arlene, all puckered up with mysterious eye-rollings and meaningful nods, "to divulge the particulars of my daughter's career. You know how people are . . . one wee little success and everyone wants to latch right onto the star."

Although Arlene wouldn't have had Arletta one inch less the budding movie star, she did keep a sideways eye on Loretta and observed the girl's maturing loveliness with grudging admiration.

"I hear that adorable Loretta of yours has got a whole string of admirers," Arlene let drop one day. Mabel saw an unwholesome glint in her eye. "I hear she's been seein' Tom Pool, that plumber boy, and Lester Moon, that poor retarded fellow that got all them girls in trouble . . . My, I sure hope your Loretta don't get all done over by a man like that . . . all stretched out and dragged down before her time like that poor Lopez girl . . . you know, the one that had all them nasty little kids so fast it was indecent. Nothing left for that girl to do but waddle around like a fat ole sow. He never did marry *her*."

"Heavens," Mabel replied through clenched teeth, "I'm not worried about a girl like Loretta. A girl like that's got respect, which's more'n I can say for some of those creatures I hear of over in Hollywood, where for two cents them Ay-rabs would grab up a poor girl like your Arletta, strip her bare, dope her up and send her off to one of those Shanghai whorehouses they got over there . . . happens all the time. Sold into slavery, if you know what I mean . . ." She had the audacity to wink at Arlene who whinnied with fear and scuttled off, leaving the field to Mabel once again.

Life in the trailer was slow for Loretta. She saw to her father's needs, she listened to her uncle Ralph talk pool, she cooked for the men and visited her old Granma Jenks, Barbara and Hetty. She was there when Mabel needed her, she was part of the life, but as yet she had no function of her own and time hung heavy on her hands.

She had enjoyed being at college. It was wonderful to walk along the campus in the throng of pretty coeds, laughing and whispering with one another in their pleated plaid skirts. She had looked like them, those shining, healthy girls, but after two years, she dropped out. On the inside, under the peaceful façade, Loretta could not feel she belonged there. She did not know where she belonged.

Close as she was to Mabel, and by now they were friends sharing the cares and satisfactions of the days, Loretta could not speak to her mother about such an alien thing. Mabel had always belonged somewhere. Even alone, she had been part of something, a continuing element in the fact of life, the family, the land.

So she kept it to herself, this sense of not belonging, and filled up the days as best she could. Flo-detta came over to the Truckstop to gossip and bemoan the doings of her kids, most of whom were drifters or in trouble with the law. Barbara Jean came, too, driving out from town to keep an eye on Maurice and to show off her new clothes to the women in the trailer.

Barbara Jean's daughters, Sue-Ellen and Baby, had blown off with the wind and no one had heard from them for several years. Barbara Jean and Flo-detta had been coming to the trailer to talk for over twenty years now. They did not have any place else to go. They were caught in that particular limbo of always wishing some new and exciting thing would happen even as they wanted the safe old ways to go on forever.

This was the way it was out at the truckstop. Things didn't change, so the place never lost its character. It was like what Loretta heard her mother tell Flo-detta one day when they were discussing Barbara Jean's face-lift: "Just as I was finally learnin' to appreciate the *old* face she goes an' confounds us with this *new* one . . . it's a cryin'-out shame when a person can't even tell who's who and what's what anymore . . ." And so any new improvements at the truckstop, few and far between as they were, went unappreciated.

"That ole fool Beamus," Mabel grumbled one day. "He's making more money each year than the president of the United States and what do you think he spends it on? Gorgeous women? A new Cadillac? Having hisself a good time? Hell, no! Why, that little toad is over there in the dirt building hisself a new fuel island and a new sewer line, and last year he dug a new cesspool out back. It's enough to drive a person crazy. I never could respect a person who couldn't have a little fun spending his money! Cesspools!"

Barbara Jean, who had to work tooth and nail to get a penny out of Beamus, was inclined to agree with her. But on most days, the meat of their conversations centered on A.A.

"Gee, I sure wish I could be an alcoholic," mourned Flo-detta enviously. For her, A.A. took on the grand aspect of a very exclusive club; Mabel was their ambassador sent out into the world to garner information and bring home food for their dreams.

Matt, Flo-detta's son, had been sent up to Brownsville to do time for passing bum checks. When he got out he was full of stories about the beatings he got there, and among the younger cousins and the women of the family he was something of a hero for a while; he gave them someone to think about. He told stories about how they had tried, in prison, to take his brain away and rearrange it; he said they had tried to hypnotize and then brainwash him so he'd be a government robot. He held out so they put him in a dark hole in the ground for twenty days and never once had he screamed to get out. Even Mabel, who saw he was no darned good, granted him a certain power.

Matt's love for Loretta endured, and she met him sometimes to drink beer and talk over the old times. He asked her to run off with him and loved her more when, laughing, she refused. Each time, before they parted, Matt told Loretta that if he ever heard of her fooling around with some man, he'd kill the man and then come for her. "You don't scare me none with your big talk," she challenged, but looking into his smiling eyes, Loretta wondered.

Matt Miller was the first member of the Jenks family to drive a diesel, and Mabel swore the boy would come to no good. Prison was one thing, but driving a rig, that was as low as you could get. After prison, Matt had bummed around some, worked in the mines and finally took to the road. His mother was proud of him. With all his rough ways and trouble with the law, he was a real man. In her eyes, that was all that mattered.

One evening as Mabel and Loretta sat discussing the books—garage accounts that Mabel juggled and controlled with the intuitive cunning of a big-time bookie—a rig roared right up to the trailer and gave a blast of the horn. Furious, Mabel leapt up to avenge her rights. Never before had anyone the audacity to drive a rig onto her private land. Taking up a pistol, which she kept in a hatbox, she went out for the confrontation.

"Hallo in there you all! Yoo hoo!" came an impertinent voice from the truck, and a moment later, Baby Jenks, Barbara Jean's daughter, jumped down from the cab. "Surprise!" she laughed and then turned and motioned to someone in the truck. "C'mon down, Matt." "Git that thing outta here," threatened Mabel with a side arm swipe of the pistol. Matt moved the rig.

Matt jumped down from the cab and grinned at Loretta. "How-'ya doing, sweetheart," he drawled, cocky as ever.

His face shone pale in the dark and Loretta spotted a few stray whisker hairs standing out on his face like weeds. He was wearing checked jeans with a black comb tucked in his back pocket, and his dark hair was worn swept up off his forehead in a free-standing mound greased back into a ducktail. Mabel took one look at him and grimaced. "Your ma know you're out with this greaser?" she demanded of Baby.

"Matt done married me!" Baby gurgled with triumph. "And I got a baby!" she finished bravely. Mabel gave them a snake-eyed glance and turned to go. "Ma's no rose!" shouted Baby. "She's been living in sin with that tub of lard for twenty years now . . . she's got nothing to say about me. I'm married good and legal." Loretta looked at Matt, but the grin was gone and he kicked the ground with the toe of his boot.

Loretta took them into the poolroom, which Mabel reserved for visitors unwelcome in the trailer. Baby kept pawing Matt and giggling and Loretta felt a dull, confusing pain down inside her gut. "What happened, Matt?" she asked. Baby had gone back out to the rig for a moment to find a snapshot of her baby girl.

"She's my cousin," he said, almost angrily. "Same as you." Loretta saw his eyes were burning.

"Well, what of it?" she answered, close to tears. "Do you love her Matt? Do you?" He stood up and paced the pool room.

"Never you mind. What's it to you, anyways? You never loved me," he spat out. "I would have waited for you, you stuck-up bitch, I would have waited forever if you'd just once, just one time, given me the time of day!" and he snatched at her and kissed her long and hard. She smelled the road coming up out of his clothes.

Baby came in, waving a photograph. She was soft and seductive, with wisps of thin blonde hair that curled against her ears and along the back of her neck. Childish, touching, hers was the kind of impudent, blue-eyed, dimpled face that wouldn't last beyond thirty. The softness of her face belied her strength. Having grown up with a slatternly, dissatisfied mother and a mean-minded older sister, Sue-Ellen, Baby had made her own way with a gentle resilience.

They started talking about trucking. "What you've got to remember in this business," said Baby, "is you're either gonna make it or you'll bust yore butt. Take Matt here. Matt an' me, we's been driving together one year and before that, Matt drove on his own for two years . . ." Loretta glanced at Matt, who, at twenty-four, looked eaten up by the road.

"We ain't made it yet, have we, hon?" Matt nodded. "We're union," Baby continued. "That's the only way folks like us kin make it . . . Take your independents, for example. The only way a guy like that kin make a nickel is to start off with money. If he buys his rig with cash and he's got a warranty on repairs, whatever he makes is his own. But your average trucker, he's in hock up to his eyeballs. Me an' Matt, we had our own rig a few months back. We're still paying off the loan Matt took out to git the rig and that was three years ago. That's a hundred and thirty-nine every month on the loan and then our finance payments ran over six hundred a month. The rig we got second-hand so there was the cost of the repairs. Then there was the lease on the trailer and waiting for the good hauls. We just couldn't make it. Matt here was driving through Illinois one night, way out in the middle of nowhere, when he smells something funny . . ."

"Smelled like sulphur," said Matt.

"That's right," Baby went on. "The rig was on fire. That's how we lost our rig."

"There was no smoke," continued Matt. "I smelled something funny, then I looks in my rear-view mirror and I see flames. It was the sleeper on fire. A short in some wires."

"Matt, he just pulled over and got out. Then the truck blew . . ."

"It was fourteen below zero that night," remembered Matt.

"Well, we learned from it." Baby smiled at Matt. "We got nothing to complain about. Take that ole Kenworth out there." She nodded in the direction of the rig outside. "That ole thing is ready for scrap but the owner, he uses it for a tax write-off. Caught on fire once with Matt and me and the baby. The baby was with us then. She's almost two." Baby showed Loretta a snapshot of a small, dough-faced creature. "I looked down and I see flames coming up through a hole in the floor. 'We're on fire Matt!' I sez, and we jumped out with the baby. We never had any accidents though, knock on wood . . . Just after I started driving, a rig hauling cattle comes along and swings out as I'm passing. He didn't see me, I guess. Knocked me right off'n the road. We chased him, remember, hon?"

"Yup," said Matt.

"That guy was about the biggest hunk of meat I ever did see. Matt backed off real quick when he seen how big he was!"

"No, I didn't."

Baby giggled and winked at Loretta.

"The thing is," she continued, "when you're hauling cattle, beef on the hoof, you just can't stop all that fast. Oh, you kin step on your brakes all right, an they're good for about ten feet. Then the trailer with all them cows starts to move onto the tractor and there's nothing on earth that'll stop you then. Matt here, he's had one little accident . . ." Baby sniggered and poked Matt.

"That's right. I run over a nigger in Waco once."

"He didn't hurt him or anything," remarked Baby, seeing Loretta was unclear as to what to make of this. "This guy pulls out to turn. He was driving a beat-up ole Chevy and Matt runs him down. They didn't book us or anything. But they took the nigger's license away."

"Yup," cracked Matt with a self-satisfied glance at Loretta.

They saw Loretta was unmoved by their joke and Baby started in again. "I never knew I was going to drive a rig. Me and Matt, we was driving down the San Diego Freeway when he pulls over and sez, 'Alright, hon, it's your turn to drive.' That was it. It was five-thirty, rush hour." Baby laughed. "The boss's wife, she don't like me to drive. Sez a woman belongs at home, not out on the road taking good jobs from the men and their families. We git twenty-five percent of every haul. Matt gits thirteen percent and I git twelve. I'm second driver so I git less, but I git just what any man would git. There's some men out there that don't like a woman driving. They say we're taking food from their families, but those guys, they're always the ones complain about something anyway. An we gotta eat too . . ."

"Bitchin' an' gripin'. There's truckers that do nothing but bitch and gripe," put in Matt.

"We got us two hundred and forty acres over near Donna, Texas," said Baby proudly. "Last time we drove through town we didn't even git home. We was pickin' up a haul and had to make time . . . I sure do miss my cats, though. And the trailer we got there. But with all them Texas mice, they won't starve. An ole lady, she takes care of my baby girl. Matt here, he needs me on the road. We got loans to pay off."

They stood up to go and Loretta walked out to the rig, a stained old Kenworth lying slack-jawed with its head hung forward. Matt got out a flashlight and some tools and tinkered with something in the engine. Loretta could see there were rosebuds on the sheets in the sleeper. The bed was unmade. A fresh blue polka dot blouse hung behind the shotgun seat on a wire hanger. Shyly, Loretta pulled her eyes away from the intimacy of the cab.

They were hauling beef on the hoof, and while the girls stood and talked, Loretta heard the monotony of restless shuffling as the cattle, sensing slaughter, nudged one another for space.

"What about you, honey?" asked Baby, glowing with the antici-pation of the night on the long road ahead. She had her arm around Loretta's waist. "When are you gonna find a good man?"

"Oh, I don't know," answered Loretta, her eyes on the ground. "I'm working on it!"

"Well, so long," said Matt, standing off from her in the dark.

"So long, Matt."

She stood to one side, against the trailer, watching in the dark as the rig heaved out onto the road with one final blast of farewell. Loretta stood a moment longer, feeling the night. The tiny red eyes of a rig going somewhere flew past, and the highway dust blew up in an angry gust and then, spent, sifted back to earth.

78

CHAPTER 7

On the day of Mabel's forty-eighth birthday, Alexander gave her a party. She had never been asked to his house before. To tell the truth, though, she had seen the house. One night she and Viola had looked up his address in the telephone book, and, finding he lived in Snob Hollow, they had cruised the place.

Over the years Snob Hollow had disintegrated, and all that was left were the decaying remnants of pink stone walls being slowly devoured by clinging vines and sticky tendrils of night-blooming jasmine. Alexander's house, looming up out of the rotting forgotten ruins of the old Elysian Gardens, once so splendid and admired, sat forbidding and alone, a dying specter of the past, in what was now the shabbiest part of town. Withered, grey as an old woman, the house sagged with memories and the exhaustion of having outlived all her stately neighbors; she had been allowed to repine into gentle decline, remaining the last grande dame in a neighborhood of down-and-out Mexicans living in adobes.

"Gol-lee!" gasped Viola, gawking up at the house. "He can't be so all-fired rich, living up there in a big ole dump like that . . . get a load of the neighborhood! This place is spooky, that's what!"

She wanted to get out of the car and peek in the windows, but Mabel restrained her. "Oh, I don't know," mused Mabel, looking askance at the spoils of the neighborhood. "A house like that is mighty impressive . . . that's *old* money you're looking at there." All the same, she couldn't quite picture Loretta living there, Snob Hollow or not.

"Old money!" echoed Viola. "Phooey on old money! Money is money, ain't it? It's all green. I'd just as soon have me some new money and live up in the foothills in one of them condominiums, a split-level with a view . . ."

Mabel drew up a careful list of friends to be invited to the party. It galled her to invite Arlene Cook, so she sent all the other invitations out and when she saw Arlene at the Club, Mabel didn't say a word about the party. In an agony of suspense, Arlene awaited her invitation. Finally, when it did not arrive, she forced herself to go down to Feigenbaum's department store and buy an impressive crystal candy dish and present Mabel with it a whole week before her birthday. After that, Mabel relented and Arlene got her invitation.

The guests arrived at seven. For most of them, it was to be the social event of the year. Fred and Betty Rudd came, along with Alma Copechne, Loretta and Ralph (Orville never went out socially), the Cooks—including Arletta who was unasked—Sweetie Pie Ramòn with the Arkansas lover boy, and Mabel and Alexander. Twelve in all.

The group was disappointed when they saw the neighborhood Alexander lived in, but this was overcome as the inside of the house surpassed their most fertile imaginings. They came in wearing party clothes. Fred Rudd had on a frontier suit and he held his hat in his hands, uncertain whether or not to lay it down on one of the gleaming inlaid tables. The women all had on their best dresses and Arlene had dredged up a moth-eaten fur piece. "Where'd you find the pole cat!" cried Mabel, tickled to death by the beady-eyed faces dangling from Arlene's skinny neck.

Mabel was standing just inside the doorway receiving her presents in the gigantic entrance hall. Seeing her there, magnificent in royal blue, standing next to Alexander who looked so wonderful and important in a bottle-green smoking jacket, made Arlene want to tear her eyes out. Shy, the others came in shuffling their feet.

It wasn't a moment before Alexander had them feeling welcome and easy. He took the men into the library to show them his great-grandfather's gun collection, and Mabel did the honors with the ladies who were not quite so well behaved and scuttled through the house with prying eyes. Breathless, Viola came galloping up to Mabel and hissed, "I found her! I seen her picture!"

"What on earth are you talking about?" demanded Mabel, holding herself a bit more erect than usual.

"The girlfriend! The cousin . . . I seen her picture! She's not all that pretty . . ."

"Viola, if you've been snooping through Alexander's private possessions, I'll see to it you never set foot in this house again," admonished Mabel. All the same, before she left that night, she too managed to get a look at the photograph.

Alexander seated himself between Mabel and Loretta, and Mabel devoted herself, heart and soul, to the food on her plate; they had creamed shrimp with peas and then Marie, who served, brought in a whipped-cream cake. Every so often, beaming with pleasure, Mabel caught snatches of Loretta and Alexander's conversation. With a sense of infinite well-being she sat back in her chair feeling how good it all was. As she watched their easy rapport and sensed rather than heard the long fine pull of their words, hovering and circling like a flock of restless birds poised just over some satisfying conclusion, Mabel thought with thrilling gratitude that perhaps the scattered pieces of her life were beginning, at last, to fit nicely, edge to edge. Every so often Alexander reached over and, without glancing up or breaking the easy flow of his conversation, squeezed Mabel's hand as if in happy recognition of her pleasure.

Tonight however, it was Loretta to whom he gave most of his attention. They had been discussing the endless pull they each felt, that of needing to be a solution for those people who loved them, and, as they talked, Alexander leaned even closer to her as if to hear each word perfectly.

"The whole thing then," he continued, one eye on Fred Rudd's empty dinner plate, "is to make oneself available. Don't you see? To figure out what it is one does best and . . ." with barely a pause in his sentence he rang the little silver bell for Marie and requested more food for Fred, "then to make oneself available for the largest needs, for filling in the blank spaces with—with whatever it is one does best. All the rest, all that performing, makes one feel so used up and . . . weary."

"That's it," she agreed, feeling for the moment the sweet relief of being understood, "The weariness. Can you imagine Mama ever being *weary?*" she chuckled. They heard Mabel call out to Marie, "I'm not going to be the one to say no to them shrimp if you're passing them round again!" and, delighted with her own greediness, she scooped up what was left on the platter.

"I've seen her plenty tired," Loretta went on, "but weary, never. People who've gotten themselves a plan to get through life, well . . . they just seem to have all the vitality in the world."

"For people like you and me, a plan is so often a trap," Alexander sighed, smiling down the table at Alma and Sweetie Pie and motioning Marie to clear away the plates.

"But if a person has a plan," persisted Loretta, allowing Marie to remove her plate, which she had hardly touched, "he has a reason for being, don't you see?"

"Of course," he agreed. "The temptation has always been to invent reasons for whatever we do. To give ourselves credibility. But there is nothing so final as an answer or a solution, is there? There are really only possibilities . . ."

"It sounds so hopeless the way you put it," she protested, feeling, for the moment, angry with him. "Look at Mama there . . . Why, she has it all . . . the possibilities and the plans!"

"Yes, but then your mother has had the great impudence to create herself as she goes along. I don't believe she cares a fig for the usual sets of rules and guidelines. They never even existed for her. Or perhaps it is that she has had such a good time manipulating them." He smiled, trying to pull Loretta back from the edge of that great sadness he had so perfectly understood in her.

"My dear, if it will really comfort you, invent a formula. Find a prescription for getting by."

82

"You mean be busy," she answered, almost contemptuously.

"Busy is such a dreary word for indolent southerners like you and me," he went on, sidestepping her disappointment easily. "One really doesn't have to be violently dedicated and get frantic about living, you know. It's not like taking the veil or swearing eternal loyalty to the Nabisco Company . . . In the end, perhaps it is enough to do one or two well chosen things nicely, nothing awesome, mind you, and leave the grandstand plays up to the experts." He stopped, seeing her dissatisfaction. "Loretta, what do you feel you do best?"

Without pause, she answered, "Wait. I'm good at waiting. I've been waiting a long long time to find something I can do that will give my life a value."

"Oh, well, we all have to wait, I suppose." Involuntarily annoyed with her sincerity, with her displeasure showing itself here at his dinner table, he beckoned to Marie and she brought out the cake.

"Some of the best people we know, my dear," he went on, after a pause of some moments, "have chosen to run the race, and of course they are very smart and absolutely right; they know what suits them best. All that has only enhanced *their* lives . . . but it would be too cruel if you and I ran ourselves ragged in all the wrong races looking for misguided solutions and disappointing ourselves all so unnecessarily, don't you think?"

"Then it really is better to wait?" she prodded, turning her candid blue eyes on him. How she hated his exhaustion!

"I don't see that there really is a choice," he shrugged, understanding her perfectly. "But I would rather call that word, that awful word *wait* something else . . . maybe it's just being available, luxuriously available for endless possibilities . . ." He smiled at the thought. "What do you think?" he asked, waiting for her to release him.

It occurred to Loretta that waiting, that being available, as Alexander put it, for the endless possibilities, was a rich man's sport and she could not afford the game. In the next moment she clearly saw from his impeccable barrier of politeness that she had gone too far, that in demanding something absolute, an opinion, a conviction, she had trespassed on his own particular sense of order. Relenting, she said at last, "You *are* a good friend, Alexander, you do things so beautifully. You make the time pass so nice and easy, you make it an art, all the little ways of just being alive . . ." He squeezed her hand gratefully and stood to lead them all out into the garden.

They sat out where it was cool and dark trying to make the moments last as long as possible. Loretta, Mabel, Fred Rudd and Sweetie Pie sang Jimmy Rodgers railroad songs, Fred hooting and howling through his cupped hands so he sounded just like the old Cotton Bowl Special rolling down the line. It gave Mabel chills, hearing it, and she thought about all the small town nights and far-off trains passing through town, going somewhere, anywhere. She remembered being little, lying in bed with the covers pulled up, waiting in the dark to hear the long satisfying wail of the 9:10 as it flew through town. She cried a little, remembering.

Alexander sang "Crazy Arms" with Loretta and everyone applauded. Arlene prodded Arletta who then gave them a show of songs from "South Pacific." Afterwards, Alexander put on a Blue Danube Waltz record and, much to Mabel's horror, Arlene got up and, still clutching the polecat, joined Alexander in a fluttering demonstration of the waltz. Mabel was embarassed but everyone else seemed to love it. It was a night no one ever forgot.

*   *   *

Arlene's ability to dance touched on a sore spot in Mabel's heart. Six months before, people noticed the old Filbert Dry Cleaners was being fixed up and painted. Several days later the Filbert sign came down and a new one went up. It showed a man and a woman dancing. They looked very glamorous and people began to be curious. Mabel, living out at the Truckstop, was unaware of these new events in town until several weeks later, and by the time she found out, it didn't suit her dignity to take part in what was to follow.

There was great excitement in the following weeks. The building was painted canary yellow and large bold letters announcing, "Victor Armando Dance Club" went up over a marquee. Yet the place was shut up tight and nobody knew what to expect. Then a man came to town and put up posters of the dancing couple in the supermarkets, outside the YWCA and in the window of the Starlight Cafe.

Finally, Victor Armando himself came to town and the dance club was opened. Besides Mr. Armando there was a Mr. Rudy and a Miss Wanda. They gave away free fruit punch and doughnuts the first night even if you only came to watch. About ten women showed up. Arlene was one of them, and they sat in a row along the wall on gilded party chairs. When Mabel finally did hear about this new club she was sick to have missed out, but since by then it was Arlene's project, she held back and waited to see what would happen.

Both Mr. Armando and Mr. Rudy took turns dancing with Miss Wanda and they put on a fine show. The old dry cleaners' had been done up with a long slippery floor, mirrors and spot lights; crepe-paper flowers and curled streamers hung from the ceiling and there was a large cut-glass punch bowl with matching cups on a card table.

When it was Victor Armando's turn to dance with Miss Wanda they disappeared behind a screen in the corner. Mr. Rudy stood in the center of the room with a microphone and made a speech.

"Ladies and gentlemen!" (There were at present no gentlemen.) "It is with great pleasure that tonight I have the honor of presenting here in person, here in your beautiful town, the *great*, the *unique*, the *world famous* and the *renowned Victor Armando!*" (Small nervous applause.) "And ladies and gentlemen! May I also say it gives me equal pleasure to announce that here tonight we have in this very town the talented, the successful, the spectacular and the beautiful Miss Wanda making her debut . . ." Mr. Rudy gestured to the dark corner where all that could be seen were four feet sticking out below the screen. "Miss Wanda doing the Kon-Tiki rhumba!" Hearty applause from Mr. Rudy.

Suddenly a blinding blue spotlight focused on the corner. The screen gave a violent twitch and out leaped an apparition completely done up in scarlet glitter. Miss Wanda, who was about forty, had uncompromising red hair pulled back into a bouffant chignon which dangled uncertainly from a jeweled, fan-shaped peacock spray at the back of her head. A pinched ruby sateen heart-shaped bodice with jeweled straps flared into a fluttering tulle skirt, knee-length and embroidered with scrolls of silver, gold and jet sequins. Black stockings twinkled up the back seams with rhinestone butterflies, and on her feet Miss Wanda wore perilous open-toe scarlet high heels.

The ladies sighed with pleasure. Miss Wanda remained frozen, head back, leg thrust forward in a fascinating moment of suspense. A crescendo of drum beats announced Victor Armando, who came out dressed completely in black. He was wearing a very daring one-piece toreador jumpsuit, which took on a rubbery glistening look along his flat belly and tight round buttocks.

They did the rhumba and then it was Mr. Armando's turn to announce Mr. Rudy, and Miss Wanda came out from behind the screen once again and in a new outfit. The performance left most of the ladies feeling dowdy and unfulfilled, and they all signed up for one free lesson and the series of twenty lessons for three hundred ninety-nine dollars.

These lessons filled a deep void in the lives of the women. They began making waltz dresses and pretty soon rivalry began to ferment in the bosoms of old friends. Other ladies joined the club and several frightened husbands were brought forth to do their duty.

The dance club met on Friday night. Each of the ladies took a turn dancing with Victor Armando and Mr. Rudy. The rest of the time they paired off and practiced with one another. Miss Wanda coached the men. Once a month was guest night and a competition was held. The members each performed their specialty alone with either Mr. Armando or Mr. Rudy for the benefit of their friends.

The competition evenings were talked of and carefully plotted out for days in advance. Great secrecy was maintained as to costume, and friends took to dropping in on each other at unexpected hours. No amount of effort was spared the design and sewing of these costumes, and amazing creations appeared on women long past their prime. Rabbit fur was passed off as chinchilla; plumes, dyed velveteens, familiar sections of lace table cloths, dimestore jewelry—all these things were ingeniously employed in the determination to outshine one another.

With a pulse of drums the performer was announced and given

a chance to appear from behind the screen. Most of the women had never felt beautiful before. All alone with a tall gliding man, out there, swaying cool and blue in the light, the quiver of chiffon and there, beyond the long shining floor, envious eyes in the dark . . . how good that moment was!

The winner of the evening was presented with a silver ribbon. When she had won three silver ribbons she earned a bronze ribbon and after that came gold. No one had ever won a gold ribbon.

Mabel decided to take her first look at the Victor Armando Dance Club on the evening Arlene was to compete for her gold ribbon. Of all the women, Arlene was the most furtive and dedicated in the matter of creating a brilliant wardrobe. Interested neighbors had detected the steady whir of her sewing machine at all hours of the night. Ed had been shut out of his room and not even Arletta was allowed into the mysteries of her mother's toilette.

Now it just so happened that on Arlene's big evening her chief competitor for the gold ribbon was a dreadful woman named Rosina Richey. Arlene and Rosina had suffered a bitter friendship over the years. Rosina claimed to be one-eighth Cherokee and it was therefore understood that she had that fiery element in her blood which inspired a born dancer.

Rosina was not above tricking the judges. She knew how to swoon at the end of a waltz and she could make peculiar suggestive noises with her tongue and cheeks during the rhumba. These disturbing sound effects had been known to sway the judges. So it was with intrepid care that Arlene prepared herself for the big night.

Arlene had seen a current picture of Ginger Rogers wearing an all-white, one-shoulder Greek tunic dress with silver sandals. She made the same outfit for herself. This was a daring move because no one in town had seen a one-shoulder dress, nor had anyone appeared in public in anything so closely resembling a nightgown.

The ladies of the dance club all arrived in long capes clutched around their mystery attire. Several ladies performed to a spattering of applause. Then it was Rosina's turn to do the tango and she made a vivid entrance in a scarlet rayon cape.

Later, out at the Truckstop, Mabel told Doris the story this way.

"Well, all I can say is, it was an evening no one could ever forget
. . . There we were, sitting in the dark, watching Rosina all lit up
with search lights. She was wearing a long, sleazy-looking red
thing and standing there in an uncomfortable, bent-over position.
One of her legs was stuck way out in front and she was leaning way
back with her arm off to one side. I never saw anything so queer.
She looked like a great red bat. Next thing, this pounding jungle
music started up—it wasn't like any tango I ever heard before—
and Rosina whips off this red cape and threw it way up in the air.
Then there was a terrible scream. It was the most awful noise I
ever heard. Still makes my flesh crawl to think of it . . ." She
shuddered. "Before anyone knew what happened, there was a
streak of something white going by real fast in the dark. The next
I knew, the two of them were out there kicking and rolling on the
floor like savages . . . you couldn't tell who was who what with all
them arms and legs thrashing that way and the two of them
dressed identical in those white get-ups . . . looked like they was
wearing their nighties—least that's what we all thought—and
pretty soon they'd ripped and clawed at those dresses so bad there
wasn't all that much left to see . . . just two old women, half-nekkid
and mean as cats. The funny thing was those two so-called gentlemen." Mabel paused here with a grimace of disgust. Doris hung
on every word.

"The two fellas (no one had ever seen the likes of them before!)
flew around screeching like chickens with their heads cut off,
'Girls! girls! please!' Oh, what a sight. No one paid them any attention. You could see they was afraid of getting scratched to bits and
finally that other one, that Miss Wanda, came out and dumped a
bucket of water over them. Rosina stormed out of the dance club
but Arlene, poor thing, she just sat there on the floor and cried.
It was awful. Then Ed came up and took her home."

"What happened after that?" asked Doris breathlessly.

"By God, I have to hand it to old Arlene. She was back at the
club the very next week and she went on to take the first gold
ribbon."

"Well, how do you like that!" exclaimed Doris.

Not long after this, Mr. Armando told the ladies there was going
to be an inter-state dance contest between all the clubs. It was

going to be held in Las Vegas and he wanted all his ladies to come since each and every one of them had so much talent. The price for entering the contest and spending two days in a big Las Vegas hotel was seven hundred fifty dollars in advance. They were to pay down their money in one week and then they would qualify for a special three-week training course before the trip.

The ladies went home buzzing with excitement. There wasn't one of them, no matter how poor, who intended to miss out on that event. Some of them borrowed from the bank or withdrew their savings. All of them paid the money down. Many of them had never been as far as Las Vegas or even been out of the state.

A period of intense concentration began as everyone worked on costumes and new dance steps. One of the ladies was eighty-three and her neighbors got up a fund so she could have a new outfit and go. This was a time of great happiness for everyone. Arletta came over to the dance club and showed the ladies how to do makeup. No one was left out.

Then a terrible thing happened. Early on the morning of their scheduled departure all the ladies were to meet Mr. Armando, Mr. Rudy and Miss Wanda at the bus depot. Their husbands and children and some of the neighbors came down to see them off. Most of the ladies were wearing corsages. They waited a long time and the Las Vegas bus came and went but the dance instructors never showed up.

Then everybody went down to the dance club. The doors were locked so one of the husbands broke into the club. No one had ever been there in the daytime. The place smelled closed up and abandoned and there were squashed cigarette butts under the golden party chairs. The punch bowl and cups were gone. The whole place looked tired and sad.

Several days later people noticed the sign of the dancing couple was gone and someone had painted out "Victor Armando Dance Studio." A truck had come in the night and taken the chairs away and nothing was left of the club but some sagging crepe-paper party streamers.

CHAPTER 8

Not long after the demise of the dance club a special meeting of the A.A. regulars in the Club was called in order to discuss a matter of some importance. At that time the group consisted of Mabel and Ralph, Aléxander, Viola, Betty and Fred Rudd, Arlene and Ed Cook and Alma Copechne, and Sweetie Pie Ramòn.

Alma Copechne, like many converts to a cause, prided herself on a particularly onerous, sinister past which she never tired of juxtaposing to her miraculous salvation in A.A. There was no pathway into sin with which Alma had not admitted a passing acquaintance, and she referred to these past shortcomings as having brushed up against the fiery touch of the devil's wings. No one was more assiduous in attending the lurid details of another alcoholic's confession of torment and crime, or more vehement in asserting that her own transgressions were even more horrid.

During a particularly gruesome moment in a fellow sufferer's revelation, with her head slumped forward in ready sympathy, nodding, rolling almost, in compassion, Alma groaned, "Praise the Lord!" and this went a long way in reassuring certain new, timorous members of proper commiseration.

There were those in the group, old-timers by now, who were sick to death of Alma's unassailable position as purveyor of sin, but nonetheless she was accorded a certain respect. On this occasion she bustled into the meeting with no small sense of self-satisfaction, and as she dawdled over coffee and settled herself, the group awaited her news.

The best that could be said for Alma's physical presence is that she was square, platinum blonde, guilty and defensive about her weight, and that always, somewhere in the world, there will be a man who finds such a woman seductive. That Alma had certainly wrung out of a number of those men every possible last drop of lust or sympathy was there to be seen on her face as a warning to any unsuspecting survivors. Beyond that, she struggled at sixty to deserve some notice as "well-preserved."

"Now then," she began. "I suppose you all want my news and I'm not going to be mean enough to hold out on any of you . . . Some of you might be very interested to know I have found not one but two worthwhile gentlemen to join our group." Here she paused to eye the ladies who all looked away instantly and affected mutual disinterest. Ralph, Ed Cook and Fred Rudd, none of whom were remotely interested in the two mystery gentlemen, were left to ask for particulars.

"One of them is a fine young man," Alma leered at Viola who was the only female present under forty, "and he's just joined the program. He's a necktie salesman at Feigenbaum's. Arthur Smolen is his name and," she paused for a long moment, "he's single."

There was absolute silence. It had long been a source of chagrin to the ladies of the group that, except for Alexander and Ralph (neither of whom seemed romantically inclined toward anyone present), not one presentable unattached man had yet been found to enliven their familiar circle. Each of them allowed herself a rapid calculation as to the merits of this Arthur Smolen. Arlene imagined a prosaic solution to Arletta's celibacy. Mabel relished the potential intrigue and desired Arthur to fall madly in love with Viola. Obligingly, Viola indulged in a voluptuous shiver of anticipation. Betty Rudd and Alma Copechne visualized Saturday nights at the Buckskin and the hot young eyes of a well-dressed admirer. Sweetie Pie hoped he was rich.

"The other person," continued Alma, who was reluctuant to part with this last morsel, "is a distinguished widower. His name is Harold Fimbers, he's a man of about fifty and there is no doubt about it, he's well-heeled. Mary Helen Morris says he owns a bank in Witchita and wears custom-made shoes."

Very few women can hear so satisfactory a description of a man, a man singled out as desirable by other women, and remain unmoved by his existence. They all agreed to admit the newcomers to their group immediately. The meeting was adjourned and each of them went off with her own particular friend to discuss this wonderful situation in depth. Mabel, Ralph, Viola and Alexander went to meet Loretta at the Truckstop Cafe and Arlene, Ed and the Rudds went to the Flamingo for coffee. Alma and Sweetie Pie went to the Stardust Cafeteria.

Once before, Alma had produced a single man for the benefit of the group. His name was Bud Cecil and, originally a construction worker, he had arrived at the first meeting with his swarthy, hairy belly hanging out from under his T-shirt and clods of mud on his shoes. Mabel and Arlene had viewed him straight off with disgust but Viola, unfortunately, had found him magnificent. At the very first meeting, as each member was introducing himself in the familiar manner ("Hello, I'm Mabel and I'm an alcoholic . . ."), Bud had said, "Hello, I'm Bud the Stud and I like my women sunny side up." It had taken them six months to rid the group of Bud and Alma never would admit he was all that bad.

A week later the next meeting was held. The two new gentlemen were introduced. Their appearances augured well. Arthur Smolen, although highly nervous and somewhat sweaty in the palm, was decidedly well dressed, and if his taste indicated a preference for the latest in department-store leisure suits, it was not a disadvantage in this group. He was wearing a brand-new waffle-textured beige suit with treated suede patches stitched onto the elbows and lapels of his jacket and onto the back pockets of his pants. His shoes were beige patent leather with dark brown stitching and chunky elevator heels. The suit was admired and Arthur acknowledged it was by Donalure, which seemed impressive enough, even if no one was quite sure who Donalure was.

Arthur was of medium height and slight build. He had a pleasant face. Naked, stripped bare of his finery, he would stand a good chance of going unnoticed. His most distinguished feature was a glorious mound of hair which had been artfully persuaded into a side sweep. He had an obliging smile and seemed reluctant to put himself forward. He was one of those men most often described as a "young man," although if the facts were to be known, he was forty-two.

Harold Fimbers was of more uncertain ilk. Probably sixty-five, he was distinguished, tractable, subdued. Since they had been told he was rich, Harold did indeed appear rich and thus what was an ordinary suit took on the proportions of a very fine suit, and his shoes, however outwardly simple, appeared costlier than other shoes. Mabel, it must be confessed, felt some disappointment that Harold Fimbers was not more conspicuously grand, and privately considered Alexander, or even Ralph, far more prepossessing.

Worn, soft in the eye and florid of complexion, Harold was entirely sympathetic. The men felt comfortable with him, although he was far too reticent in the first weeks to do more than distinguish himself with the ladies by a gentle appreciation of their costume and a modest, courtly behavior. He would no doubt have been amazed to recognize in himself the thrilling source of avid speculation within the bosoms (in some cases, the very withered ones) of his present female companions.

It wasn't until after the first three meetings that the ladies concerned could be quite sure neither of the new gentlemen had as yet shown a discernable preference for any one woman in the group. Speculation ran wild and interesting interpretations were placed on whatever hapless gesture was detected by the Argus-eyed onlookers.

Harold sank for one week in the general estimation of those who misconstrued his pleasure in Arlene's china coffee cup, only to be revived the following week when he was fortunate in noticing Mabel's new diamond ring.

Arthur, by now Arty behind his back, was considered crafty and utterly careless of Viola's feelings. Beyond a tolerably civil regard for Viola, he cannot be said to have returned her awakened passion or even to have noticed it, and in this way the women decided Arty was an adventurer. Somehow, behind that innocuous façade, lechery was detected, and unbeknownst to Arty he became a villain and a hero in barely three weeks.

Viola was set up as the fatted calf. She was taken to the Pocahantus Beauty Parlor and coiffed and to the Rose Petal and gowned, and Mabel put her on a diet. She devoted her lunch hour to chauffering Mabel to Feigenbaum's for innumerable small purchases and aimless meandering past the tie department.

Arlene had coaxed the bewildered Arty to her house for several unproductive dinners. She had plied him with obscure Cook family recipes to no avail. Stupefied by Arletta's glacial beauty, he had eaten in silence and, glutted, slunk home directly after coffee. Alma and Betty had taken him dancing and paid the bill. Still, Arty refused to make a move.

Six weeks later Viola had been driven off her diet by unrequited love and was violently eating to make up for lost time. New Year's Eve was approaching and Mabel decided to take the bull by the horns.

"Some of us are going up to the Musicade in Tucson for New Year's Eve. We got reservations." Mabel had cornered Arty in the tie department at Feigenbaum's. Arty looked wary. "What are your plans, Arthur?"

"Oh, not much, I guess. That is, I'm not sure at the moment."

"Well, then! It just so happens we need an extra man for a beautiful woman who's coming along."

"Who is it? Is it Viola?"

"What a sly one! As a matter of fact, it *is* Viola, although she's been asked out by a couple of other guys and has no idea I'm asking you. Why don't you surprise her and come along to the Musicade . . . we'll pick you up; we'll all go together."

"As a matter of fact, I told someone I'd be around that night. I remember it now. An old friend."

"Arty, I'm going to ask you something, something personal, and you don't have to answer me if you don't want to." Mabel speared Arty with a penetrating Granma Watkins look. Arty busied himself with the tie rack.

"Now, Arty, all I want to know is, do you have a preference for Viola or not. I'm not saying you have to or even that there is anything wrong with you if you don't . . ." Here, her eye fell with some disgust on a delicate young man of undetermined sexuality fussing with the mens' undergarments at the next counter. "It just seems to me all this shillyshallying around between you and Viola is unnatural if you know what I mean . . ."

Arty looked away. "Oh, my God. Now listen, Mabel, Viola's okay. I mean, she's just fine as far as that goes, but . . . well, the thing is I'm in love with somebody else. All right, I'll take Viola on New Year's Eve," and he turned away from her angrily, but he was frightened all the same.

Mabel was charming to him but could barely conceal her triumph. She patted Arthur in a fond, forgiving farewell and rushed off to gird Viola for conquest.

"Hah!" said Alma, several weeks later and after an abortive attempt to line Arthur up for herself on New Year's Eve. "So you've snared the little pipsqueak for yourself, have you!" "Wouldn't you like to know!" was all Mabel had to say. Just that day Arlene, knowing full well that Arthur was committed to Mabel, had put pressure on him to spend New Year's Eve with the Cook family.

But Mabel held firm and at last the promised evening arrived. Arthur showed up, sullen and yet resplendent in a shiny peacock-blue dinner jacket. Hollow-cheeked from dieting, Viola appeared. With a shudder, Arthur saw that she had wedged herself into a black net fishtail dress. Her heaving blue-veined breasts wobbled under the diaphanous net, and Arthur, who suspected just enough about the intimacies of female lingerie, knew she was wearing a Merry Widow corset for the occasion.

This brutal, constrictive item had given the unfortunate Viola an unusual shape; all loose flesh had been pushed either above or below the corset into a blubbery sausage roll. (Halfway through the evening she removed the Merry Widow in the ladies' room and all the flesh sank.) Arthur abandoned himself for a few gloomy moments to plans for escape. Nevertheless, the party proceeded to the Musicade.

Few things are more exciting to a country person than driving down the long highway through the desert on a bottomless black night, coming up so suddenly from out of the inky void and around the looming mountain into the lights. City lights! Reckless as a carnival beckoning with promises, spinning out a million tiny diamonds strung across the valley. And the valley, bewitched by night, hung now in a wonderful suspense between the mountains and the sky, jeweled and cloaked in a thrilling deception of gorgeous black finery.

Mabel loved the glitter of night, small-town nights. She knew the shadows in the doorways and who was home for supper as, hooded now, with shades drawn down and glowing yellow, houses pulled into themselves against the night. Without ever needing to think about it, she knew how many bulbs were burnt out in the old Fox theater marquee and the last time Baker's and Lerner's had changed their window displays, and she knew the weary faces in the Greyhound bus depot just from passing by, time after time, late at night.

Living out there in the middle of nowhere, in a place like the Truckstop where nothing ever changed, where it seemed like nothing was ever going to happen, she felt that the road to town was as seductive and unfulfilling as an old unresolved love affair. It had been years, if ever, since Mabel had seen that road as it really was. The simple fact that it led somewhere else, that it left a way open to other possibilities was enough; Later, when it came time to go home, back to the Truckstop, if she was dissatisfied she never showed it; that was just the other part of life, going home, the price one had to pay for having fun.

Full of excitement, they pulled up at last in front of the Musicade, a small hatbox of a building tucked in between a sprawling grey asphalt Woolco and Gonzalez Fish Market. A pink electric sign blinks "ROD'S MUSICADE," fades, and then flashes a tilted champagne glass with three lit-up bubbles. Nothing in the simple façade prepares you for what lies within. Groping in the dark entryway, the foursome made their way into the room, which was moist with air-conditioning and black as a cave.

Batlike, they sensed rather than saw their whereabouts and, bumping against bodies in the dark, found their way to a reserved table.

"Oooooh, isn't this something!" exuded Viola, nudging Arthur with something too soft to be a knee.

They ordered their drinks from a faceless voice in the dark. The waitress was wearing dangling lantern earrings which flickered red lights from a battery within. Viola wanted a Grasshopper but Mabel ordered coffee for her. In the next moment a surprising

96

thing happened. While no lights went on, everything white in the room lit up. Dazzling rows of teeth, eyeballs and certain shirt fronts stood out in the dark all over the room. It was a wonderful sight, a great trick, and everyone loved it. One lucky woman had worn a white dress and she wriggled with pleasure and guffawed as the light picked her out.

A voice announced *"Rod!"* and all the lights went on. There was a gasp of wonder and pleasure. The room was entirely hung with icicles, cold and silvery, clear, wet and plastic; they hung from the midnight-blue ceiling reflecting the magic light of a thousand winking stars; they oozed from the bar, the bottles, the doorways and the drinks. The entire room trembled, wet and light, as soft and moist as spindrift in the innards of a paperweight.

Rod came out. He was small, quiet as a lizard, embroidered and jeweled from head to toe. His hard little eyes watched the crowd. Against one wall an awesome organ was laid out and waiting in ceremonial splendor. The tiny man clambered up onto a stool and began to play. Fingers, hands, feet, elbows—all these things were used, although never once did Rod glance at the keyboard that curled around him on three sides. Thumping at levers hidden on the floor, tweaking buzzers and buttons, slapping his thighs, still Rod kept his cool marble eye fixed on the gaping crowd. Unmoved by their ecstasy, unbearably still within his own motion, he drove and pounded on and on, playing every request, *The Flight of the Bumble Bee, Ramona, Begin the Beguine, Onward Christian Soldiers, Hawaiian Love Call,* polkas, csardas. There was nothing he couldn't play.

Each song had a visual motif. The levers and bells, the keyboard itself triggered a kinetic jiggling and clacking all over the room as castinets, marimbas, tambourines and other noise-makers leaped to life from hidden lookouts on the walls. Clever disguises, such as navels, breasts and mule buttocks were employed in a terrifying cacophony and the audience was wild-eyed and greedy in their discovery of each new trick. Women shrieked their pleasure and some were afraid.

The consummation of the evening came with *Tiny Bubbles,* an old favorite from Hawaii. The flap in the ceiling released hundreds of tiny pink bubbles to the wonder of everyone, and then suddenly it was over and Rod was gone.

"I never saw anything so beautiful," sobbed Viola, who held to her seat, hoping for more. Arthur, exhausted and moved in spite of himself, looked about the room and was spotted and hailed by a man.

"Hey there, Rhett! Some show!" Arthur looked away.

"Who was that?" demanded Mabel. "Why'd he call you Rhett?" Arthur shrugged.

"Must've taken me for someone else. I don't know."

No one said much on the way home. Viola was too wasted to plan a technique for arousing Arthur and he was far too intrepid to allow even an accidental encounter of knees in the murky confines of the back seat. After the long drive, the four of them parted, almost disgruntled from so much excitement.

In the weeks that followed, Mabel endeavored to arrange get-togethers for Viola and Arthur, but the gentleman was elusive. He began to time his arrival at the Club meetings so that he could sit next to a different lady each week, and in this way he worked his powers on them all. Just as Viola despaired of ever being the chosen one, Arthur seemed to seek her out, and, pulling his chair next to hers, he'd whisper and tell her traveling salesman jokes. But then the next week he was distant and she imagined he was whispering about her with Arlene.

In this period, Arthur's popularity was enormous, although no one seemed to like him much. He had a way of patting the men on the back and saying, "Well, old boy, how's tricks?" and with the women he was conspiratorial, setting one woman against the others in crafty ways. When he sat with Mabel he referred to Alma as "the old warhorse" and Arlene as "her serene highness Madame Icky-Poo," Betty Rudd was "Tittle-Puss", Sweetie Pie was "Heart-Throb, Madame Virgin" and Viola was "Miss Viola." However, behind Mabel's back, Viola was "Wet-lips" and Mabel was "Goldie the Boss Lady."

It was largely Arthur who was responsible for Harold Fimber's loss of prestige within the group. Arthur began to refer to him as "Ancient Flatbottom" and said he had called Witchita only to find they had never heard of him there. Furthermore, he suspected

Harold's shoes were only Wallabees and the custom-made suits a sham, since Feigenbaum's had never carried such merchandise.

"If old Flatbottom is so rich, why does he always wear the same suit, and why hasn't he changed his socks?" Arthur pressed up against Arlene's ear. "I called Witchita and he's overdrawn there. There's something funny about that man, you'll see. He's a weirdo."

Arlene peered at Harold and perceived small, disturbing gestures for the first time. He kept his hands in his pockets too much and wore a diamond pinky ring that, seen in a certain light, appeared to be a zircon.

Harold, who in the first meetings had been treated with great deference, began now to be shunned slightly except by Mabel, Alexander, Ralph and Fred Rudd, who regarded him kindly. If he knew he was being maligned in other quarters, he bore it with touching dignity and humility. Since he never referred to his finances, it was eventually assumed he had none at all, and even those few who refused to believe ill of him were distressed to see that in fact he wore only that one suit and the same socks and shoes, week in and week out.

Harold talked of himself, of course, in a retiring way in the weekly confessionals, but all that was learned from the man himself was that his wife of thirty years, Mary Lou Fimbers, had given him five wonderful daughters and had died of a tragic inflammation of some kind. It was then that Harold took to drink and, full of shame and heartache, he left a comfortable situation and the doting daughters in Witchita to bury himself in an obscure western town.

"Haven't you ever heard of the eccentric rich?" Mabel protested one night in response to Arthur's latest diatribe against Harold. "One man I heard about was so rich he could buy and sell Texas and he used to have the hired help peel down the paper napkins so's he could get four napkins out of one. Then there's Sid Fanning, who owned Green Pastures Funeral Parlor. He made his wife save the dirty dishwater and use it again and look how rich he is. This Harold Fimbers, I'll bet he's one of your eccentric rich, and he refuses to change his socks just so's we'll think he's poor."

"He don't fool me," said Arthur hotly. "I've known plenty of rich people. They *smell* rich, for one thing; it shines right out of their eyes and sooner or later they let you know *who* they are. We've got people come into Feigenbaum's that'll drop two hundred dollars in colognes in ten minutes and they'll turn around and buy twenty ties, cash down on the spot, and then head for the suit department and walk off with suits they don't even try on. Mr. Leroy, he's my boss, he fired a guy just the other day for not noticing this dude's shoes. This grubbylooking type came up to the jewelery counter and wanted to see something nice he said, for his lady friend. Well, the guy who got fired, Randy, he pulls out the tray of five-to twenty-dollar stuff, you know, the imitation goods, and this crummy-looking dude got all insulted. Mr. Leroy fired Randy on the spot. Told Randy he should've looked at the guy's boots before he pulled out the nickle-and-dime tray. The guy was wearing white lizard-skin boots, *real* lizard, and they had rubies and emeralds going right up the side. Now there's your eccentric rich."

"We'll see," Mabel didn't like giving in too easily. Arthur, who enjoyed talking about himself in the weekly revelations, was spared the more penetrating probes of his companions. They were afraid of his powerful tongue and drew back from open assault. Then too, none of the others were as inclined to suspect such vagaries of character in Arthur as he was able to create for others.

He confided a touching history. The name Smolen came from the faraway town of Smolensk, where one of his forefathers had founded an entire city. (Arthur never referred to this illustrious personage as noble, but without a doubt each listener drew explicit conclusions of grandeur.) His grandfather, Gregory Smolenski, had as a baby been smuggled out of Russia in an attaché case and abandoned on the savage shores of Maine after a nauseating sea voyage in the confines of a mackerel trawler. This Gregory Smolenski had grown into a giant of a man, hirsute and ferocious, in the wilds of Maine where he lived off gooseberries and elk meat. A lumberjack by trade, Gregory evidently distinguished himself by being the only white-skinned man in those parts who had wrassled with a grizzly bear and ingratiated himself with a vicious pack of wild wolves.

Arthur went on to declare that Gregory, actually known as "Wolf" Smolenski, had one time ripped a lumberjack's arm right off his body in battle and (here the story grew murky and less

100

precise) was known to have descended on his mother's side from Attila the Hun, also known as the "Turk Eater."

Mabel took a good long look at Arthur during this narrative, and for the life of her all she could see was a hundred-thirty-five-pound tie salesman from Feigenbaum's.

The present-day Smolens were decent, God-fearing folk. Arthur's father was an "import-export" magnate in Bangor, Maine and his mother, an artistic woman, was according to Arthur a concert pianist. Then Arthur's story took on more personal overtones. At fourteen he was found in a compromising position with the most beautiful woman in town, a Miss Inez Merriweather, thirty years old. (The women of the group eyed one another and nodded knowingly.) Then at sixteen he had tried to elope with his cousin Missy. Found in a Seetawket motel, they were pried apart, whereupon Arthur, grief-stricken and thwarted, found himself seduced into a sex-ring of aging housewives who preyed on disappointed young boys.

A sadistic bully of a town sheriff had set a trap for the depraved Arthur, found him fornicating with his wife and tied him to an elm tree where he was publicly horsewhipped. "Praise the Lord!" moaned Alma, who was thrilled to the core by Arthur's trials. Then it was no wonder he had sought out the solace of drink. Drunk, debauched, he left his hometown and the ravishing Missy for whom he still bore an awful love. And that's how he got to Feigenbaum's.

This history was better than anyone could have hoped for on first seeing the mild-mannered Arthur. Arlene, who squirmed horribly over such words as sex-ring and the nasty images conjured up in consequence, was nonetheless reaffirmed in her desire to have the interesting young man carry off her Arletta. Ed Cook wasn't quite sure. In Viola's eyes, Arthur held more fascination than Jack the Ripper or even the Arkansas Axe Murderer, long an unrivaled source of brooding obsession in her fantasy life.

A dim yearning for unspecified carnal pleasures was awakened even in Sweetie Pie, who had "gone along" with a number of men but maintained that as long as she had refused to enjoy "it" she was unsullied and innocent. Alma, Betty and the gentlemen present all viewed Arthur with varying degrees of admiration and distaste, and in this way he remained a hero. Mabel alone was singularly unmoved by his story and she began to view Arthur as devious.

At about this time, Bud the Stud reappeared. Part of the inherent nature of this group was that although it was particular and exclusive about not encouraging any plain old Tom, Dick or Harry to join it, anyone interested enough to need its services and companionship was welcome. So when Bud walked in one Friday night he was accorded his old place within the group, however grudgingly.

It didn't take Bud long to see how the land lay. He saw Arthur was bloated with power. Bud set about showing Arthur he had spotted his type. From the beginning, Arthur was frightened of Bud but hid these feelings by appearing disdainful and aloof, leaving Bud to look ornery and low.

One night, about a month after Bud had rejoined the Club and six months after Arthur had established tenure, Arthur was regaling the group with further impassioned details of his doomed love for Missy. Bud was cleaning his fingernails with a toothpick.

"And so," continued Arthur in a swollen voice, "Missy was sent off to Australia to live with this older man, her uncle. He was forty years older than her, ugly as sin . . . I think he was deformed, and of course she was forced into marrying him." He shuddered.

There was a sigh from the group and then Bud, brandishing the soiled toothpick said, "Ever hear of Buster Damiecki?"

"I can't say that I have," condescended Arthur.

"Well, this Buster Damiecki, he's a particular friend of mine. He's three times the size of you. Wears a size thirteen shoe."

Arthur flicked a spec from his immaculate fawn trousers and yawned discreetly.

"Yup," continued Bud who lodged the toothpick into a toothy crevice, "nobody fools around with Buster Damiecki. He weighs in at two-eighty and drives a Peterbilt." Bud sucked a morsel from the toothpick.

"Well, who in hell wants to hear about Buster what's his name?" sulked Sweetie Pie. "We was hearing about Arty and Missy."

"Now hold on, toots," said Bud. "This Buster is from Bangor, Maine."

"So?"

"Buster had a run up that way just last week. Says he knows

Bangor real well. Never heard of no Arthur Smolen or anyone calling hisself Wolf Smolenski . . ."

"Who cares!" grumbled Alma. "You don't suppose folks the likes of these Smolens would know some greasy trucker, do you? You got your nerve coming in here all suspicious, sitting there like a big fat slob. It's indecent, that's what."

"Okay, Mom, calm down now. I ain't going to say another word till Buster gits back from his next run through Bangor, Maine."

Arthur smirked, but two people in the room were not fooled by his triumph. True to his word, Bud sat out the meeting in silence but he watched Arthur all the same. Mabel kept her eye on Bud and Arthur and she saw Arthur was scared.

"I've been thinking," she said that night over coffee to Viola, who sat dreamy-eyed and remote in a corner booth at the Stardust. "There's something fishy about that Arthur Smolen."

"Mabel!"

"Now listen a minute, Viola. I've done you wrong about that boy and I feel bad about it. Even that Bud Cecil is a better type than Arty." She paused. Viola was jabbing at a grapefruit half in a desultory, rebellious manner.

"I think he's cute, Mabel. He's got more class than any man I ever met and one of these days . . . well, if I lose thirty pounds and he forgets that Missy, then . . . he's the man for me!"

"Viola, have you ever met an honest-to-God degenerate?"

"You mean like Bud Cecil?"

"No. I do not mean like Bud Cecil . . . Bud's an uncouth pig of a man but he's no degenerate. I mean a real weirdo. Someone like Fatty Arbuckle."

"You mean someone like the Enema Bandit!" Viola was given to reading the crime column of the newspaper and had only the month before discovered a small paragraph about the Enema Bandit, a deviate who crept into lonely ladies' homes and after wrestling them to the floor and tying them up, proceeded to give them an enema.

"Not exactly. But that will do for starters. I mean a degenerate. Someone with *unnatural* habits."

"Oh, that," tittered Viola. "Everyone knows about that."

Mabel was not exactly sure what Viola was thinking of since, with all the utterly candid revelations of their group, no one had ever discussed or so far shown a predilection for what Mabel considered bestial, unnatural acts. These things were not discussed among her people and so, leaving Viola to her own mystified suppositions, she said, "At least I've pointed it out."

"What?" demanded Viola who was far less reticent about details.

"You know what. Just watch out. I've got my suspicions about that Arty. No point in saying more and I could be wrong. But you'd be better off looking elsewhere and that's a fact."

Nothing Mabel had said sank into Viola. Although she idolized Mabel, at moments Viola despaired of understanding so refined and genteel a brain, and not wanting to appear unworthy of this flattering friendship, she suppressed any dissension or confusion. She could only suppose Mabel had taken a delayed offense at Arthur's graphic accounts of Wolf Smolenski. There was admittedly some small confusion about the exact nature of his domestic dealings with that pack of wolves, and dwelling with uncertain pleasure on the subtleties of this matter, her mind all confused with the mating habits of wolves and exerpts from the crime column, she forgave Mabel's message.

At the very next meeting, a surprising thing happened. Arty arrived in a cowboy shirt and Levi's. Granted, the shirt was new and the Levi's, freshly laundered and pressed, were worn too high in the waist to be convincing, but all the same, his appearance was startling.

"Get a load of Tex Ritter!" Bud guffawed. He stalked Arty and whistled appreciatively. "Hubba Hubba Ding Ding!"

"Aw, cut it out, you big wart hog," said Alma, who saw Arty was dismayed.

Arthur offered Bud a Lucky Strike. Everyone there knew Arthur smoked True's but no one said anything. The meeting began with a very courteous request from Arthur to hear Bud's point of view on a matter, and then Alexander led Bud into telling something of himself.

"There isn't a whole lot to tell," Bud said simply. "I started out on the road ten years ago. That's when I was seventeen. My folks was dead and gone . . . I'd seen them buried down there in Missouri. Ma, she had blood in her lungs and then, after she died, Pa went, too. My brother Pete was doing time and the little one, Cindy, she run off. Matt, my other brother, was killed in the threshing machine, so Jimmy, he's my kid brother, he and I set off to work the railroad. We made good money. But Jimmy, he was always cold, he was a skinny kid. Didn't weigh much more'n one-twenty, but he did the work of two grown men all the same. Anyway, we came out west where Jimmy could git warm. He died just the same. Blood in the lungs. I worked on the road some and then a trucker comes along and teaches me gear-jamming . . . I'm working construction now so's I can buy my own rig. Out there on the road, things got lonely. First I started in with Wacky Tobaccy. Then it was hooch and bennies. I did it just to get by, just to get through them long nights. Well, there you are, that's my story."

There was a moment of thoughtful silence. Everyone in that room had heard that story or one just like it. They were all of them people of the land who had known hard winters and gone off on their own to make a life somewhere. There wasn't much to say, after all, about a story like Bud's. It was too close to the way life really was and they felt cheated. Most of them remembered the smell of death on the kitchen mattress. They had all lost someone and then gotten away; they were the survivors. Even Alexander, unique as he was in a group of people who had all known the compromises and humiliations of poverty, even he qualified as a kindred soul; without ever having been poor or hungry for food he knew exactly how it felt; he was able in his conscience and deep within his body to ache with the degrading loneliness of real hunger gone unappeased.

Arthur, the outsider, was the first to speak. "Well now Bud, that sure was a sad story!"

Bud glared him down. "If I wanted your pity, you little twerp, I wouldn't be here, Jesus!"

"I only wanted to say something nice. I like you," Arty whined.

"I bet you do . . . Christ!" Bud rammed his chair back and left the room. For him, Arty was an open, oozing sore.

"What'd I do wrong?" But nobody could explain something so simple to an outsider like Arthur. Even Harold Fimbers in this moment was clearly one of them, and he patted Arthur's arm and shook his head by way of explanation, but Arty shrugged him off,

105

too ashamed for consolation. The meeting ended on a cheerless note and most of them went off on their own without offering to join up for coffee.

Alexander drove Mabel back to the Truckstop. As considerable as the drive was, almost ten miles from town, he treasured the ritual, their weekly drives to and from A.A. Always, when he arrived to pick Mabel up at the Truckstop, she was on time and filled to bursting with the latest news. Mostly this had to do with her arch enemy, Maurice Beamus, land baron, truckstop tyrant, Mussolini himself over there in the grease palace, or worse, Maurice the lover, that 'ole dirt, that flap-doodle of a pathetic wrinkled rooster; who in hell does he think he is anyway! *Cesar Romero?* (Cesar Romero was It for Mabel. Later, and very grudgingly, she turned him out to pasture, but only when Anthony Quinn was found as a suitable substitute.)

Tonight, however, Mabel was worried about Loretta, and the conversation took on a more melancholy tone. Mabel had discovered, while laying down a fresh pile of papers in a corner of the pool room, so, as she put it, "my dogs kin be comfortable while I'm out galavantin' around," that holes had been cut out on the jobs wanted page. As if this weren't alarming enough, Mabel saw Loretta getting peaked, thin and sulky.

"I don't know what to think," she complained to Alexander, her wary eye glued to the road as they pulled up onto the ramp at the entrance to I10. She waited a moment, feeling his tension as he jockeyed the car, an unusual looking Alfa Romeo, one of the rare 1963 Guilia SS's, sleek as a cat, into the dim narrows between two heaving, barreling rigs. The noise was deafening. Full of the chase and feeling the gearshift pulse, almost spasm in his hand, Alexander urged the Alfa into third and then fourth; trembling, reluctant, the car held the road and then leaped to the lead. Alexander slid into fifth, taking the road in triumph.

"Anyway," continued Mabel, "what more does a girl want? She's got all the pocket money a person needs, she's got food in her belly, space to move around in, she's got a daddy who dotes on her even if he ain't worth more than a plug nickle, the ole goat; she's got family. She's got me, she's a McPheeter, she's got background and respectability for Lord's sake which is more than most people have got at twice her age. She's got an education, too. And a clean start with nothing owed. What I couldn't have done with that kind of a free ticket!" she sighed. Alexander tried to soothe her but she would have none of it.

As a rule Mabel avoided what she called depressing topics: age, death, ailments, money problems, tax deals and one's own marriage and sex life. These things simply were not discussed. Not only were they all very dark secrets to be dealt with in private, but as far as she was concerned, no person of any dignity, with even one iota of self-respect, had any business exposing things best kept in the dark. Success was what she liked to talk about. Success and gossip, alluring tidbits from other peoples' lives, these were the meat and potatoes of Mabel's conversation.

"Don't you think Loretta is just like the rest of us," ventured Alexander. "Maybe she needs a certain amount of suffering in order to support, to afford really, all that happiness, all those good things you and Orville have given her. Maybe she's searching out her own personal momentum."

"No," Mabel replied morosely, groping for a cigarrette in her crystal bead bag. "She's different from most people; that's the truth. Why, if my mama had offered me a new gown right out of the blue, I'd a snatched it up so fast it'd make your head spin! Loretta, she just hung her head and said, 'What'll I do with a new gown, Mama?' And she's full of little secrets . . . It makes me shiver, without knowing why, like when a twister's coming; you know, when something dreadful is coming your way but then nothing seems to happen and you just wait and wait . . ."

"Secrets!" he hooted. "Look who's talking!"

"Oh, well," she cackled, pleased. "At least I had something to hide."

"You're a sly one, Mabel. Your whole life is a well-armed fortress of conveniently forgotten facts and beguiled truths and irresistible realities you've seduced around to your way of thinking. Secrets!"

"I don't suppose there's anything more boring than the plain ole unimbellished truth, is there, Alexander?" He felt her smile in the dark. Signs for Benson Bisbee Tombstone Wilcox Douglas flew past. He felt the road pull; if I just follow the white lines, he thought, dreaming a little.

"Ah, you," he sighed, full of admiration. "You, of course, are free to go right on creating yourself. There are no limitations for you, not really. I am bound hand and foot to a dreary need for order which I inherited along with the family silver . . ."

"Foo!" she cried angrily. "Excuses! I sure wish I knew what good can come from taking yourself so serious all the time. You and Loretta both. Thinking, all the time making yourselves miserable by thinking. Why, I'd like to know one single thought either one of you ever had that could beat just plain ole getting things done!" she spat out.

"It's a disgusting need," he admitted. "Maybe that's why I like to warm myself near you, near your vitality, that extraordinary inner . . ."

"Watch it!" she growled, indignant. He pulled up alongside her trailer. "You think you can get me out here in the desert to talk dirty . . . Hah!" They laughed. "Will you talk to her?" Mabel asked him. "Yes," he said, following her inside.

Loretta had been waiting for them. Surprising even herself, she pretended to be engrossed in a book. Alexander came up behind her and, placing a hand on her shoulder, leaned across to see what it was that held her so rapt and pale. Loretta flung the book face-down onto the coffee table, bypassing his kindly, inquiring glance. Mabel, however, shooed them out of the trailer almost before Loretta knew what happened.

"You're cold," said Alexander, taking off his old tweed jacket. She allowed him to place it on her shoulders, but as the warm inner silk of the jacket brushed against her cool bare arm she felt that, far from a comfort, the jacket was a weighty presence unexpectedly intimate and confusing. Alexander's smell, manicured and fine like a green field of lettuce, a winter garden, clean and cared for, so surprised her that as they walked across the long dark lot, picking their way between the rigs toward the iridescent blue-white of cafe lights, Loretta felt unbearably shy.

Sensing the odd, uninvited presence of a new feeling come between them, like some tiny lewd invasion of an old, carefully guarded honor, Alexander talked to her of simple things until at last, with coffee cups pushed aside and the comfort of the cafe their easy ally, he turned their talk inward. It wasn't long before she told him that she had recently applied for four jobs, had been hired for each of them and yet, without ever actually beginning work and sickened by her own uncertainty, had quit each job.

"Then, it's not the acceptance you want," he said. She shook her head.

"No. I know that. What I want is a good reason to get up out of bed in the morning," she answered, her eyes off somewhere.

"Ah, that," he replied, without energy.

"Tell me," she asked, looking him in the eye for the first time that evening. "Did Mama ask you to talk to me?" Without waiting for his careful answer, she shook her head angrily. "God, I'm sick of being observed. I'm sick of good intentions and . . ." she broke off. "Anyway, you are *her* friend . . ."

Stung, he said, "I thought you and I . . ." He let it hang, feeling for the first time her infinite dissatisfaction. Dissatisfied women, he thought, and in that moment old thoughts of Eunice and Lily, his mother, overwhelmed him, and the memory seemed bottomless. A memory of something almost invisible but thick as velvet, soft and dangerous as that tender spot just above the long yellow teeth, there, on a horse's nose; tender fuzzy place, soft hot nostrils blowing dire little warnings, soft places, an aching reminder of the terrifying void, moist and humid with sad recollections, small betrayals. He saw Loretta looking at him curiously. Later, he remembered thinking that, in that moment she had only one eye, a soft, wet pointed eye bobbing slightly in a puddle of a face. It was a terrible moment; Loretta never knew how much anguish, in that eternity, she had evoked and Alexander had suffered.

"Look, Loretta," he said, much later, walking her home. "Venus. She points the way if only we'll let her . . . we have only to follow along gratefully without asking too much . . ."

Loretta nodded, scarcely hearing him. There was nothing so irrevocably black, she thought, as a deep night sky out in the desert, where not even the miraculous icy tracks of a billion stars amassed and a wandering vagabond moon offered the hopeful beam, the tiny lit-up clue of either a dream or a consolation.

The driver of this rig is the Colorado Kid out of Bountiful, Utah.
I asked him what he hauls and he said swingin meat, a
350 Detroit Diesel, 8 cylinders, turbo charged

The mechanics were telling me it would be a real
nice truck if it had a Cummins in it — You get a
lot more miles out of a Cummins than a Detroit Engine.
They call Detroits the "Double Breasted Yamaha" and
they're the cheapest engine to own or operate — this one here is real filthy, a 2 stroke
engine (compression & exhaust) as opposed to a 4 stroke engine (cummins) —
The four stroke engine 1. goes down & sucks in 2. pushes up compression 3. goes down
again
4. blows out exhaust — they're clean & white

This rig came limping into Jack's Diesel with
a burnt piston and a burnt valve.
It was a big job — It took over 12 hours and they had to
take half the engine apart.
The rig is extra powerful because
of the Turbo Charger — a Turbo has a
roter inside which is turned by the
exhaust gases at about 85,000 RPM's
it blows air into the intake and
gives you extra power, like
having an extra carburetor in a
car — the can on the
side is the air filter - some
are oil filled and some are Vapor.

KENWORTH

JENSEN TRUCKS
FROM BOUNTIFUL
UTAH

15

Dianne Nelson
October 1976
Jack's Diesel at the Triple T Ranch

Colorado Kid

Trucking (from Bountiful)

...me haul on the hoof and some on the hook and when you haul on
    the hook, it's swingin meat

...ut 3,000 miles a week, keeping awake on what he calls wacky tobaccy
couple of beers each stop. The truck is really something, with hand painted
...swirls on a deep navy background — red and white stripes — the Colorado Kid was
... the paint job alone cost $1,000 but he was going to sell the rig because the
...the cab is getting shabby. The truck is a 1983 and 3 years is about as long as a
...rig like this.

DETROIT DIESEL

Manifold

PART TWO

CHAPTER 9

A long time ago grass grew on this land. Sweet grasses and sorghum grew high as a horse's belly and men could live by the land. When the rains stopped coming the grass and the trees died, leaving a burnt, dried-out earth, a desert wasteland. Old men remember the grasses, and the few who are left, Navajo mostly, tell how the rains dried up when the strength of the tribe was broken.

Men went off on their own to find new gods. The power of the tribe, praying together for rain, was lost, and the earth dried up in revenge.

That was a hundred years ago. Today if you drive through this land you will find the desert, red dust and clay, stretching out to the edge of the sky. The earth has returned to the beginning of time and in places it lies barren and revealed, its belly striped mauve and yellow.

In certain places there are valleys still and new trees have been planted. If you wait long enough, until summer comes, the earth opens up and a miraculous green fuzz sprouts on the desert floor. The young trees sway with the new weight of leaves and the mesquite and palo verde, the creosote, raise up proud and yellow. Most of the grand old cottonwoods are gone now, but low down, along the desert floor, strange new plants open to life. Waxy primeval blossoms erupt at last, a year in the bearing, from the bellies of thorny, ancient survivors of the land: sahuaro, yucca, ocotilla, cholla.

The hope of this land is the rain. In June the winds come up from the desert and blow hot across the land. By July the air hangs like a shroud, heavy and awkward with the will to rain. Down in the riverbeds cows lick at the cracked earth and ranchers talk of shipping cattle to Colorado for water and sod.

Days and weeks go by and still the rains won't come. The August thunderheads move in, savage warrior clouds pulling apart the sky, roaring for power. The promise of rain is everywhere; the first desert toad appears for his night of breeding, but even he needs rain to procreate, to leave behind his tiny smell, the information of his existence lest he face the doom of extinction.

Silent warnings, fingers of light, zigzag the sky and the sky pulls into itself, sullen and miserly, until at last the burden of rain spills out in relief onto the land. The desert toads come by the thousands to caterwaul at the edge of new ponds. The urgency of the breeding chorus is heard by the female, who comes to the pond seeking her own genus and to lay the eggs at last. The dried-out riverbeds, swollen now with rain, flood with waters that pour down from the mountains; cars, trees and people are caught up in the violence of the rushing waters and in the poor parts of town trailers are swept away.

It always rains harder on the poor, thought Alexander. He liked to drive through the blurry gushing streets in the thick of the storm. Once or twice he had been flooded out and stranded but it didn't matter. The rain was his ally, an old friend from the past, and as soon as the storms came, he headed out to watch the Rillito River begin to run.

Moments alone in the desert evoked Hickman Carter, the violent earthy man who had been Alexander's stepfather in the years after his father died. It was Hickman, prowling the desert for clues to life, sniffing the earth for a scent, who had taught Alexander the feel of the land. He had told him about the desert toads, the kangaroo rats and other survivors hidden in the desert; the brutal realities which had frightened the young boy now seemed a natural part of Alexander's life.

"A kangaroo rat," said Hickman, pointing his stick at a curious beast. "Now there's a wonderful creature . . . he doesn't drink water, you know." Alexander had envisioned a skulking, parched life, trapped on the desert floor. "He pulls in moisture from the air with that ugly little tongue of his and his system converts it, uses it. His urine comes out thick as toothpaste," Hickman had continued, full of the triumph of survival. "What's the matter, boy?" he had asked, seeing Alexander's repugnance. "Not pretty enough for you, huh? Listen to me. When everything else withers up and blows away, that rat over there is going to make it. He'll hang on, no matter what. That makes him special. There's a beauty in that. Survival isn't so pretty to look at, but you've got to have respect for it all the same. You'll learn."

Driving to the Club, through the rain, for a meeting one night, Alexander thought, why is it that of all the people I've known it has to be Hickman, whom I hated, who burns deepest and lingers on alive, refusing, after all these years, to die in my memory? Why is it that the echo of this man rings forever in my ear when finally I have earned the right to silence? But Hickman Carter stayed near Alexander, and deep down he knew he would never expunge the man because, from the beginning, he had disappointed Hickman and that could never be forgotten.

Alexander clearly remembered his first trip to the ranch, the year his father died. Lily had come to bring him home from Boston. He had been gone three months. On the way home she had explained that she had closed the house in Bisbee, that there were memories there that it hurt to brush up against. She had opened the Tucson house where Agnes was waiting for them.

Alexander arrived home to find his father's old house in Snob Hollow filled with Lily's new admirers and Agnes, sour and hinting at 'goings on.' Lily, who had confined her mourning attire to delicate white dresses, drooping hats and lacy trailing parasols, was ravishing in her grief. Her mother, Mrs. Pew, who couldn't bear death, had gone off, and Lily, fragile, repining, allowed herself to be consoled by such gentlemen as the town had to offer.

Agnes brought it upon herself to act as duenna and, rigid and unrelenting in her grief, a grim specter in heavy black silks, she sat night after night in the parlor, watching Lily and these new men.

"Who's the old cat?" inquired Hickman Carter, the most persistent of Lily's admirers, referring to Agnes nodding in her chair. Alexander heard the remark and never forgave him for it, mostly because, to his great shame, he had not had the courage to defend his aunt.

"Oh!" exclaimed Lily with her sweet laugh, "you *are* a dreadful man!" and almost imperceptibly, she leaned closer to him.

"He's so *coarse,* don't you think?" Alexander said later, resorting to a word Eunice had used to describe him in a bad moment. His mother was preparing herself for bed.

"Do you think so, darling?" Lily replied, slipping her rings into a tiny porcelain snuff box on her dressing table. She began to hum a little tune to herself. It had not yet occurred to Alexander that Lily would ever remarry, that he would ever again have to share her, and he saw no reason for the men who hung about the house. "Well maybe . . ." she continued after awhile. "But he's *so* amusing," and smiling her secret, faraway smile she began to buff her nails.

Six weeks later, Lily married Hickman Carter in the Episcopalian Church. They left town on a long tour of Europe and Alexander, Agnes and Inez Hoover waited in the house for her to come home.

Although Agnes despised Hickman Carter and suspected him of not even being a gentleman, and Alexander held him in fear and loathing and Inez—even Inez—indulged herself in a condemnation of the man, the person who most thoroughly hated him was Mrs. Pew. From the very first, when she heard the news that Lily had married the man she had rushed to Arizona to be with her child, and had viewed Hickman with suspicion. Agnes and Mrs. Pew had been childhood friends in Virginia long ago and, reunited, they clove together now in this new unison of hate. They spent long hours closeted in Agnes's room, wallowing in venom. This rubbed off on Alexander and he began to see his new stepfather as a monster of iniquity.

Hickman was tall and vivid, with a shock of thick hair, black as an Indian's. His face was startling in its vigor, with strong handsome features and crinkling humorous eyes. His power, which was considerable, came not so much through any recognizeable achievements as through a remarkable vitality, a lusty appetite for life. There were those who quailed before Hickman's unflinching eye, but his humorous and unreserved capacity for intrigue and adventure made him an irresistible friend.

Hickman ran away from St. Louis when he was fifteen. He came out west to Arizona where he met a rancher named Big Red Iverson who had done time in the state penitentiary for shooting a man down at the Y Tavern in Eloy. When he got out of the penitentiary he was a peaceful man, and he went back to his ranch, which had gone to seed while he was away.

The cattle had run wild, the fences were down and a pale slippery dust had settled over everything. Big Red took Hickman in and put him to work. At the end of six long years Hickman's father died, and he took the money that came to him and bought into partnership with Big Red Iverson in the Sassabe Ranch.

When Lily and Hickman returned from their Grand Tour, they arrived at the Snob Hollow house accompanied by two burly Mexicans, employees of Hickman's, who shuffled into the house and began moving through the rooms, loading things into boxes. Agnes asked Mrs. Pew, "Who are they, dear?" in a quavering voice, but by then both Mrs. Pew and Inez Hoover were trying to shoo the men out of Lily's boudoir. There was great chaos in the house and Lily was laughing and trying to explain everything, and meanwhile, the Mexicans were loading the boxes into a pickup truck.

It appeared Hickman was moving Lily to the ranch and that Alexander was to go and they were leaving immediately. "But we can't leave the house! Not like this!" wailed Agnes.

"No one's asking you to leave!" bellowed Hickman. And then, relenting some, "You are welcome at the ranch, the two of you." He eyed the old ladies, who were clutching at one another in bewilderment. "But, if you're coming, I want you ready in an hour."

Agnes began to moan and weep but Mrs. Pew turned on him in a seething rage. "How dare you, sir! How dare you come tramping in here with these people," rolling her eyes at the two Mexicans who were now stripped down to undershirts in the heat, "and bully two ladies in the privacy of their home! Brute!" she screamed at last.

"Suit yourself," shrugged Hickman, who was vastly amused by the scene.

"Now, Mama, do come. And you, too, dear Agnes. We won't be comfortable without you . . ." Lily patted the quivering hand and Agnes began to relent. Only the day before, as the two ladies sat chastising the new husband, Agnes had bemoaned the fact that her beloved Eugene's house was going to be taken over by this man.

"Won't you spend the night here, only that?" she begged.

"I'm not spending one night in another man's house. Now get your things together and let's get the show on the road," and Hickman, beginning to be bored by it all, turned and walked out of the house to wait in the car.

"This'll be the death of me yet, see if it won't," grieved Inez Hoover, who, terrified of being left behind, had yanked up her skirt and flown upstairs to guard her room from the two sweating foreign invaders.

In a little over an hour, they were all loaded into the car with Agnes and Mrs. Pew squashed into the backseat. Morton, Lily's bulldog, and Mrs. Pew's lizard-skin jewel case were wedged in between the two stunned ladies. Alexander and Inez Hoover followed in the front seat of the pickup truck with the Mexicans. Alexander felt he should mourn the rude abandonment of his father's house, but in fact he was excited about seeing a ranch and about what might happen next, and so, holding Inez's hand in the secrecy of her skirt, he settled back for a long ride.

The approach to the Iverson-Carter ranch was a violent drive of about ten miles over a treacherous one-lane dirt road, pitted with boulders and gullies. For miles and miles, as far as the ladies

118

could see, there was nothing but scrub and wasteland, parched and dreary under the hot white eye of the sun. It was June, the hard month, full of that terrible waiting for the August monsoons. Sometimes there is a stillness, when even the air seems to have died. Then the sirocco comes, a mean June wind blowing hot and fierce over the land.

In those days there was no air-conditioning, and as an exuberant Carter, who gloried in this savage land, drove them over the endless dirt road, billows of dust poured into the car, wrapping the wretched passengers in an ominous shroud. When at last they arrived, Mrs. Pew peered out from the backseat, took one look at the ranch house and refused to get out of the car. Inez Hoover whispered something in her ear, so slowly she got out, dragging the lugubrious Morton and the jewel case.

Even Lily felt some reluctuance upon first seeing her new home. The house was low-swept and close to the ground, leaning slightly to make way for the forlorn prairie winds that year after year ravaged its dignity until at last it appeared to cower there in abject submission. It sat out in a cracked pasture of stubble and rabbit bush with nothing but a few scrawny mesquite trees and snakeweed for relief. Some pale yellow cottonwoods, limp with dying, grew along a dried-out riverbed where a herd of scraggly cows lay indolent and drowsy in the awful heat.

Behind the house were a number of low barns and a few sagging adobe shacks with curling blue-paint borders around the windows and screen-door frames. Nearby were the corrals, cattle chutes, a chicken coop, a water tank and a still, brown water hole, and then miles of desert land stretching out into the mountains and far beyond.

"Poor chile," groaned Inez, patting Lily, who she saw had assumed her brave face for the occasion. "Poor, poor chile!" And then under her breath, taking in Hickman, the weary house and the landscape all at once, "He ain't heard the last of me! Bringin' that poor chile out to a hole like this . . ."

A terrible-looking, squint-eyed, grizzled man came lurching out from the barn. "Howdy, folks!" he cackled. He seemed to find the forlorn group of ladies in their patterned summer dresses very

119

entertaining and, casting a bleary eye over them, he cracked, "Where'd ya git the fillies? Har har!" Mrs. Pew whirled on Hickman.

"Who is this disgusting creature?" The old man slapped his thigh with pleasure.

"This is Big Red Iverson," said Hickman, tickled by her outrage. "This is his spread . . . he's the boss."

Agnes, almost fainting with the horror of her new circumstances, was shown, along with Mrs. Pew, into the guesthouse in one of the crumbling adobe shacks. They saw they were evidently meant to share a room. The guestroom contained a narrow closet, two chests of drawers, two lumpy beds with striped coverlets, a rush mat, a horsehair settee, a table, a slop jar and a basin. Behind an ugly flowered curtain in the corner there was a yellow stained toilet and a sink.

"And just what is the meaning of this?!" demanded Mrs. Pew in awful tones. "You don't mean to tell me you expect a civilized human being, a *lady,* to sleep in this squatter's shack like trash!" The Mexicans were bringing her boxes in. "Suit yourself. These men'll take you back into town as soon as they're finished unloading . . ." Mrs. Pew took one grim look at the workmen and decided anything was preferable to a lonely ride through the desert with foreign desperados.

Agnes saw there was no conquering such a man in his own territory, and she went up to him and plucked at his sleeve. "Mr. Carter," she began, in a meek voice, "I know this has been confusing for us all and we appreciate your having us here to stay, but I wonder . . ." and here, her voice dropped to a whisper, "I wonder if I might request a room of my own . . . you see, never, never before have I shared a room with another person and . . ."

Hickman saw she was close to tears and so he put a friendly arm around her shoulders and gave her a brusque little squeeze of sympathy. "Miss Dautremont," he replied, taking her tone, "I do feel sorry I cannot offer you better accommodations at such short notice but the fact is, I am unprepared." It was in the back of Hickman's mind that the worse the accommodations, the sooner the two old nuisances would leave, but, relenting slightly, he continued, "I'll tell you what. If at the end of one week, you like it here on my ranch, I'll tell the boys to build another room and you'll have your own place whenever you come to visit. How's that?"

"Well," brought out Agnes, somewhat mollified, "I guess it will do."

"And what about *me?*" Mrs. Pew, arms akimbo, stood facing Hickman.

"The truck's waiting for you outside, ma'am, any time you want to go." And turning his back on her, he began to tell Agnes certain things. He asked her if she knew how to use a gun and warned her about snakes, black widows and scorpions. He told her not to worry about the "hairy ones," tarantulas or gila monsters, saying they'd only make her sick but wouldn't kill her. He also advised her not to flush the toilet often since water was scarce (here, she blushed up to the roots of her hair with shame), and then he left.

Agnes, slumped over in a heap on the horsehair settee, moaned, "What are we going to do, Mary Helen?" She was the only person left who called Mrs. Pew by her own name, except that Hickman was to take up the habit, much to her annoyance. "I want the bed by the wall," replied Mrs. Pew. The other bed was under the window, and she clearly visualized the untold evils that sooner or later would no doubt crawl in by that window. "And I'll just take this bureau," she went on, slapping her lizard jewel case down on the larger of the two chests. Then she started unpacking and prepared herself for battle.

Several years went by before Mrs. Pew was able to realize any success whatsoever in her attempts to pry Lily away from Hickman. Although Lily had no intentions of actually living within the dreary confines of the Iverson-Carter ranch, it did suit her to have it behind her as a heroic and interesting point of departure.

She imagined herself—and to her credit, occasionally she included Hickman in her fantasies—in any number of fascinating places, only swooping down on the ranch for round-up or perhaps long weekends with parties of envious friends from New York or Virginia. It never occurred to her that they were actually going to live on the ranch.

Hickman, however, was not a man to be easily assimilated by either the vitriolic proddings of his mother-in-law, the silent sufferings of Agnes or the charming maneuvers of his lovely wife. He continued to go about his ranch business with a great deal of vigorous enjoyment. When Mrs. Pew forgot herself and indulged in truculent attacks upon his character, the ranch or Big Red, Hickman sent Osie, his foreman, around with the truck to take her to the train station thirty miles away. After several grand exits and one wretched night spent sulking in the Southern Pacific Hotel in Gallup, Mrs. Pew came limping home, greatly subdued, to plot out a dreadful revenge in the sanctuary of the guest house. (Matters were not helped on her arrival home to find that Agnes had appropriated her bed and the biggest bureau.)

The situation between the two old girlhood friends had deteriorated somewhat, as friendships overexposed to the rigors of intimacy are sometimes apt to do. Agnes, determined to adapt herself to the horrors of ranch life rather than live alone for the first time in her life, had become contumacious and struggled to hold her own against Mrs. Pew. Aided by Hickman, who was greatly amused by the rivalry between the two old viragoes, as he called them, Agnes began to learn the art of survival.

Every night the two old friends played gin rummy or Chinese checkers, and Mrs. Pew cheated. They played for low stakes. Agnes, reasonable at first and caressing, would say, "Mary Helen, dear, are you *sure* you meant to do that?" eyeing a forbidden move.

"Why, whatever are you talking about, Agnes?"

And then Agnes, with pursed lips and all the outraged virtue of southern womanhood, played out her hand in suffering. Mrs. Pew, regarding her victim much as a lizard does a fly, carried on to a flamboyant victory.

Arm and arm in haughty silence the ladies went off to their room each night at ten to pursue their ritual bug hunt. They worked out a system. On all fours, armed with flashlights and moving in circular patterns, each searched her own side of the room, and then they changed sides to check one another out. Suspicions of treachery were rampant and the rigors of the hunt were heightened by the lurking fear that one of them knew of an unreported bug.

When the ladies were quite sure any vicious little marauder had been flushed out and clubbed to death, they turned off the light and, back to back, undressed in the dark. Once in bed, Mrs. Pew turned on the light and read Mickey Spillane or the crime section of the *National Enquirer* while Agnes said her prayers.

Inevitably, Mrs. Pew found a thrilling and particularly sinister murder, and she relished reading the tantalizing details aloud while Agnes, in a violent whisper, sent up a heartfelt prayer. This usually included a long inspired passage dedicated to the salvation of Mary Helen's soul. Then, radiant with serenity, Agnes rolled over to feign sleep. Mrs. Pew continued to hiss out hair-raising descriptions of elderly female tourists whose parts had been horribly dismembered and buried in lonely desert outposts.

"Oh, my God! Listen to this, Agnes dear." Silence from Agnes, except perhaps a small increase in the volume of breathing. "Woman of seventy found mangled and bloated near Gila Bend, only a few miles from here!" she continued maliciously, eyeing Agnes. "Her face horribly distorted . . . her tongue was black . . . her underwear was missing . . . Oh! How disgusting! Now you just go to sleep, Agnes dear . . . I'm sure if that nasty degenerate is anywhere out there in the dark on *this* God-forsaken ranch, that nice Osie and those Mexicans will know about it before it's too late . . ."

Sighing deeply, she turned out the light and left Agnes to her tortured ruminations. After a little while, when Agnes was certain that Mary Helen was asleep, her hand stole out and cautiously reached for the clock, which always faced Mary Helen. Slowly she slid it around so that it faced her and then, triumphant, she dozed off. Some minutes passed before Mrs. Pew pulled the clock back. Exhausted by a day of battle, the two adversaries lay rigid and uncompromising in the dark, each devoured by her own murky imaginings.

By the time Alexander was eleven they had lived on the ranch almost three years. He had not been very happy. Cosseted and nurtured in his father's sedate household, he suddenly found himself living the sparse life of any ordinary ranch boy. His mother's niceties had been of no avail and he was expected to make his own bed, rise at dawn, do chores, eat breakfast with Big Red, Hickman and the hired hands and ride horseback to school.

He had survived the terrible stench of branding and the bloody nightmare of castration as the young bulls, bellowing in fear, were wrassled to the ground and emasculated. Forced into the penalties of premature manhood, he was driven to eat the severed testicles, mountain oysters, fresh from the frying pan, and endure the brutal guffaws of the men who watched him gag and vomit forth the blubbery balls.

Pried away from the comforting security of Agnes and Inez Hoover, he was driven out on his own to appear manly, but not without a struggle. Agnes had fought for her nephew with a ferocity that amazed Hickman, but he held firm to his principles.

"Those two she-cats," he remarked to Lily, "have made a namby-pamby sissy out of the boy . . . either they've got to go, or he's got to stay clear of them till he's a man." Alexander heard, and he had no alternative but that of going off on his own.

He found hiding places and hid from the man's eye. He found ways to appear tough but he never managed to convince Hickman or Big Red he was anything but a puling, gutless sissy.

These were the pieces of himself Alexander never allowed out into the light. He meant to live his life without exposing his underbelly, the wounds and scars, the absurdities within, to the sympathy or ridicule of another human eye, lest the nakedness of being seen and known would in turn create a need. He culled that which was presentable from his past to feed the curious and concerned few, and the rest of himself he hoarded to agonize over in the dark.

CHAPTER 10

Alexander was the only person in the Club who had not shared his story. Of course, along with everyone else in A.A., he had parted with deep, aching pieces of himself as, week after week, the members shared their experiences. But it was in the Club that, in the end, the most candid revelations occurred. While hardly typical of A.A. itself, and in no way resembling the other small A.A. offshoots, the Club existed as a uniquely intimate forum for that small band of alcoholics who felt they had particular things in common. If their meetings grew more and more self-indulgent over the years, still, comfortable old intimacies had not supplanted the one essential purpose, that of being sober. If certain group members had long ago forgotten they were meant to be anonymous, they had become instead a family whose most gratifying bond was that of survival through sobriety.

Without ever parting with his own story, Alexander had, however, always given generously. He suspected it would not be long now before someone in the group succumbed to the temptation to pry; perhaps Artie who would mistakenly assume Alexander was aloof from the others because of those invisible class boundaries that Alexander himself was loathe to acknowledge, at least openly. He would entirely overlook the larger, kinder sympathy, that territorial solidarity Alexander did in fact share with the group. But that was not a thing an unrooted person like Artie could necessarily understand. Nor would he know that A.A. had saved Alexander's life, that it was the only place Alexander had come close to feeling he belonged. Of course, Alexander had means of discouraging impertinent inquiries, but even so, he did not like to think of himself as begrudging that which the others had shared with such simplicity.

It was painful enough, that separation he did continually feel between himself and all the others. How could he tell them who he really was, of the early years, of Lily and Hickman, of Grey Halls and Wind Song? He knew hollow moments when he remembered there was no one at all for whom he could gather together the fragments of his life and share the whole. They were gone now, those few he had loved, and he was left to carry on the dying race alone, at least here in this place where, one by one, all the distinctions, all the clues to his breed were dying out.

At the very next meeting, Arty cozened up to Alexander and tried to pry open the door to his past. It was inconceivable to Arthur that the honor he paid Alexander, that of being curious, might be viewed as an offense, since he was himself so dependent upon being noticed, so eager to arouse curiosity. And on that day, behind the tactful, unassuming faces of his friends, Alexander saw, scarcely veiled, the curiosity. When finally Viola blurted out, "You never got to see Alexander's house, Arty! It's bigger than the downtown Elk's Club," Alexander decided to tell them of those things in his life he could bear to part with.

"My father," he began carefully, "Eugene Dautremont, was from Virginia, but he was thought too fragile for a career and so after Harvard he was sent to live in Tucson. To the house in Snob Hollow. It was his." The room was very silent. They sat like school children afraid to scrape their chairs and he felt it. "Agnes, my aunt—she was years older than my father—was sent to look after him. When my father saw Bisbee, those wonderful mauve hills, the mines, he wanted to live there and be part of those times. The town was so wonderful then," continued Alexander, warming to the memory.

"Bisbee was seething with people from everywhere—Cornish mine workers, Serbians, Indians, Ukrainians. There were even a few Chinamen who found their way into those remote hills . . . and three-quarters of the population was Mexican. Mother told me about outdoor dances they had, in Central Park, down in the Brewery Gulch, near the saloons, on Saturday nights. There were luncheon parties and bridge for the ladies. It was a boom town then . . . lawyers, bankers, mining engineers, all those people came to work the Copper Queen and the other mines. My father told me about the Country Club outside Warren where we lived. There was a nine-hole golf course with gravel fairways, surrounded by barbed wire. The railroad ran right through it, and Father said he saw rattlesnakes there and wild horses, stray cows."

Bud began to drum his nails on the table. When this went unobserved he tapped out "Yankee Doodle Dandy" and Mabel said, "Hey! Cut it out, Bud."

"What's your problem?" he demanded. Three or four of the women said, "Shhhhhh!" good and loud and there was silence.

"Every fourth of July," continued Alexander quietly, "there was a mine-drilling contest. The man who drilled the fastest was king for the day. The men ran wild; they shot their guns into the air. I remember it. I remember that and the parade down Brewery Gulch and—" he broke off. Bud was humming under his breath.

"All right," shouted Alma, "I've just about had it. You're jealous, that's what. Jealous of Alexander." She banged her fist on the table under Bud's nose.

"Who is this guy?" argued Bud. "Well, answer me! Who the hell is he that the bunch of you sit there lappin' up all this lah-de-dah stuff about a country club and the fourth of July? Jesus!" Bud pushed his chair back and glowered at them all.

"He listened to you, Bud Cecil, when you was goin' on about your folks an' all. He's a gentleman, which you *ain't!*" cried Sweetie Pie. Bud was the only one there who didn't need Alexander in some way to pad out his existence. He resisted Alexander, not because he was rich or because the others admired him so, nor even because he couldn't begin to understand him. Bud didn't like Alexander simply because he thought he took up too much space.

He couldn't understand how elegance or even courtesy could have weight when stacked up next to the reality of things.

"It's as plain a case of jealousy as I ever saw," decided Mabel.

"Aw, hell," said Bud, looking at Alexander. "Why's *he* so important? He don't earn his living. He don't fight to keep alive. If he don't do that, he don't do anything!" Everybody began to talk at once until finally Alexander rapped on his glass.

"In a funny way," he said, smiling, "I agree with him. But," and here he turned to look at Bud, "it's a tricky business, this needing to weigh and measure a man's life. I don't suppose, in the long run, you know a hell of a lot more about it than I do. And then . . . well, my life's not over yet. I was trying somehow to justify myself, to set the mood for what I am, to tell you about Bisbee where I was born, about the way things were . . . I'm not like you Bud, free, in transit . . . I'm tied in with my surroundings, I'm standing still . . ." He saw they didn't understand and so, shifting, he gave them what they wanted. The whole of his life he cut and pared so that, once unfolded, it looked like a paper chain of dolls, linked and dancing, hand and foot.

Giving his story to Mabel and Bud, the last survivor and the new breed, he began to dwell on the years after Harvard, on the wasted days and years in Italy, in New York, glimpses of solitude seen from Bellosguardo where, high up on the hill, immured in a stone citadel, he mixed the paints he never used, slept and drank, the stench of the Arno, yellow mud, boozy, lost days.

New York, the people bought and sold, the hotel rooms, nights alone when, driven and afraid, he had telephoned eight, ten friends to have a drink, to be somewhere else, the degredation of being turned down, the promises of calls returned that never came. He told them how he came to loathe the desk clerk, witness to his empty box, purveyor of messages that never came. He became so afraid of being seen alone when he went out that, paralyzed, he ate alone in his room and drank.

"Well, what about the cousin?" asked Viola, referring to Eunice who she knew lived in New York. She was almost afraid to hear more for fear Alexander would cease to exist altogether, that he would destroy the last of her illusions. If the rich weren't happy, who could be?

"Eunice?" asked Alexander, startled out of his reverie. "She was married to someone, she wasn't there . . ." He slipped past it quickly. In fact Eunice had been there; she was married to Drew Peabody, his roomate from Deerfield and Harvard, his best friend. After the first three months, when she had sent flowers and messages and expensive-smelling parcels to his suite at the Pierre, when they had exhausted themselves in luncheons and evenings out, when she had finally seen that once again he needed her, she had stopped coming to the phone.

He alluded to drunken debaucheries and let them imagine what they would, and finally he told them how his mother had sent a male nurse for him and had him brought home. Bloated, drunken beyond recognition, he was sent to dry out in a sanitarium and then was propped up, cleaned out and returned to Tucson to get on with the business of living.

"Praise the Lord!" breathed Alma, satisfied by at least one reference to debaucheries. He saw things were all right with the group, that Bud was silent, that he was still one of them, and yet, how great is the ache of holding back. "It's the things I haven't done, it's what I held back," Lily had said to him once. "Those are the little stinginesses in myself that I do regret . . . it's all the ideas that I murdered along the way, all the thoughts and words I strangled in their sleep, for fear they would betray me . . ."

"He's a small man, a common man," said Mabel later, talking of Bud Cecil. After the meeting she had gone to have a cup of coffee alone with Alexander. Burning still, she needed to vindicate her friend. "No," said Alexander, "You've missed the point. He's his own man, a maverick really. He's the solution. He's what comes next . . ."

"What? That pot-bellied trucker? A man like that, he's no hope for the future! Why, he's the dregs of the past, he's what's left from the crumbs on the table!"

"The land is dying out, Mabel. It's these new people who will own the land, the highway people. People without memories."

"Not as long as I'm still around to fight for it!" answered Mabel and, eyeing Alexander, she thought, "Sometimes that man's got some pretty funny ideas . . ."

Later, alone inside his own head, Alexander thought with unbearable clarity of the years to come. He let himself into his house and slowly walked through the dining room to get his pie and milk and then, clutching Ruth's notes, made his way upstairs. He lay in bed thinking of the enormous stretch of time yawning ahead, of the days and years of sameness, and, panicking a little, he began to make plans. Paris, Turkey, Madrid. But then, wormlike, termites from the past wriggled into place, and he focused on the terrible evening in Siena when, all alone, he had pried himself away from his hotel room to dine as other people did, in public.

Even now he shuddered with the memory of the gay red walls, the smiling, leering faces, the clatter of forks, the difficulty of chewing the veal and of swallowing, the heat of the room, of being alone and finally, escape. He had wept outside in the street. Back in his hotel room, he had suspected himself of going mad.

No, I won't go to Europe, he decided. His eye fell on the grey hooked rug and he resolved to throw it away, to carpet the room with something else, red or blue. He thought of his breakfast, the boiled egg, and decided to have French toast or waffles, and then, last of all, and most painfully, he thought of Eunice, alone in New York.

He had been twelve years old the first time Eunice had come to visit at the ranch. She had stepped down from the train and then turned to help her grandmother maneuver the steps. Wearing a small neat cloche, grey with a smooth feather cockade, she carried a fur muff. She looks a lot older than me, Alexander had thought to himself, hanging back until Mrs. Pew was safely settled on firm ground.

Lily rushed forward. "Mother! Darling!" and Alexander just heard Mrs. Pew, his grandmother, say, "Don't crush me, dear. I have a new hat!" before he was swallowed up within the vortex of furs and feathers and tweed coats. Pressed for a moment to his grandmother's uncompromising breast, he saw his cousin watching him. Why, she's laughing at me, he thought, confused and dismayed.

"And here is your divine cousin," Lily exclaimed, presenting Eunice. "You look very grand, my dear," she said to the girl, who hardly seemed his own age. "And very sweet. And you are lovely to come all this way to visit us." Turning away to help her mother, Lily left Eunice to Alexander. They had met once before, just after Alexander's father had died, when he had been sent to Boston to visit his aunt Nanine. They did not like each other.

"Well," Eunice remarked, looking around. "So this is Tucson." She said it oddly, pronouncing "Tucson" with a slur so that it sounded like a punishment and not at all like the holiday it was meant to be.

"Yes," he assented, running a little to catch up with her. "There's so much to see . . . have you ever seen an Indian?" he panted, rushing to hold the station door for her.

"Certainly not!" she replied. "Why ever should I?" and she let the door go in his face.

His mother had sent him off to find a porter and, feeling important, he disappeared. The same age as Eunice, but undersized, he looked ten and was ashamed of his small stature. Perhaps because she was his cousin and therefore bound to him forever, or perhaps it was because he lived out on a ranch and had no friends of his own, that he thought of Eunice as his friend and was determined therefore to overlook the indignities she inflicted on him. Lonely, he could not afford the see the plain truth of her and so, undaunted, he planned ways to please her.

"Heavens, child, what took you so long?" demanded his grandmother. She was sitting on her trunk.

"I stopped for a moment at the gift shop," he explained, holding a bag behind his back. "Here." He thrust the bag at Eunice just as the others began collecting their coats.

"What is it?" she asked, suspicious.

"It's for you."

She looked into the bag. Inside there was a chunky lavender rock specimen attatched to a polished board on which was inscribed, "Welcome to the Grand Canyon State."

"What is it?" she asked again.

"A paperweight," he replied, feeling its ugliness all of a sudden. He had spent his entire allowance on it.

"Oh," she said, closing the bag. "How amusing."

"Come along, you two, plenty of time to visit later," Lily called out. "We have three whole weeks ahead of us. What fun. And fifty miles to go before dark." She attempted a laugh.

Eunice and Alexander climbed into the front seat with Osie the foreman. Eunice sat slightly foreward, unwilling to touch against either the grizzled, bemused old man or her cousin.

"Have you ever been on a working ranch before?" asked Alexander.

"I've been to a farm," she answered. "In Virginia."

Osie laughed. "This ain't no farm, missie. It's a cattle ranch. Santa Gertrudis. Beef," he said, his eye on the road. She refused to dignify him with a response and appeared to shut her eyes in infinite weariness against the long road and the ring of violet smoking mountains rising up massive and fierce out of nowhere. "Easterners!" said the old man, half under his breath. He saw Alexander's eye on him. "You weren't much better yourself, young whippersnapper," he chuckled. "What a dude! Hah!"

"We're here." announced Osie without ceremony. Alexander had fallen asleep and awoke parched, tasting dust in his mouth. He glanced at Eunice. Apparently, while he was asleep, she had decided to placate the old man, because he saw things were different between them and Osie had left off calling her "missie."

"Here you go, Miss," and he helped her out. Eunice looked with disfavor on the ranch, much as Mrs. Pew, her grandmother had done before her. "Where am I going to sleep?" she inquired.

Lily took her off to her room and Alexander, who had envisioned long cozy conversations while lying on the foot of his cousin's bed, laughter in the dark when the lights were out, shared secrets, whispers, was in no uncertain terms invited to stay out of her domain. "Can't I come in?" he begged.

"No. I need my privacy," and the door was closed.

Dinnertime was painful. As always, it was the worst time in Alexander's day. Hickman and Big Red were meat-and-potatoes men, and they always had a side dish of chiles and beans, no matter what else was served. An enormous roast was brought out, glistening and black with overcooking. When left to his own resources, Alexander had a delicate appetite and preferred breast of chicken and breads with the crust cut off, but Hickman meant him to eat like a man.

Invariably Hickman served him a mountain of thick meat slabs, potatoes smothered in gravy and beans with chiles. When the others had eaten, Hickman looked down the table to examine Alexander's plate. It had barely been touched. "Eat up, son! Eat up all that good red meat!"

"It's mostly gristle, sir," whispered Alexander, flushed and miserable. He saw Eunice watching.

"Nonsense, my boy. *Eat!*" Alexander began to stab and peck at his food.

At this point, Inez slipped out of the kitchen and attempted to remove Alexander's plate. Hickman roared down the table, "Leave that goddamn plate where it is, you meddling old hag! Now, eat up, goddamn your hide!" Inez shot through the pantry door and Hickman, rising to full height, stood directly behind Alexander's chair and waited until the boy choked down the last piece of gristle and gagged over the fiery chile.

Then the family, all cowed by the violence of the scene—except for Eunice whose eyes gleamed with intrigue—arose to take coffee in the living room. As Big Red and Hickman discussed the business of the day and Agnes and Mrs. Pew began to play cards, Alexander stole off to his room. After a while there was a knock on his door, and Eunice appeared.

"Why do you sit in the dark?" she asked.

"I'm not afraid of it," he answered, hostile.

"I wouldn't let anyone speak to me that way. He's only your stepfather. You don't have to take it." She sat down.

"I hate his guts," he boasted.

"You're scared of him," she continued, toying with her hair.

"You would be, too . . . everyone's scared of Hickman. He and that other one, Big Red, they killed a guy once. In cold blood."

"Phooey," she scorned and, getting up, turned on the lights.

Alexander watched her. She stood before his mirror, entranced at what she saw. She isn't even pretty, he thought and, wanting her to see him, he came and stood beside her. She moved away.

"I think he's wonderful. I'm not afraid of anybody," she said, and turning off the light, she left him there alone.

His mother came in to say goodnight just as he was beginning to sleep. Bending over him, she stroked his head and whispered caressing little words into his ear, but he could not share his hatred for Hickman with her and so he pretended to be asleep. Hearing her sigh and turn to go, he was left alone in the dark with the enormity of his loneliness, inconsolable, afraid.

In the days that followed, very little happened on the ranch that Eunice missed. She was like an enormous eye watching them all, and as her contempt for Alexander grew, as she saw how alien he felt from the very thing he claimed as his own, the land, the sprawling desert, she seemed to thrive on the harsh challenge of the environment. Afraid of nothing, she demanded the meanest horses and rode with a vengeance that won the respect of every man on the place. She practiced roping, spent a day mending fences with Osie, ate like a stevedore and rose at dawn. In three weeks she was able to accomplish all that Alexander had struggled to achieve in four years, and he who loathed horses and dreaded the dawn stood by and watched her amazing success.

"My dear, you've burned your hands and ruined your lovely complexion," said Lily, attempting to help Eunice pack. It was her last night at the ranch. "Your mother will never forgive me. Oh dear," she sighed, "You were such a lady when you came . . . all that energy. Heavens."

"Are you ever coming back?" asked Alexander, lost in admiration as he watched her deft brown fingers fold her riding clothes and wedge them into the suitcase. She had left the lavender paperweight on the bureau and he brought it to her.

She shrugged. "I've been asked to Bermuda for spring vacation . . . I'll be going to Farmington in the fall."

"Oh," said Alexander. He felt her slipping away and he wanted to tell her things, to share something with her. When his mother left the room he began to tell her things at random, and in a moment of weakness he told her about Green Song and Wind

Song and the riverbed. He felt as if his secrets were being pulled from him one by one on a long thread, and as soon as they were out and had touched the open air, he wanted them back; he felt he had betrayed his inner soul. She snapped the suitcase shut.

"If you ask me," she said, appearing not to have heard his confidences, "you'd better start packing yourself."

"What do you mean by that?"

"Hickman's going to leave your mother, that's what. Anyone can see that. He's tired of her," and she faced him at last.

"I don't understand. It isn't true," he protested, feeling violated.

"Suit yourself. But I warned you. Your mother drinks. She locks herself up in her room and drinks."

"You're lying!" he shouted, feeling sick.

"Listen, silly, I've seen things here. The other day when I went to Nogales with Hickman . . . well, he met a woman there, a Mexican. He's got someone else, I tell you. You'll see." She stood watching him, and he felt everything inside himself crumple before her cold eye.

"I hate you," he said, but by then it didn't matter because she knew Alexander needed her.

She left the next day, and it was several years before he saw her again. Before she had been gone a week he had forgotten to hate her. By then he was far too preoccupied with his search for the truth about Hickman and his mother. Each day at four, after he returned from school, his mother shut herself in her room. She had begun to drink, absinthe at first and then other sweet deadly liquers. While she never disgraced herself by appearing drunk, she floated in a demure, inaccessible twilight all her own. Her smell had changed and like a young animal, Alexander began to sense her changes.

In the late afternoons, Hickman, thick with the dust of the day's work, abounding in vitality, came into their room to find her there, limp, translucent in the dark, sunk in amongst the linens and lace of her bed. Pulling up the shades, he said, "My God, Lily, what are you doing alone in the dark?" and he threw open the windows. "The air in here is old, worn out . . . what have you done today?" he asked, knowing.

There was a faint motion from the bed, a tiny resettling of silks.

"Oh, I don't know, darling . . . not much, I guess. It's so hot . . ." Hickman came to stand over her and reached for her soft hand. "You know," he began, "Marge Thompkin is making jellies and putting up pickles and relish over at Sinvaca." He paused. "She could use some help. It might be fun. Some of the other girls are going over to help tomorrow. I could have Osie take you in the truck . . . " He saw he had lost her again.

"Oh, darling. Marge is so clever, I know! I do so wish I was good at making jellies and darning socks and doing all those useful things, but . . . well, I'm just not, that's all. If only it weren't such a dreadful bore . . ." And he let her hand drop back into its fluffy cocoon.

Alexander brooded about Lily but there wasn't much he could do. He stayed close to her; he watched over her; he attempted to make little amusements that would distract her, beguile her away from the pain. One night as he lay in bed, he felt a curious new ridge of hair along his upper lip and, thrilled, he ran to show her.

"Look!" he burst out, arching his lip.

"Don't, dear. It makes you look so foolish."

"Don't you see? It's a mustache!"

"Oh, God!" she cried, "No!" and she wept against his shoulder.

The summer days crawled by, hot and futile. In the fall he was sent away to school in New England, and he spent his holidays with his aunt Nanine, where sometimes his mother came to join them. Hickman came just once to visit him at school and was much admired as a romantic figure by the other boys, who were impressed by his Stetson hat and cowboy boots. He took Alexander and a group of his friends out to dinner and asked them how their grades were and told them stories about the West, about Big Red Iverson and cattle drives, and this increased Alexander's prestige in school. But he hated to owe anything to Hickman.

In his freshman year at Deerfield, Lily telephoned him to say she had left Hickman. "Shall you mind terribly, dearest?" she asked in her silvery voice. "I know these things are annoying and so unsettling but I think it's time to do something else . . ."

"Why can't we just open up Pa's house in Tucson?" asked Alexander.

"Well, darling, we'll see . . ."

Two months later he got an envelope postmarked Farmington, Connecticut. Full of excitement and thinking it was a letter from Eunice, he ripped open the envelope. There was no letter, only a newspaper clipping from the Tucson newspaper. It said, "Rancher Plans To Marry Local Girl," and there below the headline was a small article about Hickman Carter who planned to marry one Chata Hernandez, as soon as his divorce was final. Eunice, of course, had been right.

Tomorrow, he thought as he began to sleep, tomorrow I'll ask her to marry me.

CHAPTER 11

Saturday night Bud asked Viola to go dancing at the Maverick in Tucson. Only a few months ago nothing would have satisfied Viola more than riding pressed up close to Bud, listening with unrestrained enthusiasm to the low-bellied rumble of his pickup truck. How she had loved being squeezed tight up into his big chest against the smooth, clean Saturday-night shirt, smelling ever so slightly of ironing board and thick healthy animal smells. She loved rocking against his big belly in the dark of the dance hall, nocturnal rubbings, fingering the defiant little prickles on the back of his neck where the barber had missed his mark.

In those days the finest thing that had ever happened to her was an encounter in the ladies' room of the Maverick. The most popular girl there, a blonde named Queenie, had asked her in front of the other girls if she was Bud's girl. "I don't know," she had replied, too late to reap the benefits of the enormous question. There was nobody so handsome as Bud Cecil at the Maverick.

On this particular Saturday night, all these months later, she felt a date with Bud was nothing compared to that thrilling ride in the back of the Cadillac, alone in the dark backseat with Arthur Smolen. But she went anyway. She had nothing better to do.

"C'mon, Bud, get your hands off," she said, not more than ten miles out of town.

"What's eating you, hon?" asked Bud, who had not suspected this new dimension of Viola.

"What makes you so sure every girl you meet likes getting pawed on the first date," snapped Viola, righteous and indignant.

"Who you kidding, anyway? Last time you and me went out I had to fight you off with a brick bat . . . so good ole Bud's not good enough for the virgin queen, huh? Don't tell me you're stuck on that weenie runt, Mr. Bangor, Maine?"

"You ain't worth a lick of his little toe, Bud. Oh, you're okay and all that, but you're uncouth, Bud. It's as plain as day."

And then, afraid she had hurt his feelings, she reached out for his hand, scrubbed clean for Saturday night, and she rubbed it against her cheek. It smelled of Dial soap. Bud yanked it away and, without saying another word, turned his truck around and drove her home.

In looking back, Mabel supposed it was this unhappy encounter between Viola and Bud, which of course Viola revealed in full detail, that finally triggered the unfortunate events of the next meeting. In the days that followed that meeting she felt terrible about her own influence on Viola and brought herself to speak very plainly to her. Mabel saw that Viola had somehow come around to thinking she was too good for anyone but the disinterested Arthur Smolen and knew this was an unwholesome conflict for a hot-blooded creature like Viola.

Arty strolled into the next meeting, to the embarrassment of one and all, in a T-shirt. It was odd how none of them had noticed before how thin his arms were. Thin and white. He had his hair worn differently, too. It was swept back and wild, à la Conway Twitty. Bud snorted and looked away. Even Viola had misgivings.

Looking straight at Artie, who seemed to have withered in his new attire, Bud started things off. "Guess who's in town?" he challenged.

"Gloria Swanson?" said Artie. "How should I know. I don't even know who your friends are," he sulked.

"Well, I know who some of your friends are," snapped Bud, "and they ain't exactly wholesome, if you know what I mean." Artie flushed up.

"We can't *all* have those attractive truckers you're always going on about for our best friends, now can we?"

"Who're his friends?" begged Viola. "Gangsters?" She tittered. "I always wanted to know a real gangster . . ."

"Arlene can help you out there . . . get her to introduce you to that adorable Vito Faldutto she knows," cracked Mabel.

Arlene was preparing for a crushing revenge when Alma spoke up. "Why are you always picking on Artie? What's it to you who he sees?"

"I don't like him, I don't like him giving me the hot eye, that's what. It ain't decent. It stinks."

"Hot eye! The nerve!" squawked Artie. "Don't you *wish!*"

"Just what is that supposed to mean?" roared Bud, but Artie had fallen silent. "I'll tell you what it means. I've been hearing a thing or two about you. I've been asking around. Buster Damiecki's back in town."

"So?"

"So you ain't no son of a prince, that's what. Your father's the postman in Bangor, Maine and your mother plays the piano weekends at the Ramada Inn. You ain't no big deal!" shouted Bud.

For a moment there was stunned silence in the room and then Viola shouted out, "You made this up, Bud Cecil! I turned you down and you're mad. So he made it all up," she went on, turning to the others. She felt like a heroine.

"You can talk about this later," began Alexander, looking wretched, but he was interrupted.

"You mean your grandfather wasn't royalty? You mean there was no Wolf Smolenski who ate the Turks and that stuff about the wolves wasn't true?" demanded Alma in a dreadful voice. She was beginning to feel cheated beyond all description and nothing but the interesting thought of what might come next kept her from viciously clubbing Arty with her pocketbook.

"He was a goddamn mackerel fisherman," said Bud. "He weren't no royalty!"

"He came from Maine!" protested Arty, "and that was his name. It was Wolf Smolenski. He was from Russia. It was true." He looked around and cowered before their eyes, before the distrust he saw

140

there. "Well, anyway, *part* of it was true. I don't know about the wolves . . ." he whispered.

"And Missy, the beautiful cousin?" asked Viola, almost panting.

"Can't you get it through your thick head? Can't you see there weren't no Missy," said Bud contemptuously. Viola started to moan, but still she looked to Arthur for the truth and Arthur, despising her for the adulation, saw her as the enemy.

"Why can't you leave me alone? I'm so sick of you I could die, I'm sick to death of your big fat cow eyes following me around. You started this, you horny bitch! I never wanted you! Can't you take a hint, for Christ sakes?" he almost screamed at her.

"Now hold on a minute," said Mabel and Alexander leaned across to change the subject by speaking to Fred Rudd.

"It ain't no secret," interrupted Viola with something akin to pride in her voice. "I think Artie's real fine, so what's wrong with that," she challenged.

"The only thing that's wrong with it," said Bud, pounding his fist on the table, "is you've picked a pervert, a dirty pervert to go and fall in love with!"

"I beg your pardon!" demurred Arlene but Bud persisted.

"Ask him why he left Bangor, Maine! Sex ring! Hah! He calls hisself Rhett Butler up in town and he got caught doin' it with a colored janitor in the school basement. That's why he left Maine and it's a well-known fact! Sex ring! Ask him what kind!"

There was a dreadful noise—a shriek, almost—from Artie, and turning a blotched, livid face on them he stood up and shouted, "Are you trying to tell me I'm a *homo?*"

"Praise the Lord! A Sodomite! Son of Sodom!" bellowed Alma.

"Shut up, Fathead," said Mabel. "This is disgusting. Pull yourself together, Arthur. And you, Bud Cecil, you're a mean sonofabitch if I ever saw one."

"It isn't true," cried Artie, to anyone who would listen, but everyone had begun to shuffle nervously in their chairs and Arlene began to jabber about Arletta's new beau and then she broke off guiltily remembering how she'd pushed Arty on her daughter. Fred Rudd started to talk to Alexander about the market for last year's steers and then grew confused, thinking, almost out loud, hell, the last thing some poor guy with a sex problem wants to hear about is steers, and so finally it was left to Harold Fimbers and Alexander to discover a neutral ground for conversation. The women were no help. Betty Rudd, Alma and Sweetie Pie tried to tear their eyes from Artie's defiant face, but a bug in a bottle couldn't have become more fascinating and they held to him, riveted. After some moments, Artie, close to tears, stood up to go.

"You all believed him," he whined, "It isn't fair. It's a lie."

"That's enough now, leave it alone, kid," soothed Bud.

"We've all had sex," began Alma.

"Speak for yourself!" cried Sweetie Pie, indignant.

"All except Miss Virgin here," continued Alma, warming to the subject, "and some of us has felt the fiery brush of the devil's wing in the heat of the night,"

"Oh, for God's sake, Alma, cut it out," interrupted Mabel, putting on her coat. "Why not call a spade a spade. I'm not going to mention names but certain persons here, they raised some hopes and that ain't fair. The fact is not one of us in this room kin say he's better than anyone else . . . or worse. So I say we bury the hatchet and leave what's meant to be private, stay private."

"Amen," said Alexander.

They all went off for coffee. Ed Cook and Fred Rudd wanted to ask Artie to join them, but they felt awkward about it and wondered if Arty would think they were making unnatural overtures toward him. In the end, Alexander took Artie home. Alexander had been so horrified by the evening's revelations he could scarcely speak on the way home, and they talked of other things as Artie, wretched, ashamed, slumped against the passenger window.

"I don't see that anything's really changed," said Viola hopefully as she discussed her own prospects with Artie.

"Oh, my God," Mabel groaned. "Listen Viola, you'd better leave Arty alone. If Bud Cecil ever asks you out again, I'd go . . ."

* * *

A year went by. Bud dropped out of the group. He bought his rig at last and was out on the road, hauling beef. Mabel saw him sometimes, out at the Truckstop. Whenever Bud came through town he stopped off at Jenks' Diesel if he needed repairs, and he would pass the time in the back room with Orville and Ralph, chewing the fat, telling them road stories. He would always ask after Mabel, and once or twice he had seen her sitting in the corner booth at the Truckstop Cafe. Since there wasn't much of a welcome in her glance, he usually just nodded and passed on.

The Truckstop was becoming a great sprawling empire. A tire chain had opened up a franchise next door and Beamus now had six separate fuel islands going. The awful roar of rigs pulling in at all hours of the day or night, hooting, blasting horns, backing, grinding up the back lot with their huge hauls and radios ajitter was a disgrace, complained Mabel, who thought of herself as getting sedate. It had been ten years since she and Ruby had roared through that back lot themselves, the top down, fur flying and Fats Domino belting out "My Girl Josephine" at the top of his lungs. Those were the days, mourned Ruby, who swore she'd just as soon die as "move over or slow down."

She had nothing good to say about A.A. and thought Mabel was a darn fool for letting it crowd her style. But Mabel didn't let Ruby worry her; as far as she was concerned, the program had not only saved her life, it had given her friends. Best of all, it had given her Alexander. Besides Bud, the other member to drop out of the group in that last year was Artie. For a while he had simply avoided them; then he disappeared completely. Viola had gone down to Feigenbaum's only to find he had been fired.

Then one night Mabel got called out on a Twelve-Step call. The night janitor at the Geronimo Hotel had called to say some crazy drunk was asking for her. He also warned her to come armed. This loony had been standing naked as a jaybird out on his balcony, the janitor said, where he'd "flapped his member" and, calling out nasty words, peed on a passerby.

Meeting her at the door, the janitor had walked with Mabel through the soiled hallway where he abandoned her in front of room 101. She went in and found Arthur Smolen weeping and afraid. Half-dead, wretched, he had crawled off to the Geronimo to die. Carefully removing his false teeth, which he left grinning in a glass of gin beside his sleazy bed, naked except for crumpled jockey shorts, he had lain down and taken an overdose of Nembu-tal. Mabel found a sordid compromising note addressed to some-one called "Scarlett" who was apparently a man. She burned the note.

Later, back on the wagon and restored to the group, Arthur explained to them about losing the job at Feigenbaum's and told them he had been employed as a hairdresser (Beauty Operator, he called it) at Roberto's in Tucson. He lost that job and then got hustled by a couple of traveling faggots in the door-to-door cos-metic business. After that, things had gone from bad to worse and nothing was left but suicide when the one person he'd ever truly cared for (Scarlett?) had passed him over for a younger man.

As soon as Arty was back on his feet he revived his old hostility for Harold Fimbers. Now in all this long time, this year which had passed, the group had come to value Harold. His quiet unpreten-tious ways had prevailed and yet still no one knew how much money he had or even where he lived. Somehow, no one had ever thought to question him as to the particulars of his existence.

Arty, who had nothing left to hide, or so everyone hoped, took it upon himself to question Harold, little by little. He phrased his questions so as to trick Harold.

"Well, old man, Christmas is on the way. You got family com-ing?"

"Not this year."

"Must get lonely, living all alone . . ."

"It suits me fine."

"It's not often you find a man with a clear conscience living all alone . . . where exactly did you say you live, Harold?"

"I didn't say, Arthur."

"You got something to hide?"

"No more than anyone else, my friend."

Flushing angrily, Arthur planned his next attack. As the others grew defensive and supported Harold, Arthur grew angrier.

"What have you got against poor Harold?" asked Mabel.

"I don't like his goodness," replied Arty, petulant. "It makes me nervous. Nobody's that good."

144

"You wouldn't like Harold any better if he was bad," said Mabel.

"Maybe you're right. I'd despise him more. But nobody has a right to be so good. It's his stupid normalcy I can't stand. I'd like to find out he's a pervert."

"What difference would that make? Harold is Harold no matter what you find out about him. You can't change that." Mabel wearied of Arthur's venom.

A few weeks later Arty borrowed a friend's car and followed Harold after the meeting. First Harold stopped at the drugstore on South Main street and bought a newspaper and a package of chewing gum. Then he stopped off at Molina's to buy a bottle of cranberry juice. At last he turned his car, a grey Plymouth Duster, east on the old highway and headed in the general direction of Benson. He drove steadily some thirty miles when finally, to Arty's relief, he stopped.

Harold parked in front of a diner and went inside. He ordered what appeared to Arty (who was crouching just outside the window in a wiry clump of mesquite) to be a combination platter of tacos, enchiladas and refried beans. He ate leisurely, wiping his plate with a morsel of tortilla and glanced up occasionally from his newspaper to address some remark to the only other occupant of the diner, a dark-skinned older man with a soiled apron tied about his waist.

Up to this point Arty's endurance was dedicated. But when Harold pushed back his chair, cleared his place and put a quarter in the jukebox, Arty gnashed his teeth and, cursing inwardly, clutched himself against the mean desert night, cold now and starless.

How clearly he heard the tiny febrile rubbings, the high dry crackle of a thousand furtive creatures buzzing in age-old ceremony. Nighttime rituals, desert song. The night sounds came to him isolated, estranged, even as the juke box rippled to life with a sonorous, jubilant "Jambolaya."

The man in the apron pulled out a greasy pack of cards and Harold sat down to play gin rummy with him.

"Goddamn his ugly hide, goddamn turd," said Arty, shivering in his fear of the black desert. But he had come this far, he couldn't turn back. Prancing in place, he stuck his hands in his armpits to keep warm and then discovered in the pocket of his cardigan a half-eaten Mounds candy bar. He gobbled it down, giggling with nervous gratitude, and then licked the wrapper clean.

The man in the apron pulled the shades and Arty, alone with the night, was afraid to sit down, for he imagined the barren earth was writhing with scorpions and centipedes. Rocking in place, he dozed, and then at last the door slammed and Harold came out. He drove off and Arty scurried down the road to where his car was parked in a ravine.

The car would not start. Arty screamed with frustration, then the car started, but the tires whirred and spun in the shifting sandy ravine. Arty shook the steering wheel and savagely gunned the motor, blowing a frenzy of sand up around the car. Then he got out and, heaving with sobs, grunting, he rooted the car out of the holes and put rocks and bits of mesquite into the pit beneath each tire. Slowly, with the careful patience of a madman, Arty got the car out of the ravine.

This took time and Harold was gone. Arty spent several hours driving up and down the highway, stopping to check the occasional mailbox strung out in the desert, miles and miles from even a light. The moon was up and he saw thin stretches of road trailing like dirty pink ribbons through the desert brush. But Harold Fimbers was gone.

Several days later Arty was home alone watching television when the phone rang. It was Mabel. Harold Fimbers was dead. They had found his body about forty-five miles east of town in a shabby little homestead. He had been shot through the head, murdered. The police wanted to talk to Arty and all the rest of the group, so they were meeting at Mabel's house.

Arty was terrified. No one knew he had followed Harold, but then everyone knew he had hated the man. He went down to the bus depot and bought a one-way ticket for Chicago. He hid the ticket and a hundred dollars in a satchel with clean underwear and a shirt and checked them at the bus station. Then he decided to go to Mabel's.

The group had gathered, and Arlene, Sweetie Pie and Viola were weeping and consoling one another with mournful lamentations about Harold. Very white in the face, Mabel, Alma and the others sat quietly listening to the sheriff, Alf Moroney.

"What we can't figure out," Alf was saying, "was why anyone would want to kill an old man like that . . . he had nothing in the house you could steal, not even a flashlight or a radio. Nothing. There was a portable burner and a couple of soup cans, one tin plate, some coffee and a cook-fire pot. There were a couple of *National Geographics* in the room and two books. One of them was something called *Puddin' Head Wilson* and the other was by a fellow called Theodore Dreiser. *Sister Carrie* it was. There was nothing else except the mattress he was lying on . . . the bullet blew him face-down. There were some flowered curtains I guess he'd made out of some of those El Molina flour sacks. And this . . ." Alf held up two photographs. "I found these tacked up on the wall. Anyone here ever seen these people before?"

They passed the photographs around, peering closely at the faded imprint in each picture of a blonde woman sitting on the top step of a front porch behind a group of young girls. They were wearing summer dresses.

"This must be Mary Lou!" cried Alma. "And the girls."

"They're two different people," noted Alexander. "Look here. The woman in this picture has darker hair and she's a bit plump. See. And the girls. They don't look the same. They're similar. But not the same."

"Lemme see," exclaimed Betty Rudd. "Maybe she's dyed her hair." But they all agreed the pictures were of two entirely different women. In one picture there were five little girls and in the other there were three.

"This picture was taken a long time ago," Mabel observed. "You can tell by the shoes . . . she's got on those funny old shoes people used to wear. And in this other picture, the lady is wearing the shoes we wore about ten years ago."

"You know, the houses are so much the same I thought they were . . ." added Arlene. "But lookit here," and it was seen the houses were different also.

"Who would want to go and do a thing like that to a kind old man?" cried Alma, and she broke down again and wept.

And then somehow every eye in the room was on Arthur, and even Alf looked at him with interest. Under their callous glare he whimpered and turned clammy.

"Well, what was he doing out there all by himself anyway?" demanded Arthur. "If he was so rich and important, what was he doing out there living alone in that hovel?"

"Why, he was a pig farmer," said Alf. "He raised pigs. He'd built a little stick-fence corral and he had about twenty-five pigs holed up in there. A big ole sow and a new litter as well," he added, wistfully.

"A *pig* farmer!" screamed Arty. He looked around at his friends, triumphant. "A pig farmer for Christ sakes!" He began to howl.

"Beat it," said Mabel. "I want you out of this house." Alf took Arthur by the arm and led him to the sheriff's car.

"Did he do it?" wailed Viola, glassy-eyed. She turned to the others. "Arty murdered Harold, I know it was him!"

"Nope." said Fred Rudd. "A worm like that hasn't got the guts. He didn't do it any more than I did."

"I hope they lock him up all the same," Arlene volunteered. She had never forgiven Arty for the perverted fantasies suffered in his honor.

"He'll get his due, one way or another," said Mabel.

Arty was held for questioning, released and followed for some weeks by a deputy. He lost the few friends he had outside the group, mostly a frightened band of shifty-eyed men who were not going to risk being seen with him now. He clung to the group, feeling despised.

One might suppose Arty was allowed back into the Club not just because he was an alcoholic needing help but also because the group wanted to make amends for having encouraged Arty's meanness. But no one knows. Most of them saw themselves as old sinners to begin with, and what more fitting place for Arty was there than among a group of reformed sinners? So he was allowed to be with them.

Once Arty had shown himself to be despicable he persisted in being despicable, and the group, having confronted Arty's lowness, his low-down craftiness, took the attitude that, given a fair chance, there was bound to be some good in the man. No one in that group wanted to write off a man's character for once and for all.

But a few of them took too much pleasure in suspecting Arty of murder to let go of the idea, and for Viola, it was as if all her maudlin fantasies had finally paid off. Here at last, in their town, was someone as heinous and fearsome as the Arkansas axe murderer! She for one intended to stay on his good side, although further intimacies were of course now out of the question.

A few months after the tragedy the crime was still unsolved, and Alf Moroney dropped by the Club one night to talk to them once more.

Of course everyone entertained his own opinion about Harold Fimbers. Ed and Arlene suspected he was a CIA agent on a secret mission and he'd been murdered by his own suspect. They never for a moment believed he was a common, ordinary pig farmer. Mabel and Ralph believed he had a past, perhaps debts or a little small-time swindling. Betty, Sweetie Pie and Alma were sure he had come to town for surreptitious, romantic reasons. . . . maybe he was one of them gigolo fellows (whatever *that* meant) hiding out from an enflamed admirer. Maybe he'd come to the desert to find God. Arty and Viola were convinced he was a confidence man or a gangster doing reconnaissance work in the area under the sly guise of pig farmer. Alexander and Fred Rudd felt he was simply a pig farmer.

"We're no closer to the truth about the man today than we were three months ago," Alf was saying. "We run some checks on him and we found out who he was and all, but no one knows why he come here or what he was after . . . or why anyone would kill a man like that."

"Who was he, anyway?" asked Alma.

"Well, he was Harold Fimbers all right. No doubt about that. But it almost looks like there was two or three Harold Fimbers."

The group members eyed one another knowingly. "Who's ever seen a pig farmer in a custom-made suit!" offered Betty.

"Well, now," said Alf, "Harold Fimbers had a right to that suit same as you or me . . . the fact is, Fimbers was a druggist from Spokane, Washington." There was a moment of disappointment. "Go on," said Mabel.

"This Fimbers married a woman named Mary Lou Rasmussen in Spokane, forty-five years ago in 1930. They was married in the United Methodist church. Then they had five daughters . . . Peggy, Sara, Nancy, Judy and Diana. All five girls are alive today, and Mary Lou, too." Here there were surprised murmurs and a clucking sound from Arthur.

"They were good girls, too. Peggy was class valedictorian when she graduated from Spokane High. She sent us a picture." Alf produced a blurred photograph of a serious young woman squinting into the sun. She was wearing a pointed flat black cap and a black gown. Then he showed them pictures of several of the other girls, all fine, serious young women. One of them was holding up a piece of paper (Alf explained it was a certificate for "Homemaker of the Year Award, Spokane 1949"), and she was pointing to it, pleased and proud.

"All this time, Fimbers was a druggist. He bought his own pharmacy. Fimbers Drugstore on Elm Street. Then a strange thing happened." Alf shook his head, bewildered. "Mary Lou, the wife, she says she went upstairs to call Harold down for dinner on the night after their twentieth anniversary. That was back in 1950. They were having pot roast. Harold was gone. There was a note stuck on the mirror over his bureau. She kept it all these years. Here's what it said: 'All I have is yours now. Don't come after me. The keys to the Plymouth are in the bureau drawer. The warranty on the freezer runs out in June. Kiss the girls goodbye. Their allowance is in the soap dish. There's money for the new hat you've been wanting. So long, Mary Lou. God bless you and keep you. Harold.' Mary Lou says she screamed and screamed but Harold was gone and they never saw him again."

"Why, that dirty ole bum!" cried Betty. "Nothing's too bad for filth like that!" and she turned on Fred accusingly.

"Now hold on," continued Alf. "The girls told us that until he run off there wasn't a sweeter man alive than this Harold. Year in

150

and year out he gave every one of them anything they wanted. He never bought a thing for himself. Mary Lou, she was a God-fearing, law-abiding citizen. She ran the bake sale committee for the PTA, she was one of them Daughters of Shriners United and a DAR and she founded something called AMAS, American Mothers Against Sin.

"Godalmighty!" said Mabel.

"P-U!" said Alma, holding her nose. Blowing, she gave vent to a wet, horrible noise.

"None of them could figure out why he ran off. He disappeared completely. Three years later he showed up in Mason City, Iowa where he married a woman named Ina Whipple. She's one of them Latter Day Saints . . . they got married in that church. Harold went to work in a drugstore again and pretty soon he bought out Ely Drugstore on Washburn Street. They had three kids, daughters. Now here's the funny part of it. He names these daughters Peggy, Sara and Nancy, same as the last set!"

"Who would have believed it!" gasped Arlene.

"God, a bigamist!" whispered Sweetie Pie, awed.

"Three fine girls. Here's their pictures." Alf held up snapshots of three amiable young women. "So finally we got to talk to this Mrs. Fimbers, Ina Whipple. Seems she has these terrible migraine headaches. Pete flew over to Mason City to meet her. Said she was nice enough but he couldn't tell much because she spends her time lying in the dark with one of those Hallowe'en eyeshades over her eyes. He had to whisper the whole time. She told Pete that Harold was a good gentle man, that he'd nursed her in her bed of pain for twenty years. She'd had nothing but sickness from the day she was born. Then she sez, Harold run off, just disappeared the day after their twentieth anniversary, leaving a note and all the money and the drugstore. It almost killed her. The only thing he took was the Plymouth, but I guess he figured an invalid like that wouldn't have much use for a car . . ." Alf paused.

"We found a will." There was a buzz of excitement. "He kept it under his bed. But none of us could figure it out so we sent it over to the county clerk and he sent it on to some lawyer in Mason City. But nothing ever came of it." said Alf, apologetically.

"What was in it, was he rich?" they all asked.

"Well, that's the funny thing. No one rightly knows. I brought a copy of the will. He left something to every one of you."

There was a gasp of surprise, a wonderful moment of expectation. After a struggle they agreed Alma should read the will out loud, since she had been the lucky one to have brought Harold into the Club. Here is the will.

"I, Harold Fimbers do hereby solemnly bequeath Mary Lou Rasmussen her sacred due—a new washing machine and a place up in heaven at the right-hand side of God. To my darling girls by Mary Lou I humbly bequeath a toaster, a crockpot, a garbage dispose-all, a portable Hoover and a lifelong subscription to *Family Circle* magazine. To Frank ("Who's Frank?" everyone said), I rejoice that it is within my power to leave you my dearest worldly treasures: my copy of *Puddin' Head Wilson,* the Andrew Wyeth (this was a reproduction of *Christina's World*) and the combination to the lock on the cellar door, I–I8–I940."

"That's where he keeps all the riches, I bet," cried Sweetie Pie.

"Hold on, Alma. What's all this about?" asked Mabel.

"Sounds like his shopping list . . ." sniggered Arthur.

"Danged if I know," said Alma, and she continued.

"To my precious Ina Whipple, I tenderly bequeath a peach satin boudoir and bedroom slippers with feathers on the toes. And an angel of mercy to guide and protect you and hold you close. To my darling girls by Ina, I humbly bequeath a toaster, a crockpot and a garbage disposal. To my wise friend Ignacio Hernandez (the dirty-looking man in the apron, thought Arthur) I lovingly bequeath my suit. To my good friends in A.A., I give (at this point a delicious tremor went through the room):

"To Ralph, one night in Moline.

"To Mabel, a hurdy-gurdy and a monkey.

"To Arlene, one pair of real silk stockings." (Arlene flushed up with pleasure. How had he known?)

"To Alexander—this is a man who has everything but one thing, so I leave him that one thing."

Alma paused and read ahead to herself, her lips moving madly, searching for the "one thing."

"Well?" demanded Sweetie Pie. "What's the one thing? What'd he git?" But there was no answer except a terrible frown from Alma, who began to drone on.

"To Ed, a silver bugle.

"To Alma, hot nights with a handsome stranger." (Alma paused here, thrilled to bits, and then slowly the bitter emptiness of it broke through. Her voice grew flat and dissatisfied.)

"To Arthur I leave my social security number and my soul.

("The nerve!" screamed Arty. "What the hell'd he mean by that!")

"To Bud I leave the highway and the nights.

"To Viola I leave a hot apple pie on the kitchen table.

"To Sweetie Pie, the golden goose.

"To Betty I leave Fast Eddy and the Rodeo Kings.

"To Fred Rudd, last but not least, I leave my land, the sow and her litter."

"Amen. Praise the Lord!" finished Alma, with something less than her usual fervor. She was totally mystified and disgruntled with her own bequest.

"What's a golden goose?" asked Sweetie Pie.

"Who knows? It sounds like something dirty to me," gloated Viola, who felt she'd come off rather well with an apple pie. "When do we get the stuff?" she asked.

"Jesus, Viola! You make me sick," crabbed Arthur. "Can't you see he's played us a dirty trick? He's gone off and died and he got the last word. It's all a trick!" Arthur kicked the table in his rage.

"He left me silk stockings," said Arlene dreamily. "It wasn't a trick . . ."

They all looked to Alexander, figuring he must know something. "He could have been the Pied Piper," sighed Alexander at last. "He was so quiet, so modest, if only I'd known . . ."

"Known what?" demanded Artie. "What? What was there to know! He was invisible, he wasn't anybody!"

"No, no," said Alexander, "that was only his power. It was there all along. I missed it," and he stood up to go. He saw the others watching him, surprised by his confusion and discomfort. "I thought he was only a clay pot, a simple, useful, unremarkable old clay pot. He was like a mirror! You looked into him and saw only yourself, only what you wanted to see! He gave us back our own reflections . . . I feel sick about it," he said, his hand on the door. "I should have been able to see more . . ." and he left them.

"Well!" complained Betty Rudd.

Nobody knew what to say or what to make of the will and Harold Fimbers. Arthur was the most depressed, and he clung to the feeling that this was an evil man, a pervert even. Everyone wanted to know an answer, to be told something more.

But there was no more to be told about Harold Fimbers. They were left to go home feeling confused and dissatisfied. All except Fred Rudd. He mourned the man and kept silent.

CHAPTER 12

Not long after Harold was murdered, Alexander got a call that Hickman Carter was dying. His wife, Chata, asked Alexander to come down to the ranch and see him.

"He's pretty bad off and talking about the old days. He wants to see you. It'll do him some good." Unable to rid himself of Hickman's spell, to exorcize his power, Alexander had seen him occasionally over the years. Once or twice he had gone so far as to seek him out. Deciding to go to the ranch and unable to face it alone, he asked Fred Rudd to go with him. Fred had ranched in that valley and it seemed their memories could best be braved by going there together.

They chose a Saturday in May and left early, before the heat took over the day. An interminable blue china-bowl sky rose up over the yellow flats of earth and horizon, leaving the mountains, aloof, bold as they were, truncated and diminished.

"Seems like I come alive," said Fred, his eye feeding on the land, "when I head for this valley. Like an old horse turnin' for home," he sighed. Alexander was driving. "Hardly seems right," he continued, wistfully, "to think something as small and soft as a man could eat into a mountain, tear it down that way." He pointed to a fresh pink scar torn into the haughty upper edge of a jagged mountain range. "Strip mining," he spat out contemptuously.

"We're not too far from your old ranch," observed Alexander. "Do you want to swing by and take a look at it?"

Fred pulled into himself. "Nope. Not today." Afraid he had sounded rude, he added, "I hear they changed things there. No point seein' what they done to it . . . it ain't mine no more. Nope." He shook his head.

They cut off the Nogales Highway, heading through the village of Continental on rough dirt roads, winding up into the mountains through Greaterville, a ramshackle skeleton of a settlement hidden within a gulch. Ten signs pointed to Greaterville and they all led nowhere. A cow straggled out onto the road and, incredulous, unblinking, stood to watch their approach.

"Stop a bit," said Fred, and he got out and stood beside the car. "Look!" He pointed at the sky. Alexander saw the silent white finned arc of a jet high overhead, its smooth silver belly spread along the rim of the sky.

"God, how wonderful." Fred strained to see the last of it. "I never can get used to them things."

"Have you ever flown?" asked Alexander, moved by the old man's wonder.

"Not me!" said Fred. "I never been in an airplane. It wouldn't seem right somehow," he finished.

"I've flown," said Alexander. "It's the most exciting thing in the world, floating free through those clouds. Hickman took me flying when I was little. He was in the civil air patrol. He loved to fly. Even when it rained and the lightning came, he'd beat against the sky, laughing his head off, like a kid, roaring with excitement, 'Go ahead! Rain, you sonofabitch, rain!' he'd say."

"Scare me to death," Fred remarked, looking at Alexander.

"Yes, well . . . sometimes it was scary," and Alexander got back into the car. It had been one of the tests, the survival Hickman had goaded him through. He remembered the sickening smell of fuel flooding in on him as the plane, a single-engine Beechcraft, spluttered to life; he remembered strapping himself in, feeling small. He always sat just behind Hickman and kept his eyes pinned to the man's enormous strong back. He couldn't bear to look out the window, not even when Hickman, hooting with glee, circled the ranch, swooping like a buzzard until Lily, flimsy, preposterous, a tiny stick figure, ran flapping out of the house and along the driveway.

"This is what life's all about!" he had shouted from the front seat. "This is being alive, goddamnit!" he howled, bucking the wind. Hearing no reply, he contorted in his seat to see Alexander crouched low, his eyes closed. "If you're going to vomit, do it in that can, damn your hide!" Hickman always handed Alexander a large coffee can to hold, just in case. Invariably the boy spent the entire trip hunched over the can waiting for the gorge to rise and then missed the can when the dreadful moment came. Once he had thrown up in Hickman's Stetson hat and another time vomit had sprayed all over his stepfather's head and shoulders, and he had been beaten for it and made to scrub out the entire airplane, sick as he was, after they landed.

Alexander drove Fred along the narrow rutted back roads and out onto the Patagonia Highway, leaving the ragged mountains behind. Hairy with wild grasses, the hills grew humped, one upon the other, soft and round in coats of blue violet, and dwindled down into the lowlands of Sonoita.

"We're almost there," said Alexander, feeling tight inside. He felt a sudden yearning to lean on Fred, to extract a bond of sympathy in preparation for the meeting with his stepfather.

"Did you ever feel your life was bound up even before you were born, Fred? Did you ever feel you were owned by a destiny, that you had been given away before you had a chance to begin?" He looked at Fred, wanting a truth.

"No, I can't say I ever did feel that way," answered Fred. "I'm a simple man, you know. Nothing fancy about me," he apologized. He felt he owed Alexander something but he didn't know what.

"You see," he said kindly, "I was born to be what I am. I knew who I was. It didn't take no thinking out. I've never been one for thinking much. There wasn't time. There was the work to get done and I did it. It wouldn't have done no good to say, 'Fred, maybe you should go to college or make a big name for yourself, in the city somewheres.' It wouldn't have been the truth. I was born plain Fred Rudd and that was always good enough for me. That was enough."

"Yes," sighed Alexander, "that was enough. There's something clean and fine about it."

"You've got a good life," said Fred, feeling Alexander's regrets. "You've got comfort all around you. You've got an education, money in the bank, friends. People know who you are. You're young yet . . ."

"Young!" exclaimed Alexander, surprised. "I never was young! I was born with a conscience, a terrible great shadow of a conscience that hung over me like a phantom, whispering things, little obscenities, in my ears. It was like an eye that never slept, a memory that never varied or dreamed or erased itself; it carried the records, all the obscure, obsolete moments of my life, open and gaping inside my head for me to see, over and over again. Imagine having the minutiae of your life read out endlessly, like the minutes of a meeting, so that nothing you do is free of the weight of a history that precedes you, that orders your existence, your behavior, even before it happens!" The minute he said it, Alexander wished he could have it back. He saw Fred twist his hat in his hands and then fumble for a limp Chesterfield which he extracted from a crumpled packette.

"Well," offered Fred at last, lighting the cigarette, "I can't say as I know much about these things. I always thought you was happy. You always *looked* happy," he faltered, unable to glance at this man who had so startlingly exposed himself. Alexander began to curse the man inwardly. "I mean," persisted Fred, "we all know the difference between right and wrong. It's not like you've done wrong, killed a man or something. Can't you just turn your back on this eye you say is there? Can't you just go on about your business like it wasn't there? Maybe it isn't there," he suggested hopefully. "Maybe it's just like a little kid being scared of the dark . . . well, maybe you never learned how to turn off the lights and face the dark. It isn't too late. There's always time."

Alexander sat silent, wanting to end it. The old man looked at him expectantly, ready to give whatever was needed.

"Sometimes I feel like I'm living out a story that has already been told. The chapters end, the book ends, but there never is an ending." Alexander said, finally.

"Hell," began Fred, struggling against the clumsiness of words, "Maybe what you need is to forget who you are and just let yourself be someone . . . someone ordinary who does what has to be done. Maybe you got caught up in the importance of things. Thinking never did most people a damn bit of good. No siree. Give me a good day's work and a hot meal. That's what counts. As long as the body works, well . . . thinking would be all right if it added a thing or two, if it gave something you could hang on to. It's like them mines we saw. You take something away from the mountain and you leave a hole, you strip something off that matters, a piece of the rock, and there's no way to put it back again. The mountain stops being a mountain and you got yourself a rock pile, nothing but loose rocks that don't mean nothing special. Why do you want to peel yourself down, to take away the innards that hold you up when, in the long run, you'll end up being who you are, who you were meant to be all along. Anyway," continued Fred, with something like a challenge in his voice, "it never is who you are that counts. It's what you do with yourself. That's what matters . . ."

"We're almost there," cut in Alexander pleasantly. He left the old man's words sighing in the wind, severed from their mark.

He tricked me, mourned Fred to himself. He asked me for something and then when I gave it, when I told the truth, he pulled back. He pulls strings on people, decided Fred, growing angry, feeling the twitch as Alexander yanked at another string.

"I'm so glad you could come today. I didn't want to do it alone." He smiled into Fred's eyes and parked the car in front of a rambling adobe house. Feeling used up, Fred saw it all at last. I'm here as a decoy. I wasn't meant to *say* anything or be a problem or see too much. I'm here because I know one piece of beef from the other and I've got my uses, same as anyone else. Slapping on his hat, Fred followed Alexander into the house.

"There you are!" smiled Chata, a small wiry woman who bustled into the deep cool gloom of the long hallway, talking all the while. She took Alexander's hand as if to gird him against the dragon snoring in the next room. Unafraid, she threw open the doors on

Hickman who was lying half-asleep in a maroon leather chair in the study. "Wake up! Wake up, they're here!" she chattered, tugging at a cushion behind his head and giving it a vigorous whack back into place.

"Who?" demanded Hickman, peering at the interlopers.

"Don't be an old grumpy!" Chata laughed. "You know who it is." Turning to the others, she said, "You see! Tricks, all the time little tricks. What a bad boy!" and she leaned down and gently bit his ear. Hickman's hand slid around her plump bottom and, taking a handful, he squeezed. Alexander looked away.

"So it's you! Come to pay your respects to the devil, hah?" snorted Hickman, eyeing Alexander. "I suppose he told you I'm the bogeyman, eh?" he continued, speaking to Fred. "Scared to come alone, I see. Who's your friend?"

"He's so mean!" laughed Chata, full of admiration.

"This is my friend, Fred Rudd. He was a rancher in these parts," answered Alexander, ignoring the bait.

"Well, I havn't left you a goddamn thing in my will, so you're not going to get a dime out of this good deed, my good man, but I'm always glad to see you, just the same," and standing, he shook Fred's hand and allowed his hand to rest a tentative moment on Alexander's shoulder. He's small, thought Alexander, shrunken. Hickman seemed to sag beneath a pair of droop-bottomed khakis and a threadbare sweater; his breath smelled of old age and disappointments.

"Come," said Chata, "we'll have some lunch in the zaguan where there's a little breeze." She led the way, strutting like a circus rider who, unused to firm ground, swayed with the roll of the horse, her black chignon bobbing from a long bone pin. There were chiles rellenos and a shredded pile of fried beef jerky covered in limes on a platter, frijoles, tortillas, a bowl of hot sauce. No wonder he's ill, thought Alexander, recoiling from the food.

"Eat up, my boy!" shouted the man. "These chiles'll put hair on your gizzard, get your juices going!"

"Now there's a fine spread!" enthused Fred. "A man could do worse for himself." He heaped a portion of the hot sauce over his plate and smiled gratefully at Chata as though she were a mysterious foreign deity, unable to speak his language.

Hickman and Fred began to talk ranching, and it wasn't long before Fred's whole story came out and Hickman was working up a plot to get the ranch back from Larry Slade.

"My little tiger over there, the she-wolf," Hickman held forth, grimacing at Chata who, eyes glowing, was watching the men eat, "She thinks I'm dying! Never admit it," he waggled his finger at Fred, "never! Take an old gristle like me. Or you, for that matter. We've done a thing or two that a man can be proud of. Not like these smart young pretty boys who read all the books and know all the answers and still can't tell when the wind's in the east or a bitch is in heat . . . Now they're talking about giving it all back to the Indians," snorted Hickman, glowering at Alexander. "It's easy for them. Doesn't cost nothing to give away what you got for free. It was men like us, like Fred here, who worked the land. We've got a right to it. We earned it. No Indian's going to get his foot on *my* land. Let him earn it, same as me. Bah!" he cursed, beginning to cough. "I get so sick of these gutless thinkers who put off living until it's too late, who talk all night and feel they've lived and lie in bed waiting to die. The good men die off one by one leaving all this to a race of cowards. Cowards and voyeurs, peeping toms! Jesus!" he spat out, between the hacking coughs.

"Heh! hey, what do you want, you go and ruin a fine lunch for ugly talk like this. You see!" the woman chided, wrapping him in her thin arm.

"I always wanted a son," he answered. Her arm fell. "I could have left a son something that mattered . . ."

Alexander stood up. "Oh, don't go getting oversensitive on me. No one's talking about you. You always were your mother's son. There never was anything I could do about that, although God knows I tried," Hickman muttered. He saw Alexander preparing to go and tried to hold him. "How's business? When are you going to marry that little tornado? He's got a cousin," he went on, turning to Fred. "You never saw a woman could ride like that. Full of spunk. Pretty too. If I were ten years younger," he complained, following them to the door, "I'd marry her myself. Don't go. What's your hurry?" he fretted, pushing Chata to one side. "There's still time. I've got things to say."

He watched Alexander throw his jacket into the backseat and

roll down the window, calling out, "I'll be back soon; the lunch was wonderful! Take care of him, Chata!" Turning back into the house, Hickman allowed Chata to help him back to bed. "They're two of a kind," he said to the woman as she tucked him in. He was thinking of Alexander and remembering Lily. "He never will amount to much . . ."

"Now, now," she soothed him. "They can't all be a big honcho, like you. There isn't room," and she slid her hand down under the bedclothes.

"Aren't you driving a little fast?" volunteered Fred as Alexander took a hairpin curve and the car squealed out in protest. "I'm sorry Fred." Alexander was unable to look at the man. "I'm sorry you had to meet him like this. He was something once, an amazing man, so strong. There weren't many like Hickman Carter," he finished, with pride.

"Why, I thought he was wonderful!" said Fred. "He's the kind of man I understand. It must have been a fine thing to have a stepfather like that," he trailed off.

"Yes . . ." Alexander remembered something. He had been hiding up in the hayloft when he heard the heavy wooden door slide open and a shaft of light—speckled with dust, aquiver, dancing like flies in the heat—severed the dark of the barn. Eunice laughed, a dusky silhouette in the eye of the doorway, and then, reaching for Hickman, stepped into the barn. Alexander buried his nose in the bittersweet tickle of hay and his head and neck began to itch and prickle.

"I'm never going to call you anything *but* Mr. Carter," he heard his cousin say, "and you know perfectly well why."

"I had you figured out from the first," Hickman's voice was husky, low. "You didn't fool me with that cute little fur muff . . ."

"How old are you?" she challenged.

"Old enough," he sulked.

"You're a dirty old man," she triumphed, "I wouldn't give you the time of day. Why should I?" She began to curry the buckskin, who rippled his back and paced within his stall. Alexander heard his heavy shoes thud into the sod and knock the wooden slats.

"I suppose you're saving yourself for little Lord Fauntleroy, then?" inquired Hickman, his hand on the gelding's rump.

"You're jealous of him, you know," she taunted. Alexander held his breath. "You're mean as dirt to that boy." He soaked in the sweetness of the moment.

"Fat lot you know about it," scoffed Hickman, unperturbed. She bent to rub along the belly of the horse, who stood tight and still, allowing her young fingers to caress the soft veins, the smooth balding skin.

"Of course," she continued, careless of the buckskin's pleasure, "there is something about that boy, something so soft and helpless. It makes a person mean. I wouldn't want either one of you, that's for sure." She stood up, slapping the brushes together, raising the dust.

"We'll see," said Hickman and he followed her out of the barn.

Afraid to move, Alexander held himself frozen and still until long after they left. He saw the light at the crack in the door settle from white to amber and climbed down from the loft and crept out of the barn to wash up for dinner.

"I could drive for a while if you're tired," volunteered Fred.

"I'm all right," he replied, resenting the man's intrusion.

All the same, he allowed the old man to drone on about his ranch, about the changes in the landscape picked out and lamented as they drove home through the failing light. Feeling like an imposter, alienated as he was at this moment, shut out from a right to the land and his own custom-made childhood memories, he gave himself over to the void and placated Fred.

"I feel like a new man," insisted Fred, buoyed up by the day. "I never should have given up the ranch. A man has to hold on to something till the end. You've done me a good turn, bringing me down to the valley today. That Hickman Carter is quite a man." Fred looked to Alexander for affirmation. The light was gone. Alexander pulled into Fred's driveway and shone his headlights onto the scaly, prickled stucco house, no bigger than a bungalow and closed in by twenty identical houses, synthetic, airless, squatting in formation, all in a row. Alexander saw a light go on behind a nubbled green linen curtain at the plate-glass window and Betty peered out.

"Christ!" she shouted from the door, "Where'ya been? The macaroni's burnt. Serves you right. I never git to go anywhere." She padded out to the car in a pair of hairy, shocking pink, flapping bedroom slippers.

"We've had a wonderful day," said Alexander.

"I'll bet," she complained. "I thought maybe the ole coot went and died on you or something. I can't ask you in. The house ain't been cleaned." She stood by the car and then went back into the house.

"You sure you don't want to come in?" ventured Fred. He looked old again like someone had shut out the light inside. "It was a fine day," he mumbled, fussing with the car door and then he was gone.

A week later, Fred Rudd took sick. He went into the hospital and then the nursing home. Alexander meant to visit him there; Mabel told him Fred was lonely and depressed and wanted to talk over their day in the valley. He had John Hatch send him some books on breeding and the *Farmer's Almanac,* but he never could get himself to phone the old man or go see him.

His neglect of Fred caused a cool spot between Mabel and Alexander, the first small taint of imperfection. She was one of the few people who dared to criticize Alexander to his face, and for a moment she saw the bare man.

"I thought you and Fred was such good friends . . . it's not like you to leave him lying there, asking for you."

"I don't want to see him. There's nothing to say."

"You've turned on him, then," she pronounced, full of the disappointment.

He turned a cool eye on her. "When I look at Fred Rudd, I see one thing. I see a man who saw me at my worst. He was generous enough to forgive me, to look the other way. His generosity makes me feel like a miser. When I look at Fred, I see my own failure. He was able to give more than I was, that's all, and I don't ever want to be reminded of it," he finished, shutting her out.

"There's still time, you can give him something yet," she remonstrated, but it was too late. Not long after that, Fred Rudd died and Alexander never mentioned him again.

164

CHAPTER 13

With Harold Fimbers and Fred Rudd gone, the feverish activities and even the closeness of the Club dropped off some. Bud Cecil was still out on the road and Viola was off the wagon and out on the prowl like an alley cat on a hot summer night. Sweetie Pie Ramón was visiting Hawaii with her man from Arkansas, and Alexander was busy with visitors from back east.

In the middle of this slow-moving time, Doris pulled into the Truckstop and joined Mabel one night at the Truckstop Cafe. Sly Fox and Tommy Buffalo were there and the cafe was humming with excitement. The news had just come through that Pete Gorodnitzky had got it at last.

"Who's this Pete Grodsky?" asked Mabel.

"Gorodnitzky," said Doris, "was the meanest low-down varmit that ever put on a uniform. He was a cop."

"That's right," added Sly Fox. "He worked the Pennsylvania Turnpike."

"That was one real sick weirdo," growled Lorraine, passing by at top speed with a teetering deck of hot apple pies.

"The thing is," continued Doris, "this Gorodnitzky killed a couple of guys. Truckers. He hated truckers and he lay in wait for them, hidden in the bushes alongside the pike."

165

"Killed Joey Toms and Nick Greco both," said Tommy Buffalo, shaking his head over the memory.

"He got Orway Miller, too," added Sly Fox.

"That guy sure could drive, though," reminisced Tommy Buffalo.

"Well, what happened?" asked Mabel who was beginning to feel cheated out of the facts.

"Gorodnitzky was a little pig-eyed man, no taller than this," Doris held her hand up to about four feet nine. "He'd come up behind the truckers in an unmarked car and he'd hassle them into doing something."

"I seen him follow a guy for forty miles once," explained Sly Fox. "He'd honk his horn pretty near the whole durned way, then he'd pull outta lane to pass and cut truckers off, push 'em clean off the road. That's how Orway got it. Gorodnitzky pushed him into the side of a mountain . . . he was hauling flammables and his rig caught on fire. Burned right down to the bone."

"Me and Ron," continued Doris, "was rolling hot down the 'Pike one time when this copper starts on us. He gits six inches behind the trailer—we was hauling garbage at the time—and I sez to Ron, 'I'll just bet that's ole sicko we got on us, hold onto the double nickel.' But he stays right on us. Then he pulls out real close to the trailer and passes, cutting us off, but Ron, he held onto the wheel so the cop speeds up, slams on his brakes, lets us pass him and just as we pull out to git around him, he swings out to pass. We clean near got it that time."

"That's the way he got them other guys, on the pull-out to pass, rammed 'em off the road," said Tommy Buffalo.

"He's been at this now for over ten years," Doris went on, "But there wasn't a dang thing anyone could do about it. Shorty Morton tried reporting him but that didn't do no good . . ."

Lorraine darted up to the table, her eyes flashing with excitement. "Guess who it was! Guess who got him!"

"Who?" they all exclaimed.

"It was Bud Cecil and some trucker called the Blue Streak! Bud's a hometown boy!" Lorraine boasted. "Dick Young's got it on his CB." She flew off, leaving them full of wonder.

"That Bud Cecil is no damned good. Looks like it's all over for him," observed Mabel with mixed feelings.

"Bud Cecil! Why, I met him in the Fresno truckstop," exclaimed Doris. "He's a fine hunk of a man! Built like an ox," she enthused.

"Hmmph," said Mabel.

Lorraine came back with the story. "They squashed him like a bug. He was tailing the Blue Streak when Bud comes up on him from the rear and he steps on it just as the Blue Streak jams his brakes. They squashed him like a bug!" she crowed.

"Well, by gum!" said Sly Fox.

"Goddamn!" echoed Doris "What a man!" and she rushed off to the Garage to tell Ron.

The word spread and Bud and the Blue Streak became underground heros. They were pulled in for questioning but nothing ever came of it. It just so happened the next time Bud pulled into the Truckstop, Mabel, Doris and Loretta were having dinner there. They saw him come into the cafe and some of the truckers got up and shook his hand. Others held back but they all looked at him with kindly eyes.

Doris jumped up. "You come right on over here and sit with us, Bud Cecil," and she led him over to the table.

"Is it all right with you?" asked Bud, looking Mabel square in the eye.

"Help yourself," she replied, none too friendly.

"Don't mind if I do," He seated himself next to Loretta.

"Kin you tell us what happened on the 'Pike?" asked Doris.

"No," he answered, taking the menu from Lorraine, whose eyes were filled with something suspiciously close to love. "I don't rightly think I kin talk about that," he drawled and the women respected his silence and talked of other things.

In spite of her mother's ban on truckers, it was curious that Loretta, growing up as she had in a truckstop, knew so few. Of course, her mother's prejudice had insulated her from contact with truckers, and there had been so many of them, nameless, faceless transients coming in for an hour or two, that they had for her no value, even as a curiosity; they were simply a familiar grey blur, a functional piece of the landscape, separate from her dream of life, her vision of things. The only truckers she knew personally were Doris, Baby and Matt. As Bud and Doris talked of trucking and Bud and Mabel talked of the Club and old times, Loretta found herself conscious of the bulk of Bud's thigh, tight and strong, next to her own, under the table.

Mabel rose to go. "Better git on home, Loretta," she said.

"I think I'll stay awhile, Mama."

Mabel hovered, uncertain about whether or not to sit back down and then, feeling foolish, she took herself off.

"I'll bring her home," volunteered Doris, attuned to Mabel's disapproval.

"She don't go for me one bit," chuckled Bud, winking at Loretta. "Can't say as I blame her," he finished. Loretta savored the sweetness of the moment.

"Who would believe a big stupid like that could be a hero?" complained Mabel, the next morning.

"Oh, I don't know, Mama . . . he's not so stupid," said Loretta. Mabel took a good look at Loretta.

"Now don't go getting yourself mixed up with trash, girl!" admonished Mabel.

"Now, Mama!" and at that moment Loretta looked so cool and fine that Mabel chuckled to herself and laid the thought aside.

Later, refusing to let go of her dislike of the man, she talked to Alexander about Bud.

"What's everyone see in an oaf like that? What's he got?" she asked.

"He's got life in him," answered Alexander.

"What's that supposed to mean? I got life in me! You got life . . . You got style too, that's something nobody kin buy."

"Oh," replied Alexander, "style . . . It's life that matters. You've got it, Mabel, and Bud, he has it, too. But I don't have it . . . people like me, we're here, that's all. Taking up space. Waiting to die."

"God, don't say things like that. Sometimes you scare me," said Mabel, mourning her friend, not understanding.

She had begun to think he might never marry Loretta after all. All this talk about dying. Alexander had turned forty-four and still he wasn't married. If only people like that would get together, she thought, picturing her daughter and Alexander, this land would never die out; this place would go on just the way it was meant to be. Loretta was twenty-nine, almost past her prime, and still she was waiting to leave home, waiting to find her place in the order of things.

Alone in her room, Mabel allowed herself to think on things that no one, not even Loretta, was able to share. She thought about growing old and the new pains in her breast and belly. Switching on the vanity-table light she took a good look at what she saw there, and then, bewildered by the image, the decay, she turned off the light and pushed the sight of the old woman with hanging jowls away.

Memories crowded in on her. She saw a plump young woman with golden hair in a polka-dot dress and a brown young man in baggy trousers. They were in front of the trailer. She remembered Orville, eyeing the scrawny rows of cypress still in their tubs, saying, "What are them things for?" Proudly she had shown him the picture of a massive, full-grown cypress on a seed packet. "We're going to plant things here that nobody ever seen before," she said. And she had.

But then, lowering herself into a chair, for her arches had fallen and her back ached with the weight she bore, she thought of Orville, black as a coal miner with the work of the years, and Ralph, innocent still with his uncanny resistance against growing up, stooped now and yet childlike, bewildered by the ravages of time. She thought of Flo-detta, Barbara Jean, Viola, Sweetie Pie, Arlene and all the people she knew, and in the ache of one clear moment she knew not one of them had gotten fulfilled, that finally, they would all die off, unsatisfied. She broke out in a cold sweat of fear thinking this, and then, almost savage in her will to survive, to gobble up the last moments left, she got on with the invigorating business of living.

"Are you always going to be a trucker?" Loretta asked one day when she went driving with Bud. "No such thing as always," Bud answered. She studied his profile out of the corner of her eye and, impressed, saw him slide into sixteenth gear with the ease of an old-timer. He saw her looking. "I got two more payments on this baby and then, she's mine," he said, his eye on the road.

"Your ma know you come with me today?" he asked, his eyes crinkled now against the sunset. "No," she answered. They drove to the Crystal Palace in Tombstone and danced, ate tacos and drank beer. Afterwards he asked her if she wanted to drive to Bisbee to see the moonlight on the old Lavender Pit mine, abandoned now and lying idle. "I'll go," she said. They drove around town. Brewery Gulch and the old saloons had gone to seed. They could see sheets flapping on the line next to a house in Warren, but the porches hung and weeds had grown in at the windows of most of the grand old houses.

"Loretta," said Bud, "you can come on down the road with me to Douglas, or I can take you home." He paused, unable to see her in the dark of the cab. "Which is it going to be?" He could hear her breathing quietly and then she spoke, "I guess I'll go on home." He turned the rig around and with a sweet chuckle started for home. "I'll see you next time through," he promised, leaving her off at the trailer. She stood and watched his tail lights swallowed up into the highway.

"Where you been, honey?" her mother asked, turning on all the lights.

"Out with a friend," answered Loretta, touching her mother's arm and brushing past. Then she went into her room and had a good cry.

Barbara Jean was over the next day, full of news. "That dirty ole pervert is getting married again!" she wailed and threw herself on Mabel, sobbing with rage. Mascara dribbled a crack through her face powder and Mabel thought, "Poor thing, she looks older than God."

"I'll git him this time, see if I don't," and, wild-eyed, Barbara Jean looked around for Mabel's pistol.

"Now there," said Mabel, "you take it easy. That isn't the way to git a man like Beamus." She opened a fresh box of doughnuts and, momentarily distracted, Barbara Jean hovered over the box, hunting for the biggest one.

"The thing is," she went on, dabbing at her full mouth with scarlet lacquered nails, "he promised it would be me if there ever

170

was a next time . . . he promised," she screamed and then fell back into the chair, moaning, "I stayed with him all these years. I gave my best years to that hog. I risked my good reputation and the welfare of my kids. I stuck with him even though he ain't so hot as a lover, let me tell you!" She gave Mabel a meaningful look. Mabel clearly remembered years of innuendos, smirking and self-satisfied, dropped from Barbara Jean in reference to Maurice's prowess. She let that slip by. "That man's a pig in bed, I'll tell you that much," continued Barbara Jean, who had evidently forgotten herself in the heat of her rage. "He ain't got a dinkie any bigger than this," she gloated, wiggling a pudgy little finger.

"Hold on now," protested Mabel, revolted. "Where's your dignity, Barbara Jean?"

"Dignity! Who's worried about dignity at a time like this . . . I'm gonna shoot that ole goat right where it counts, right in the dink."

"And give him satisfaction?" asked Mabel, who privately thought it was a suitable ending for Beamus. "Let him see you carried off kicking to the state pen?"

Barbara Jean sat silent. After a while she said, "What's out there for us, Mabel?"

"What do you mean?"

"I mean," said Barbara Jean angrily, "what's gonna happen to us? We're not getting any younger. It seems like life passed us by."

"Speak for yourself, woman," glowered Mabel. "You went after what you wanted . . . you got what you asked for. What made you take up with a man like Beamus? Why, you went and sold yourself like a bundle of goods . . . what'd it get you?" And plain as day, Barbara Jean saw herself in Mabel's eyes; fat and sagging, she felt the wobble of her flesh corseted and held together by the rumpled armor of her shiny flowered dress. Her scalp itched from peroxide, her soul itched from the weariness of staying young, holding together, waiting for the phone to ring, waiting for Beamus, the man she hated, to take her up once again and use her. And in that moment, her hatred for Beamus was second only to her hatred for Mabel, who saw her so nakedly.

"I got a house, a real house, not just an ole trailer parked along the highway . . . a house with a fence around it, and a fur coat and

171

bonds in the bank. I've been to Las Vegas, too," she threw in, knowing Mabel had always wanted to go there. "I'm fifty years old. That's not so old. I've got good years ahead of me yet."

"Sure you do," said Mabel.

"And what've you got?" demanded Barbara Jean. "Nothing but this trailer and that ole man out there," (nodding toward the garage) "and that girl of yours who's been raised up to think she's too good for the rest of us and she's not married yet! What've you got?" Panting like an animal, Barbara Jean glowered at Mabel.

"I got self-respect," said Mabel, who stood up and opened the door so Barbara Jean would leave.

"Self-respect," grunted Barbara Jean. "Phooey on your self-respect. You can't eat it! It don't keep you warm! It don't lie alongside you in the night. It ain't gonna pay the bills and scare away old age and come along with you in the ambulance when they drag you off to die," shouted Barbara Jean, and she sailed out the door.

Beamus went ahead and got married and Mabel saw the new Mrs. Beamus holding forth in the Truckstop. By and large, Barbara Jean had the sympathy of the family, but Mabel felt she got what she deserved. Barbara Jean lay in wait and plotted her revenge. One night she hid in the bushes near the Beamus house, and when Mrs. Beamus came along, Barbara Jean leapt out and hit her in the face with a shovel. A week later, Maurice came over to her house and beat her up. He took the diamond ring he'd given her and ripped out all her rose bushes and left them lying mangled and torn in the driveway.

Mabel and Flo-detta went over to help her clean up the rose bushes. "Why do you help her, Mama?" asked Loretta. "She means you harm. She's no good. One of these days she'll do you a bad turn."

"Maybe," said Mabel. "She's got no one; she's family. You can't turn your back on family."

Even Orville, who had retreated into almost total silence, warned Mabel about seeing too much of Barbara Jean. "I'd be careful if I was you. That Barbara Jean's passing around bad words about you . . . ."

"I'll look out for myself," Mabel persisted.

She had a lot on her mind these days. Alexander had out-of-town guests and he seemed remote, inaccessible. It wasn't that he was rude; his very politeness had come as a barrier between them. Sometimes, she thought to herself, betraying all her principles, I wish he weren't quite so much the gentleman. Ashamed of herself after such a thought, she restored Alexander to his inviolable place of honor alongside Loretta as nearly perfect in his destiny.

She managed to take the rough edges of his history, his drinking, the floundering years, his own self-doubts, as tokens of his courage; what could be more oppressive than an idol without a history? For Mabel, he shone forth as the final refinement on the best civilization had to offer, he was the hope for a finer breed to come, and if only, she thought, the fruition of her strong blood could mingle with the fineness of his, she could rest in peace.

At this time, much to everybody's surprise, Arletta Cook's engagement was announced. This caused a great soreness in Mabel. Arletta was to marry a successful young banker called Jason Bottomley, a man of no small social prestige in town. Bloated with this news, Arlene was insufferable. Mabel was tempted to drop out of the Club, so low did she feel, but pride kept her rooted to the group.

The Club meetings were full of the happy commotion of wedding talk. Mabel was utterly sick of hearing about the cake, the presents, Arletta's dress and everything else.

"Nobody wears the half-veil anymore," Mabel heard Arty say as she entered the meeting one evening. "It's definitely *out.*" Producing a current issue of *Town and Country* magazine, Arty leaned over Arlene and they whispered, studying the photograph of a smug young debutant in wedding attire. Arty had long since defected to the Cook camp rather than be left off the guest list for the wedding. Mabel shot him a terrible look. At any other time, such a look would have sizzled Arty into the ground but, turning his back on her, he continued, in high form. "When Marina Vanderbilt married Brownie Auchincloss, she wore a divine little coronet of tiger lilies with a cascade . . ." he broke off with a glance at the group who hung on every word. Lowering his voice, he continued in an enticing whisper, shutting them out.

Flushed and triumphant, Arlene allowed the bitter dregs of her glory to settle on Mabel in full. "Mabel, dear," she cooed, "I'm sure you've got lots of saved up wedding ideas of your own . . . How many guests do you think we should have?" She paused, savoring Mabel's rage. "Of course, we're only inviting *real* friends of the bride and groom," she continued, leering horribly at Mabel. "People who have loved her through the years . . . The mayor is coming, and two congressmen and all of Jason's friends from Yale. My, I do hope they don't look down their noses at us provincials with our funny clothes . . ."

"I've got me a real cute sheath dress all picked out. It's orange," volunteered Sweetie Pie, excited.

"And who *are* Arletta's friends?" inquired Mabel in a dangerously sweet voice. She was ready to forever abandon any hope of an invitation rather than endure this.

"Well, of course there's Patrick Epstein, her producer, and that nice Mickey Grigolino, her director, and—"

"Foreigners!" Mabel interrupted. "How about Victor 'the Weasel' Faldutto?" she demanded. "Aren't the Faldutto's close old friends of Arletta's? Maybe he'll be out of prison in time for the nuptials." Arlene had just curled her lip for a stinging reply when Ralph leaned across Mabel and addressed Ed Cook. "I'd sure like to know what happened to the plain ole discussions about drinking . . ."

"They went out of style ten years ago, you ole dummy," snapped Betty, glaring him down.

"We kin talk about drinking any ole time," complained Sweetie Pie. "How many times do we get to hear about a genuine society wedding with out of town guests and a catered buffet table? Men just don't know beans, do they honey?" She winked at Arlene, feeling the thrilling solidarity. Arlene rewarded her with a flicker of warmth, not letting her get too close. Watching, Artie wriggled with satisfaction.

The day of the wedding came around and Mabel had still not received an invitation. She had, however gone out and bought a wedding outfit. The phone rang and it was Arlene, breathless with the excitement of the wedding.

174

"Mabel dear," she drawled. "We were wondering why we haven't received an answer to your invitation . . . are you coming, dear?"

"Why, Arlene! Now that's funny. I did send you an answer and a present over a week ago. Haven't you received it?"

There was a profound silence as Arlene, dumbfounded, tried to remember whether somehow, quite by accident, she had indeed sent Mabel an invitation. Suspecting a trick, she answered guardedly, "Well, so many presents have poured in, I just haven't had a chance to open the local packages . . . but do come!"

"I'd love to," said Mabel, "but don't worry about me if I'm late. I have another wedding to go to *before* Arletta's, but I'll try."

"Whose?" barked Arlene. But Mabel had hung up.

Mabel arrived one hour late and found the festive little group in Arlene's backyard. A redwood picnic table was laid out with the presents, which were being watched over by an armed guard. Curious, Mabel pushed up to the table to examine the things. There was a toaster, a set of gilt plastic Japanese rice bowls with red and gold chopsticks (the Hollywood people, thought Mabel), several electric frying pans, a cuckoo clock, one very simple silver bowl (Alexander, thought Mabel), some gold and white china, six dinner plates, three luncheon plates, nine soup bowls, and four place settings in silver flatware. Two Waterford goblets stood in the center of the display, and propped up next to them was a magazine photograph of an entire set of Waterford crystal glasses in various sizes.

"Big deal," said Mabel under her breath as she passed the guard.

A strange assortment of guests stood separate from one another in clumps. Mabel caught sight of a curious group of pale young men with spots on their chins, all wearing black coats. Undertakers, she thought, seeing the Yale men. They looked unsure about what to do with themselves and they made up for it by telling jokes and laughing too loud. She noticed a nervous-faced woman in navy blue pumps and a navy and white printed silk dress, wearing white gloves and pearls, standing with Arlene. The mother of the groom, guessed Mabel.

Arlene was very grand in a cloud of swirling baby-blue chiffon with silver shoes and a corsage of spider orchids hanging off her front, like a growth. Off to one side, Congressman Alcindor and his wife Lucille sat in what appeared to be the only chairs. A maid in white stockings brought them plates heaped with deviled eggs, canapes with strips of pimento and wedges of cheese stuck with toothpicks.

A small group clustered around the buffet table—Alma, Betty Rudd, Ed Cook, Arty, and Sweetie Pie Ramón, wearing a flamingo-pink sateen dress of an iridescent hue, matching dyed satin shoes and the long dangling lavender earrings. She was talking to a squat bald fellow in a tight silk suit. He was mopping the sweat off his forehead with his cocktail napkin. The Arkansas lover boy, shuddered Mabel.

A few of the ladies from the Victor Armando Dance Club stood around smiling at people as they passed, and in the middle of the yellow patches of lawn, Mabel saw Alexander talking to a handful of men in grey suits and ladies wearing sensible shoes and pearls. There was a gay outburst from under the olive tree and Mabel spotted Arletta, dazzling in dotted swiss (Little Bo-Peep, thought Mabel), hanging on the arm of a serious young man in black. They were laughing and talking to three curly-haired men wearing sateen cowboy shirts, studded denim pants suits and fancy cowboy boots. Those don't look like any movie tycoons I ever saw, mumbled Mabel to herself.

A small boy with missing teeth played "Here Comes the Bride" over and over on his harmonica until finally one of the movie men went up and giving him a dollar, asked him if he knew anything else. The boy played "Up against the Wall, Red-Neck Mother" several times and then looked around for another dollar, but the man had gone off.

Arlene flew by the group at the buffet table and gurgled, "Isn't this wonderful! Having fun?" "Where's the governor?" shouted Mabel, but Arlene had flitted on to the next group. Somebody opened the window into the living room and started up the record player. Strains of Perry Como floated out, and then the needle was yanked off and the volume was turned up loud on "Leroy Brown." Everybody laughed and Arletta danced on the brick portion of the patio with Ed Cook, who looked miserable. Ed watched his daughter do something called "the Jerk," and finally, after a few spasmodic jiggles, he gave up and stood around, grinning and foolish. No one could find the groom, so one of the curly-haired men in denim jumped out on the floor and, taking Arletta in his arms, began a tight slow rhumba, pressing himself into her skirt and gyrating his buttocks.

"Get a load of Miss Bo-Peep and Rubirosa over there," commented Mabel to nobody in particular, but Arlene heard and rushed off to find Jason Bottomley.

Somebody put on the "Beerbarrel Polka." Arlene danced with Artie, and Alexander led a tall, very thin woman out onto the floor. Mabel's heart stopped in her throat as she saw how well they danced together. The woman was taller than Alexander but she carried herself in a curious, graceful slouch, an effortless posture of splendid disdain. She was wearing a simple brown matte silk jersey dress which moved about her tanned legs as though part of her, a long silken flow of hair, swaying with the dance. She wore tiny summer shoes and her head was thrown back with her hair hanging loose and free, brown as her dress, and she was laughing and looking into Alexander's face with a teasing, amused smile.

"Who is she?" asked Mabel, standing in the grass next to Sweetie Pie.

"Oh, her. That's the cousin, Eunice Peabody from New York."

Mabel went up to Alexander when the dance was over. Smiling, she said, "I'd like to meet your cousin, Alexander."

"So you are the wonderful Mabel," Eunice replied, taking her by the arm as if they were old dear friends. "Tell me, my dear. Who *are* these amazing people?" she laughed. "Alexei says they are his very best friends, but I don't believe him, do you?"

For a moment Mabel was speechless, and then, pulling herself together, she spoke. "My dear," and she dropped her voice to a whisper, "being as you're from the east, you might not have noticed but every last one of these people packs a pistol and if I was you, I'd watch my step . . ." Bowing slightly, she stormed off.

"Heaven!" said Eunice, turning to Alexander with her bemused half-smile, "What divine friends you have . . . and now Alexei, darling, I think I've had enough of the floor show. Shall we go?" Extending a weary hand to Arlene, she departed, flashing the pleasantest of farewell smiles.

"Isn't she wonderful!" raved Arlene, who had sidled up to Mabel to watch Eunice sweep out. "What style! Now *there's* a woman with class . . ." and she sighed. "She'll be perfect for him!"

"She looks rented to me," said Mabel.

"Rented! A woman like that, rented! What *do* you mean?" Stung, Arlene looked at Mabel in disbelief.

"She looks like she borrowed herself out of a book, that's what I mean. She isn't real. I seen pictures of women like that. Only this one's got a cobra smile. She's a snake."

"Real!" spluttered Arlene. "Real for you is what I call low-class. There's your 'real' " She motioned to Sweetie Pie, whose heaving bosoms were just poised for flight from her dress. Caught in the act of popping an entire deviled egg into her mouth, she licked her fingers and waved at them.

"I think it's refreshing to meet a real lady now and again," said Arlene, pulling herself up.

"Not if the price is too high to pay," objected Mabel. She saw Arlene had no idea what she was talking about. "Anyway," she went on, patting her arm, "I do think it's nice to meet a real woman now and again." And then, Mabel went home.

CHAPTER 14

The very next week there was a large picture of Eunice Peabody in the social page of the newspaper. Arlene telephoned Mabel, whom she knew went weeks without seeing a paper.

"Have you seen it?" she almost screamed.

"What?" Mabel's antennae began to prickle unpleasantly.

"Eunice Peabody! Big as life. It sez here," babbled Arlene, reading, " 'Glamorous New York socialite to wed distinguished second-generation Arizonan, Alexander Beal Dautremont.' "

"No!" cried Mabel. She put down the receiver, weak with the pain of it.

What a waste of a good man, she thought bitterly. And then, in her anguish, she indulged in bitter thoughts about Alexander. The rich get richer, she thought, fighting back tears of self-pity. They stick to their own kind and the blood of this land gets watered down and dried up till there's nothing left but half-breeds and fat tourists. Feeling utterly impoverished, she took a savage kick at the chair.

Six years wasted, waiting for that snot to marry my girl, she thought, and rising slowly, bowed down with the weight of it, she went off to her room and locked the door. She almost began to believe that Alexander had deliberately played with her hopes, that catlike he had seduced her dreams and come in the night to steal away her future. Mourning for Loretta, she sat in the dark rocking her pain like a baby, holding it close.

There was a gentle knock on the door. "You in there, Mama?"

"Oh, God," Mabel groaned. This will break my poor girl's heart, she thought. "I'm here." Opening the door, she clutched Loretta to herself, saying, "Oh, my baby, I wanted things so fine for you! I wanted you to have the best and to leave your mark." And, for the first time in her life, she cried in front of her daughter.

"What is it Mama?" begged Loretta, frightened.

"He's gone off and married that skinny snot of a girl," Mabel wept.

"Who has, Mama? I don't understand . . ." Stunned, Mabel stopped crying and looked her daughter in the eye, but what she saw there was so clear, so unsuspecting, that she sucked in her breath with amazement.

"Why, Alexander, that's who!" she brought out at last. Loretta was silent, trying to figure her mother out, and then, at last, she began to perceive the truth.

"Oh, Mama!" she cried, close to laughter with the surprise of it. "No, never. Never!" and then she did laugh. "Didn't you realize?"

"Realize what?" demanded Mabel, outraged, and bitterly disappointed in Loretta for not having had the good taste, the romantic determination to have loved the man. If a woman couldn't see a man like Alexander and recognize him for what he was, so fine and gold and shining rare, better than any two-bit hero or fairy-tale Romeo, then what hope was there? The moment was bitter.

"Why, I never could love a person like that," Loretta said quietly, amazed by the ferocity in her mother's face.

"Like what?" roared Mabel. "Why, *I* could have loved him!" she went on passionately. "We all ought to get down on our knees and thank God there's still someone left around here who's got a little quality! Loved him!" she moaned. Suddenly they fell silent. Each was filled with the wonder of having so misunderstood the other, of having felt so sure, all along, they had really known one another.

Alexander had left town after the announcement, so it was several weeks before Mabel saw him. He called to ask her to a party given in Eunice's honor, and since by then she had seen her way to forgiving him, she went.

Mabel arrived at the party and saw Alexander standing with Eunice in a crowd of people. He had lost weight and looked pale. Eunice, exuberant in white silk, with a white cashmere sweater trimmed in white satin rosettes thrown over her shoulders, floated up to Mabel.

"You were very naughty to me, you know," began Eunice, turning her cheek and pressing Mabel into her flat body in a brittle squeeze hello. An extravagant dry smell rose up out of her clothes —orchids growing in the dark, thought Mabel, recoiling. No one she knew would have dared press himself onto a stranger that way; among her people, a touch still meant something.

"You must be sweet to me now," continued Eunice. Her eyes were yellow and glowed disturbingly. "We're going to be the best of friends, aren't we?" Mabel grunted. "Look," she persisted, dancing up to Alexander with Mabel in tow. On her hand, Mabel spotted a simple, square-cut sapphire, large, in an old-fashioned setting. "Isn't it heavenly?" Eunice patted Alexander like a dog. "It was Lily's," she boasted.

Alexander turned toward them and Mabel saw with a gasp that his eyes were dead and glassy. He was drunk. Coming over, he put his arm around her. They moved away from the others and, putting his finger to his lips, Alexander went, "Shhhhh!" Giggling, his eyes as crooked as a wicked child's, he whispered, "Don't get mad at me, Mabel. Don't tell on me. I feel absolutely wonderful you know." He looked away from Mabel's sad eyes.

"I'm not going to tell on you. What's going on, Alexander?" she demanded indignantly with a glance for Eunice who was watching them.

"Been auctioned off," he snickered.

"Don't give me any of that stuff. I want to know in plain English what in hell you're doing."

"I've joined up." He tried to look her in the eye. "I've joined the breeding chorus." He saw she was baffled. "You know," he almost wept, "I've come out by the pond to leave the seed. Otherwise, the race will be extinct; otherwise, I'll die off. Hickman knows. It's what I always should have done." He reached down behind the bench and pulled out a glass of something. Mabel smelled Scotch.

"What about that?" she asked, her eye on the glass.

"It's only for a day or two, then I'll quit. A man doesn't seal his destiny every old day of the year, you know . . ." He hid the glass.

"Listen to me, Alexander. I have to tell you something. Do you want the naked truth or a kindly lie?"

"The kindly lie."

"All right then," She decided to slip the truth in anyway, but not so naked. "You're not going to die, not that way . . . you've left your smell on the land as it is, and not even a million years of wind and rain can take away your tracks. You've earned this land and it's earned you. If you've gotta leave seeds do it straight and clean, leave a seed that'll grow here. Not some watered-down foreign plant that'll ask for too much water and too much shade and suck up the vitality out of the land . . . don't you see? Leave something behind that will really grow here in this soil . . ."

"She's my flesh and blood, Mabel. She's got all the impurities of her race, but she's my own kind, my genus." and he stood up to go.

On her way home, Mabel thought, she'll kill him off for sure; just like the black widow spider, she'll kill him off. And then she began to understand Alexander; she knew now what he meant by dying; she knew that by clinging to the old ways, the old blood, he was dying. Mourning him, she saw that in spite of everything, he had chosen to die, to sacrifice his life on an obsolete altar. For nothing, she thought, he's giving it all up for nothing! Her sympathy began to unravel into rage until, contemptuous of the waste, the deliberate, martyred waste of a good life, she swore to stay true to her life, to the land she came from.

Thinking of Loretta, she marveled over her girl knowing about Alexander, about his having chosen to die out, and had she gone with him she too would have been lost. Filled with pride in her girl, Mabel found peace in the thought and began anew to plan and dream for Loretta.

Later that night, when all the guests were gone, Alexander went to his room, locked the door and crawled into bed. Twenty minutes later, there was a small knock on the door. Turning off his light, he waited in the dark.

"Alexander." There was a pause. "Alexander, I know you're in there." There was another knock, louder this time. "Goddamnit! Open this door!"

He got up and opened the door, pulling his bathrobe on. "What do you want, Lolly?" he asked unsteadily.

"I want to see you, silly," she said, pushing past him. He turned on the light and saw she was wearing a pink chiffon negligée banded in satin.

"It's late, Lolly. I need to sleep." She lit a cigarette and sat at the foot of his bed. "C'mon, damn you, let me alone." He began to sweat.

"Do you love me, Alexei?"

"Yes, you know I do," he replied irritably.

"I mean really love me. Passionately, with a burning fire."

"Lolly, I love you. I promise," he swore.

"Do you love me better than anyone else? Better than that old warhorse?"

"Who?" he demanded, knowing she meant Mabel.

"That creature from the Truckstop, whatshername." Her eyes flickered yellow with little spots.

"Don't be ridiculous."

"I don't believe you." She stood to go, dropping her cigarette into the glass beside his bed. Stalling a moment, she glanced through the books on his night table and then said, "It doesn't really matter . . . I don't know if I love you either." She patted his arm and smiled. "Alexei my love, do be a dear. Get me a drink, I'm afraid to go downstairs alone . . . this house gives me the creeps. Then I promise I'll be a good girl and go to bed."

He waited a moment, filled up with the pain of her. Perhaps I do love her, he thought, and he went downstairs to get her a drink. When he returned, she was going through the things on his bureau.

"Do you remember the last time I asked you to marry me?" he asked, handing her the drink. She laughed.

"Of course I do. It was in the bar at the Sherry Netherland, the Polo Lounge."

"I had just graduated from Harvard, remember?"

"Yes," she yawned, turning to go. He followed her out into the hall.

"You were wearing a blue linen dress," he added, weakened by the memory. She reached the door to her room.

"And I told you I was going to marry Drew instead." She laughed again. "Drew had more money. . . . Goodnight, Alexei darling." And she shut the door.

She was sleeping in his mother's room and he stood a moment, overcome by memories. He could hear Lolly preparing for bed. No one had slept there since Lily died, but Lolly had insisted on having that room. "It's so absolutely quaint, so amusingly froo-froo," she had said, pulling open all the cupboard doors, peeking into the tiny painted secretary, tweaking the fine old lace of the bedclothes. Then, seeing he was offended, she appeased him. "Darling, it's absolutely heavenly. I'm enchanted with the whole thing . . . you know I am," and he had forgiven her.

He remembered the day Lily had moved into that room. Sweeping aside the musty old hangings with her hand, she had said, "Oh, Alexander, I'm going to make this room everything I've ever wanted! It's going to be my secret bower, my treehouse in the woods." And, hugging him, she whispered, "You can come see me here, but no one else, ever again."

"What about the money?" asked Agnes, watching this scene through grudging eyes. She was unwilling to have anything her brother had chosen ever changed. "Money?" laughed Lily. "I've got pots of money! I can do anything I want now!"

"We'll see," Agnes warned through pursed lips.

After her divorce from Hickman Carter, Lily had drifted around Europe for a year. Alexander joined her for holidays in Positano, Venice, St. Paul de Vence. It was then that she had decided he should paint, and she had given him a beautiful oak box full of paints from Senelier. Together they had gone sketching in the hills behind Vence. He had loved to see how happy she was in those days.

"Let's stay this way always," he had said, one night over dinner in the Colombe d'Or.

"Oh, if only we could," she sighed. "But don't you ever worry," she went on, "that a great finger in the sky will find us . . . that it will circle around and around over our heads and then fall . . . squash us like bugs. We're too happy," she trailed off, and then, seeing she had frightened him, she ordered more wine and stroked his arm to erase the fear.

When he was a sophomore at Deerfield she sent him a telegram from London saying, "Have married the most divine man. Talk to you soon. Love Lily."

It was Christmas vacation when she arrived in New York, and Alexander went down to the Queen Mary to meet her. He saw her leaning against the railing. She was wearing a brown velvet hat and her face was nestled into her furs. Standing next to her he noticed a short sturdy man wearing a heavy sealskin coat and a fedora.

That can't be him, thought Alexander. Why he's old!

"Darling!" cried his mother, flying into his arms. After a moment she turned and said, "and this is Alfonso . . . my husband. Alfonso Gaspari. Isn't he wonderful!" and Alexander looked into the eyes of his new stepfather. God, he's an animal, he thought to himself. A rapacious old animal.

They took a suite of rooms at the Carlyle until Lily found an apartment. The suite was filled with anemones, cineraria, freesia, heather and lilacs, which Alfonso bought in huge quantities and showered on Lily. Unopened baskets of fruit slowly suffocating in cellophane cages, boxes of half-eaten Godiva chocolates, magazines, *Europeo* and *Oggi*—all these things were left lying about the suite. The room smelled thick with Gitanes, and the tiny refrigerator was crammed with Dom Perignon, fresh figs and prosciutto.

Alfonso liked to strut about the suite barefooted in a silk shirt opened to his waist and a pair of black bikini underpants. He had a magnificent build, thick and muscular, with a large tight belly matted with hair. He sat, almost naked, his brown legs spread, on a pale lemon-colored silk chair, smoking, talking with Alexander, but all the time watching Lily with burning eyes.

"See this," he'd say to Alexander, lifting his shirt and pointing with his thumb to a place on his back. Alexander saw a terrible deep gash, about eighteen inches long. "Palermo," he grunted. "During the war."

"Oh," said Alexander, "the war."

"That's right," continued Alfonso, unbuttoning his shirt. "I was a partisan. I fought for your country. Take a look at that," and he pulled off his shirt and, jabbing with his thumb, pointed to a deep red welt burned into the hairs on his belly.

"Wow," said Alexander.

Then, closing one eye in a dreadful wink, Alfonso gestured down towards his crotch. "That too," he bragged, bobbing his head and looking downward with great satisfaction. "They got that too. Nothing sacred for the Nazis. But he still works good!" he confided, reaching down with his hand to give his groin an admiring tug. Oh God, thought Alexander.

Lily drifted in. "What are you two darlings whispering about?" Alfonso snorted. "Guess!" he roared, slapping her bottom.

In the night, Alexander heard horrible noises across the suite. He heard the bed heaving with the weight of the man, he heard the grunts of an animal and the low moans that followed. Her moans. At first he was terrified, and one night he stole out into the living room, near their door, perhaps with the idea of protecting Lily, or maybe just to be near her. He stood frozen, listening to the violent, wet sounds of their passion, and then, sick with the confusion of it all, he heard his mother sob, "Never leave me, never leave me, my man, oh God, how I love you. Hold me."

Dazed and sickened, Alexander crept back to his room and pulling the sheets, blanket and pillow over his head, he wept.

Alfonso was a great artist, a painter. He took Alexander to the museums, where he was forced to run through the rooms in order to keep up with Alfonso, who never looked to the right or the left until his sensitve radar led him, almost by remote control, to a painting he approved of. Moving very fast, pointing with his thumbs, he would say, as they passed whole rooms full of paintings, "Don't look! It's shit!" and then finally, when he stopped, "Ah!" he would sigh, "Now *that* is a work!" He explained to Alexander what made it good, using his thumb to carve out sweeping, descriptive images. If he brushed against the canvas and the guard rushed up to restrain him, he bellowed, "Stand back, *idioto!* Do you know who I am? Porca miseria!" and he grimaced horribly at the guard, who shrank back in fear.

One day, as Alfonso and Alexander were awaiting Lily's arrival for lunch (they were at Romeo Salta's), Alfonso nudged Alexander with his elbow, winked and said, "Eh! and what about you . . . you get rid of the virginity yet?" Alexander turned scarlet.

"No," he whispered. "I don't think so . . ."

"Think so! And what is this think so?" roared Alfonso, bent backwards with laughter. People began to notice from the nearby tables and the waiter snickered.

"Take my advice," said Alfonso, leaning close with his face pressed into Alexander's. "Do it quick. Find a nice girl, clean, and . . ." leering at Alexander, he made a circle of his thumb and index finger and with the other hand jabbed his index finger through the hole repeatedly. "Hah hah!" He continued, "You wait too long, the other side gets you." He looked meaningfully at Alexander.

"What other side?" the boy asked.

"The fairies!" The man grimaced. "You gotta watch out every time for the fairies, a pretty boy like you!" and pinching Alexander's cheek, he muttered, "Bah! *Che schiffo!*"

"I'm only sixteen," protested Alexander.

"Sixteen!" Alfonso grunted. "Sixteen! Listen to me. By the time I was sixteen I had two children. I did it when I was a baby, twelve, thirteen, out in the field with the bulls and the horses, I did it first time with Stefania Cicci, the neighbor lady. She was forty, a big lady," and carving her out of the air with his hands, he continued, "let me tell you, I was something. I used to watch my sister make peepee," and he threw back his head and howled. Then, stopping as suddenly as he had begun, he turned on Alexander, prodding him with his finger. "You. Take my advice. Do it now. What's the wait? Do it," and he stood up to pull out Lily's chair.

By the time they moved to their apartment in New York, Lily had begun to weary of Alfonso. Alexander saw little signs. His mother began to go more often to the hair dresser and she dawdled over her errands, straggling home hours late. This unleashed a terrible rage in Alfonso, who paced the floor of their apartment, lighting Gitanes, cursing and grinding the cigarette butts out on the floor. Beating on Alexander's bedroom door, he shouted, "Where did she go? Where is she!" Alexander opened the door a crack.

"She's at the hairdresser's. Arden's."

"Dial me the number," demanded Alfonso, and so once again, Alexander called Arden's. "Mrs. Gaspari is gone." They heard the key in the door and, slinking off to his room, Alexander awaited the inevitable scene.

"Where have you been, *putana* whore!" he heard Alfonso bellow. He pronounced whore "hoor." And then there were violent, bitter words, the soft sound of his mother's voice, pleading, the walls shuddered with slamming doors, drawers being ripped out of their sockets. Alfonso is packing again, thought Alexander, hearing his mother's sobs.

Sometimes Alfonso actually left. Once or twice he flew back to Italy, and his mother shut herself in her room, in the dark. There would be telephone calls in the night, long conversations to Rome, whispers, laughter, and then Alfonso would come home.

This went on for three years, until Alexander was a freshman at Harvard. He came to New York for Lily's thirty-eighth birthday party and saw lines in her face that had never been there before. She was nervous and fearful-looking, and Alexander knew she was wretched.

"Leave him, Ma," he begged her.

"I can't." Weeping, she put her hands over her face. "He said he would kill me if I did," Lily shuddered. "I know he will, I know it."

Hating himself for his fear of the man, unable to rid his mother's life of this presence, Alexander did the only thing he could. He telephoned Hickman Carter.

Three days later, Hickman flew into New York and brought Lily back to Tucson, to the house in Snob Hollow. He got her a manservant, one Jesus Jimenez, a bricklayer and a great hulk of a man who watched over her night and day. She had her name legally changed from Gaspari to Dautremont again and, much to the displeasure of Agnes, talked of settling in Tucson.

It wasn't long before Lily fought bitterly with Agnes. Her mother had abandoned Tucson for Virginia, so she had only the one old lady to appease, but Agnes was inexorable.

"I don't want men in this house," she insisted. "I want to end my days in peace and dignity."

"It's not your house, Agnes. You're welcome to stay here of course, as long as you like. But it's not your house."

"What would Eugene say!" wept Agnes, puckering and watery. "God forgive you for turning an old lady out of her family home . . . after all these years. He (her eyes flew heavenward) would roll over in his grave to see your carryings on. All those men," she continued, referring to Hickman and Alfonso, "all those dreadful coarse men . . ." and wringing her hands, she bemoaned her lot.

Whenever Lily did have a caller, Agnes sat posted in the front hall till he left, and whenever Lily drove away from the house, she saw the upstairs curtain move in the window of Agnes's room.

Several years went by in this fashion, and although Lily traveled, she made the house in Snob Hollow her home. Agnes, as decayed as a rotten apple, had sunk and withered into herself, and night after night she and Lily sat opposite one another in the large dining room in silence. Inez Hoover was the only person Agnes had to talk to. Her few friends had died off and she was left to await Mrs. Pew's arrival with avid excitement whenever her old friend chose to come. Alexander had disappointed her by defending his mother, and slowly she soured on him as well as on Lily.

When Alexander graduated from Harvard she sent him his father's gold pocketwatch and a long letter full of complaints about Lily. She intimated that Lily, whom she referred to as "that woman," was having unwholesome relations with her manservant, Jesus Jimenez. She begged Alexander to come home and hinted that it might be necessary to have Lily "put away" somewhere. Angry, Alexander never answered her letter, and it was three years before he returned home. By then, Agnes was dead.

He arrived home when he was twenty-five, a recovered alcoholic. Full of the loneliness of New York, the disillusionment of

Italy, and the lost, drunken years, he arrived home ready to begin his life anew. He had only left one thing behind, his cousin Eunice, Lolly, married to Drew, and he yearned for her.

He felt the thrill of coming home, of flying low over the pitted brown hollows of desert land, pockmarked and furrowed mauve and pink, coming home at last. The earth had waited, stretched out, round and yielding as a lover. His mother sent a car and driver to the airport. Driving home, the man told him his mother was ill. Hardly able to recognize his house, the abandoned neighborhood, he arrived to find the shutters hanging warped and dismembered from their hinges. A wild hairy green vine had devoured the front of the house, and the windows gaped down with empty sockets onto the straggling garden. Awnings flapped like ragged petticoats torn loose from their moorings.

He ran up the steps, and Inez threw open the door and took him in her arms, rocking him like a baby.

"Where is she?" he cried.

"Up there." Inez rolled her eyes upwards. He climbed the stairs two at a time, shouting, "Ma! I'm home!" But the only answer was silence. Inez came running up after him.

"Wait a minute," she panted.

"No," he said, and pushing her aside he stepped into his mother's room.

Her room was almost dark, with nothing but a dim grey light broken by curved amber shadows, yellowed stripes of light, seeping in at a crack in the shutters to weave oblique patterns across the bed and the floor. A curious, stale medicinal smell disfigured the memory of Lily's own delicate faraway perfume, and it was that at first which frightened Alexander. He stopped altogether and very quietly called her name. But the only sound in the room was the slow swishing of the fan overhead.

He went to the bed and leaned over her. "Ma!" he whispered. "Ma, I've come home!" She was lying on her back with her head twisted. Her mouth was open and as he bent over to take her in his arms, he smelled her stale, putrid breath and pulled back. Her hair was matted, and along the edge of her hairline he saw a glisten of sweat. He pulled the sheet up to cover her thin white thigh, blue-veined and held at a crooked angle like the leg of a broken doll lying twisted in a heap. Her nightgown was soiled and smelled faintly of urine.

"Ma!" he cried, shaking her. "Lily! Lily!" He shook her until her head wobbled on its stem and Inez came up from behind and pulled him away.

"What's the matter with her?" he sobbed.

"It's them drugs, chile; it's the morphine," she moaned, tears running down her face. She pulled open the night table drawer and he saw hypodermic needles and bottles, the old thrown in with the new, all in a jumble. "It's them friends of hers that brings it, She cain't live without it no more," and tenderly she led Alexander out of the room.

In the next year Alexander had Inez dress Lily in a pegnoir each day at five and then he carried her down to the front parlor. Laying her down on the red damask couch, he made her tea and read to her. He read her everything—Jane Austen, Dickens, Trollope, Balzac—but best of all, she liked to be read fairy tales.

She couldn't bear the light, so he kept the curtains pulled and read by candlelight. She liked to talk of her childhood, of the farm in Virginia, of climbing trees and hiding from her sisters in the woodshed. She giggled like a schoolgirl over her memories, and there was no mention of the later years, of Eugene or Hickman or Alfonso. Hickman came to see her once or twice, bringing her huge bunches of cornflowers, always her favorites, but she did not seem to know who he was.

Alexander tried carrying her into the dining room for dinner, but she dribbled her food and was frightened by the furniture which she saw as dark and menacing. In that period, he hardly left the house and discouraged people from coming there. He got her morphine and left her in peace.

Inez came into his room one night and stood at the edge of his bed. He opened his eye and saw her there, dark and still. "She's dead and gone," she said at last, and then gently, ever so gently, she tucked in the sheets around Alexander's feet and arms.

CHAPTER 15

Alexander married Eunice in the same Episcopalian church in which Lily had married Hickman Carter so many years ago. Nanine Brown, Alexander's aunt from Boston, arrived for the wedding along with her sister Lydia, Eunice's mother. Eunice's brothers, tall men with serious faces, important bankers and stockbrokers from the east, came bringing their wives. It was not, however, a joyful crowd. Loretta arrived with Mabel, the only friend Alexander had invited from the Club. Alexander had dropped out of A.A. and drifted away from the others.

"Well, Alexander! I can hardly say welcome to the family and give you the sort of pep talk the occasion merits, now can I, old boy, hah hah!" quipped the stockbroker, slapping Alexander a great fraternal blow on the back.

"So you did it at last!" roared the banker, evidently finding more humor than anything else in the situation. "The old girl's a real handful. I don't envy you . . ." he sniggered.

Nanine squeezed her nephew affectionately. "Well, dear boy, you got what you wanted. I can't pretend to understand you but you're so awfully clever, I'm sure it will be just fine . . ." Chuckling, she patted Alexander's hands in her own. And then, turning to Mabel, Nanine said, "You are Mabel, of course. And I am the old dragon of an aunt. What do you make of all this?" She took in the crowd of well-wishers with an unimpressed eye. Mabel liked her.

"Do you like my niece?" Nanine inquired, drawing Mabel off for a stroll.

"I can't say I do."

"She's a cold-blooded fish if ever I saw one," Nanine sighed.

"But then why'd he do it?" mourned Mabel.

"Ah . . . ! Why do any of us mess up our lives? He always wanted her. She was the one thing he couldn't really have. A symbol, I suppose, maybe even a mockery. Of course he wanted her desperately when she chose his roommate . . . now I suppose he thinks he has her. But you'll see, worse luck. She'll eat him alive . . . she'll revenge herself on him."

"Revenge?"

"Oh, well, perhaps nothing so odious as revenge," relented Nanine. "But our poor dear boy will have to pay dearly for all her disappointments . . ." and, appearing vastly entertained by the whole situation, she wandered off.

Mabel passed Eunice and overheard her saying to a small group of women, "Of course, the whole place has to be re-done. God, can you imagine living in this mausoleum! Alexander won't sell it so we'll just have to make do. But of course, we'll probably end up in Greenwich like everyone else. My dears," she continued, keeping one eye on Mabel and lowering her voice only slightly, "you simply cannot imagine some of the funny, curious people Alexander has introduced me to here." Mabel walked on.

Loretta stood talking with Alexander. It had suited him to avoid her since Eunice had come to town: knowing he owed Loretta nothing had not absolved him from the futile feeling that he should have given her something. It was his fear of the expectations he either genuinely perceived in others or attributed to them that had constricted him all his life. The tiresome, self-inflicted burden of being a man for each and every fantasy except, perhaps, one's own. Even so, it was not in his nature to alienate Loretta.

"Well, my dear, do say you forgive me for not quite proving . . . consistent, at least. I was hardly the beau ideal, I'm afraid," he threw out, somewhat carelessly. He was very drunk.

"I don't know what you mean," she replied in even tones.

"No, no!" he protested, feeling at that moment such a thorough distaste for himself that the sight of her infuriated him. "Let me at least be contrite if for no other reason than the good it does me. I loathe misunderstandings, don't you? I always wanted us to be perfect friends and I only meant that, in the end, I found myself needing to do that very thing I remember once advising you against . . ." Too generous to let him see she understood, Loretta waited until he finished. Appalled by the look of infinite weariness in his eye, she felt, for the first time, a deep love for him.

"Maybe you think I sold out and got a thirty-year plan or whatever," he went on, stubbing out his cigarette in a pot of geraniums, "but it really doesn't matter, you see. I did exactly what I was always meant to do, just a little bit late, that's all, but I *have* done it, you see . . ." He avoided her eye.

"Nobody ever gave me what you did," she offered tenderly, touching his arm. "You gave me more than I ever hoped for, you understood me after all . . . you made me feel so . . . admired. I never wanted more . . ."

"You *are* good," he smiled wearily, reaching for his drink. He suspected she was telling the truth, but it didn't matter; he was not in the mood to believe her words and he felt wasted by her generosity. Seeing the love there in her eyes, he felt indebted. "I just want things to be right," he murmured at last, and patting her arm, turned away.

Mabel was standing close by, waiting to say goodbye. Alexander was going to France on his honeymoon and Mabel felt he was passing out of her life. As if anticipating her thoughts, he took her hand, saying, "It will only be for a little while, Mabel. And then I'll be back, and we'll meet at the Club, and afterwards we'll go down to the Starlight or out to the Truckstop and talk about our friends . . . you'll see. I want to know everything about Viola and Artie and especially Arlene when I get back." Mabel was silent. "Hold on to it for me. Don't let it go." Then, before she could wish him well, he was gone.

In the days to come, Mabel dragged herself around the trailer, heavy with loneliness. Except for one postcard from someplace

she had never heard of, she had no r
to remember how she had managed
along, but those days were so remote
more. Loretta saw her mother grieve,
amuse her, so she sat with her for l
television set and tried to think of th
emptiness and talked to her of the old
her sad. Orville crept in and out of the
he too, mourned her loss.

Flo-detta and Barbara Jean started
Loretta encouraged it, thinking that perh
rivalries would sparkle her mother to life.

a fur coat and l
house . . .”
“If I w
smirke

..на от old

"What's happened to all your highfalutin friends?" asked Barbara Jean, plunking herself down next to Mabel and looking
around the room as if, any moment now, she expected to see Mrs.
Rockefeller herself step out from behind the curtains. Even this
didn't get a rise out of Mabel.

"Rich people," echoed Flo-detta. "They're the worst. Fair-
weather friends, all of them." This was meant to be sympathetic,
but it galled Mabel.

"And just how many rich people do *you* know, Miss Know-it-
All?"

"You might as well come down off'n your high horse," snapped
Barbara Jean. "Fat lotta good it's done you hobnobbing with them
fancy folk," and she huffed over to the door. "C'mon, Flo-detta,
let's go git us a Dr. Pepper over at the station."

Things at the Club weren't much better. Seeing Mabel was
down, Arty abandoned her and joined up with Arlene. He had
been in awe of her as long as Alexander was around to cast his light
over Mabel, but now he thought, she's just ordinary, like the rest
of us.

Arlene was full of tidbits about the newlyweds, Arletta and
Jason. "Can you imagine," she said to Arty one evening, loud
enough for Mabel to hear, "the monthly down-payments on that
new ranch house of theirs are more than most people's rent for a
year!" Silence from Mabel.

"Shoot," spoke up Sweetie Pie, "I'd a whole lot rather have me ve in a hotel room than shell out money for a

re in *your* situation, I guess I'd feel that way too,"
Arlene. Arty tittered.

What's *that* supposed to mean?" demanded Sweetie Pie,
nowing perfectly well.

"Oh, leave it alone," Mabel muttered.

"Well! Get a load of Miss Goody-Two-Shoes!" prodded Alma,
hoping for a good fight. But Mabel wasn't ready to do battle yet,
and she sat drinking her coffee in gloomy silence.

"It's like a morgue in here," observed Arty, to fill up the silence.
"I wish Bud would come back, or even Viola . . ."

"Bud's a hero these days. He don't need us," said Alma.

"Even hero's have to go to the bathroom," cracked Arty,
pleased with himself. He looked around. No one was amused.
"He's got a new girlfriend, anyway," he sulked.

"Who?" asked Sweetie Pie.

"Never you mind, Miss Snoop!" Nobody seemed interested, so
Arty was driven beyond his ordinary boundaries of courage. "She's
a real princess, this new girlfriend . . ."

"What in God's name are you rattling on about?" asked Alma.
"How do you know what Bud Cecil does?"

"Oh, I know all right," Arty said, nettled. "I seen him twice at
the Maverick up in Tucson, all smoochy-smoochy with this girl.
She's someone we all know," he brought out at last.

"Okay, who is it then?" demanded Alma. Artie's courage gave
out and he hid behind sly smiles. Winking at Arlene, he wrote a
name down on a piece of paper and passed it to her. She flushed
up with pleasure and, looking directly at Mabel, toyed with the
paper. Quick as a snake, Alma leapt to grab the paper, but Arlene
stuffed it into her blouse. Heaving and angry, Alma wrassled it
away from her, reaching right down into her blouse to get it. Artie
turned purple with the pleasure of the moment, and even Mabel
was pleased.

Arlene, quivering with outrage, stood up and shouted across the
table at Mabel, "Go ahead and laugh, you old bag, but it's your
daughter who's been sneaking around town with a greasy old
trucker!"

196

"Liar!" said Mabel. Puffing from the skirmish, Alma yelled out, "Arlene wears falsies!" Triumphant, she flapped something pointed and white.

"She's false clear through, if you ask me," scorned Mabel, come to life.

"Lemme have it!" howled Artie, grabbing for the odd little contraption.

"Pervert!" screamed Arlene, and turning to Ed who was blinking in confusion, she demanded, in her most awful tones, "Get me out of this place. *Now.* I want to go home."

She sailed out the door dragging Ed. Artie, thrilled with his mischief, sidled up to Mabel, thinking that perhaps it behooved him to stay on her side. But she would have none of him and turned away in disgust. Betty Rudd came in late but nobody spoke to her.

"What's going on?" she demanded, looking around at the sour faces.

"Oh, Betty!" began Sweetie Pie. "You missed the most wonderful thing!"

"Goodnight everyone," snapped Mabel, and she left the room. "Now, what's eating her, anyway?" she heard Sweetie Pie say to the others. When she got home Mabel saw that Loretta was out. Turning on the T.V., she sat in the dark, waiting. At about two in the morning she heard the air brakes on a diesel, close to the house. Loretta came in, tousled and glowing.

"Where you been?" asked Mabel, in the dark.

"Mama! What are you doing here all alone?" Loretta reached for the light.

"I asked you a question, girl!" Loretta stood a moment, unsure of her mother's voice.

"I've been out, Mama. Dancing. What's wrong?" she asked, afraid. There was a terrible stillness in the room as the two women waited for something to break the spell. Finally, loathing the smell of her own fear, Loretta spoke up.

"It was Bud Cecil, Mama." Still, the silence. Loretta felt the hairs on her neck begin to prickle, but she went on. "I love him. We're getting married." Just as Loretta was preparing an apology, just as she was thinking how to tell her mother how it happened, Mabel

197

came up out of the dark and slapped the girl, hard. Then, turning, Mabel went to her room.

"You can't do that to me!" Loretta sobbed, outside her mother's door. She had never been hit before; she had never known anything but her mother's tough, gentle ways. Orville came out, scratching his eyes.

"What is it, girl?" he asked, frightened to see her this way. She wept out her story, sitting on the end of his bed in the dark. Mabel heard it all through the wall, and turning into her pillow, she rocked herself to sleep.

No one spoke of the matter the next day. It lay buried in their lives like a deep, troublesome growth, and there was a new, unfamiliar silence in the house as the women went about their work. Mabel was feeling poorly and she stuck to her bed most of the day.

Loretta went over to the Truckstop and called Bud and told him how things were at home. They decided to get married soon. A week later, Mabel saw that Loretta was wearing a wedding ring but still she kept silent. She knew Bud must be off on a run; otherwise the girl would be gone by now.

"We're going to lose her, Mabel, if you go on like this," said Orville one night. His tired face was full of the pain.

"We have lost her," she answered.

"No, it's you who's doing this to us. You're driving her away." Hating Mabel, he turned from her.

Those were bad days. Mabel stopped going to the Club and Orville, too depressed to come home, stayed away. Ralph hung around the trailer looking scared, and finally Loretta left.

Ralph heard from Loretta that she was out on the road with Bud, but he was afraid to tell Mabel so he and Orville whispered about it in the garage. Then he heard she had settled for the time in El Paso and he gave Mabel her address, but Mabel tucked it away somewhere and refused to write her.

At last, since there was nothing else left to do, Mabel got sick. She lay in her room and it hurt to breathe. At first she refused to get a doctor, but Orville and Ralph were so worried about her they called one in to see her. She had pneumonia. They moved her to

198

the hospital in town where, disgruntled and crabby, she bullied the nurses. It's a good sign, everyone said. Mabel's coming around.

Barbara Jean went to visit Mabel three times, and when at last, after hours of unproductive waiting, Mabel had not yet mentioned her will, Barbara Jean decided to take the bull by the horns.

"Mabel," she said one day, "You're not going to hold things against me now, close as we've been, are you?"

"What in tarnation you talkin' about?" grumbled Mabel.

"I've done my duty by you, there's no disputing that," continued Barbara Jean, her eye fixed on Mabel's diamond ring. "I've come over here to this terrible place to see you day after day in the hopes we kin let bygones be bygones . . . Never mind the time it took me to git here all those days. That don't matter, nor the cost of the gas neither. It ain't *that* I'm worried about or even the possibility of catching some horrible disease, risking myself like I am, to come here and see my best friend . . ." She paused to allow the weight of this new avowal sink in properly. "What matters to me is that you don't sit here alone. Especially not if you're really going to die or something." She gave Mabel a penetrating glance.

"Just what is it you want?" inquired Mabel, knowing exactly.

"Why, I don't want anything except to be friends!" protested Barbara Jean.

"Well, that's just as well," commented Mabel, " 'cause that's all you're going to git."

"What's that supposed to mean?"

"Just that. It means I ain't going to leave the stuff to you. No reason why I should." She rolled over with her back to Barbara Jean.

"Now you lissen here, you ole bitch!" screamed Barbara Jean. She ran around to the other side of the bed. "You ain't no better than anyone else. You're goin to die jes' like plain folks—"

"Her time ain't up yet!" cracked a voice from the doorway. "You'd better clear out before I get it into my head to do you some harm." Barbara Jean turned to face Doris. There was a deep chuckle from the bed.

"I wouldn't mess around with no trucker," Mabel warned Barbara Jean. "That lady there drives a White Freightliner and she's a real pistol. Mean as all get-out," she concluded, hoping for a showdown. But Barbara Jean didn't need to be told twice and she shot out of the room.

"Who's the battle-ax?" Doris plumped herself down into a chair.

"The buzzards have started to circle the carcass," grumbled Mabel.

Doris laughed. "The best way to find out who your friends are, "is to go broke, clean house or break a leg . . . I guess you're just finding out things ain't no better than you knew they were."

"I don't like needing people," complained Mabel.

"Oh, you can need people all right," asserted Doris. "It just doesn't make sense to count on them, that's all."

"I'd like to be able to count on something. I'll tell you one thing. When I get out of this place, the first thing I'm going to do is find me something I kin count on. I never looked before," Mabel admitted.

"What about the land? You always had the land, and you've got Loretta," Doris ventured.

"The land is a lonely thing sometimes. It holds you down. Fenced-in land, it owns you and the other land . . . well, it ain't mine. And Loretta, she's gone."

"Listen." Doris laid a hand on the bed. "Life ain't worth a fig without belonging to *something* . . . sometimes I say to Ron, 'Let's find us a spot and settle down. Let's git us some land and build something that will be there the day after tomorrow . . . After a while, one road can git to look pretty much like the next. I git tired out there, day after day.' But Ron, he sez, 'One more haul, hon. Then we'll look.' You see," Doris went on, looking Mabel in the eye, "we ain't so free either. We've put our best years into that road. It owns us, piece by piece. We belong out there." She waited a moment. "Mabel. In all these years I never butt into your business, never once. But something's on my mind. I'd like to say my piece and then I'll be on my way. It's about that girl of yours, about Loretta." She saw the resistance in Mabel's face.

"It's always better to hold off a little and wait and see what a

200

person's gonna do before you make up your mind about them. There's always something left unfinished. We never do git to finish," she put in, reluctuantly. "Loretta's young yet. Oh, I know she let you down and I ain't saying she was right or wrong. She did what she had to, that's all." She saw the tight line of Mabel's mouth. "I saw her last week. In El Paso. Bud's out on the road and she's staying in some motel, a regular dump, and things is lonely for her. She's alone for the first time in her life."

"I knew she shouldn't have married him," Mabel said bitterly.

"Mabel, remember what it was like in those first years? Remember how getting married seemed so exciting and free, and it seemed like we was going to be taken care of, we was going to have someone to talk to. Someone of our own. It's like a woman saves up things all her life to talk about with her husband. And then, when she sees he don't really want to listen, that all those years he'd just as soon spend the time in silence, near her maybe, but in silence, it comes as an awful shock. There ain't no lonelier time in the world, those first few years of marriage, don't you remember?"

"I remember," said Mabel.

"She could learn from you," pleaded Doris. "Loretta needs to know that her loneliness is a part of life, that she ain't alone, that it's happened to the rest of us—that part of being a woman is never getting enough, learning to live with the silence in a man, the things they never hear or say. You could tell her. And now," her voice trailed off and she stood to go, "I guess I'll hit the road. So long, now."

"So long," said Mabel, watching her go. She began to ache for Loretta.

The day before Mabel was supposed to go home the doctor came into her room to see her.

"How'm I doing, doc? I'm feeling mean, so I must be doing fine," she laughed. There was something in his eyes that bothered her. Like an animal sensing an enemy in the brush, she circled and held him off. "I'm all packed and ready to git outta here, Nothing's going to stop me now."

"Mabel," he began.

"I don't want to hear it, doc," and she turned away.

"I got your x-rays here. They don't look too good." He paused. She was looking wild-eyed and trapped. He put a hand on her but she shoved it away. "Get out of here," she threatened.

"It's cancer, Mabel. I'm sorry." He stood and waited but she was frozen, staring at the ceiling.

"Well?" she spat out at last. "What are you waiting for? Go on. Clear out." He left. Mabel turned her face to the wall and lay there for a long time without moving. Fifty, she thought. I'm only fifty. And then, after a while, she got out of bed and dressed. She telephoned Ralph and sat on the edge of the bed, waiting for him to come get her.

CHAPTER 16

When Alexander arrived home from Europe, the first thing he saw was a stack of notes bound up in a rubber band and, lying next to them on the hall table, a single note. It was from Loretta. She had never called the house before and Alexander knew it was important.

Eunice was using the telephone. Upon arrival, she had taken a look through the veranda door and gone straight to the phone to call Whitaker Pools and complain about some detail in the new pool they had built while she was gone. Hanging up, she called a New York decorator and arranged for him to fly out immediately. Then she called her best friend, Deezie Lawrence, in New Canaan.

Quietly letting himself out of the house, Alexander got into his car and drove out to the Truckstop. It was fall, October in the desert; the young green fuzz had died off the desert floor and the waxy blossoms had blackened, shriveling back into the earth. It didn't rain here, he thought, mourning the earth.

Eunice had wanted to stay a few weeks in New York to shop and have lunches and see her friends, but Alexander insisted on going home. She sulked on the airplane, but he had ways of appearing not to notice. It doesn't matter, he thought with loathing. I have her now, I have done my part, she can do what she wants. She had resettled herself with her shoulder in his face; smelling the cloying department-store scent of hair spray and perfume, he reached up to turn on his air nozzle.

There was no part of her that did not offend him now; his senses revolted at her nearness, at the candid openess of her very pores, oozing out unabashed impurities. Her smallest gestures were calculated to excrete and expose that which a woman who valued herself would demur from revealing, sparing him somehow from the appalling assault on his keen sensibilities.

He remembered now that first afternoon in Cannes, when he had gone down to the front desk to buy a newspaper and cigarettes and returned to find her naked, sitting on the bed, filing her toenails. He had excused himself foolishly and gone to sit out on the balcony, but just the same he saw her there, bent over, spread apart, angled in the mirror. She knew he watched her.

"You don't have to sit out there leering like a peeping tom," she called to him, laughing that peculiar, hard laugh of hers. Getting up, she moved about the room, all the time watching herself in the mirror with the tired eyes of an old, old voyeur. There is nothing innocent or even decent about her nakedness, he thought, watching her strut with the articulate indiscretion of a Via Veneto slut. And yet, try as he might, he was unable to pull his eyes away from the offending sight.

"Well?" she teased, coming to the door of the balcony and pulling the delicate glass curtain across herself like a dancer's veil. Alexander could see her thin brown breasts with their hard nipples flattened through the glass of the door. Poached eggs, he thought. She had the tight lean body, the sinewy arms of a golfer. Her legs were thin, so thin and taut that there was a horseshoe-shaped hollow below her groin where normally the round flesh of a woman's inner thighs comes together to shield the secret place from the mockery and openess so revealed in Eunice.

She waited. Afraid she could be seen from the street below, he stood. "Aren't you coming to carry me off and ravish me?" She laughed, but her eyes were cold. "You've waited twenty years . . . more." She turned and he saw the helpless droop of her buttocks, flat and small as they were. Flopping onto the bed, she lit a cigarette and flat-eyed, detached, stroked her belly.

He walked to the door and opened it. Without looking back, he escaped into the hall, shutting the door very quietly behind himself. He walked along the esplanade for several hours and then went to the hotel desk and called his room. "Come down and join me for a drink," he said to Eunice. "It's so amusing. There's a marvelous group of American tourists haggling over their luggage on the sidewalk in front of the hotel," and he hung up.

They meant to be gone three months, but at the end of three weeks, Eunice said she wanted to go home. "Let's go stay at the Carlyle. We can see people and *do* things. I'm so goddamn bored here I could die."

"You can go," he replied, "but I'm going to stay. I'm never coming back here. This is the last time."

"What do you mean by that?" she had asked.

"I mean just that. I'm going to do this now while I'm here and then I won't need to do it ever again. I want to go home and stay there until I die. You can suit yourself, go or stay. You can do what you want. You are free."

"More of that crap about dying," she ridiculed. "If you think I'm going to bury myself alive in that dump in the desert, you're mistaken! It would kill me, living there. Look at what it did to Lily. Look at yourself . . ." But all the same, she stayed.

They moved from place to place, and when they were staying at the Colombe d'Or in St. Paul de Vence, Alexander took his paintbox out into the hills. Eunice never saw any of his sketches. He kept them hidden in a portfolio and she did not ask to see them. One afternoon he returned and found her sleeping nude, rumpled, sweating slightly, and a new, acrid smell rose from the bed.

The next day he left to paint and waited in the hall, hidden in an alcove, until he saw a small, dark-skinned waiter slip up to his room and knock softly. It doesn't matter, he thought, nothing really matters.

When the ache for the land, for home, got to be too much, they came back. As they flew in low over Tucson Alexander shook

Eunice gently to awaken her. "Look!" He pointed out the mottled desert curve, the sweep of mountains rising from nowhere. She leaned across him to look and fell back, exhausted.

"It's barren," she yawned, "Like me."

Alexander reached the Truckstop and drove through the back lot, past the gleaming rows of diesels, slumbering, prehistoric. He never felt, as Mabel did, that they were a violation of the land. They belong here, he thought admiringly, seeing them there, parked row after row, desert beasts, dragon flies, violet dancer, mantis. An old Kenworth pulled out of the line-up, crawling with the bulk of its load, a worker ant bearing the burden, and slowly made its way out to the highway.

Loretta met him at the door. Without asking him in, she stepped outside to talk.

"Mama's real sick. I'm glad you're home. She's as low down as she's ever been." She waited a moment. "It's cancer," she brought out at last, in a flat voice.

"Is she going to live?" he asked, shading his eyes from the sun.

"If anyone will," Loretta said quietly, "it'll be her," and she led him into the house.

Mabel was propped up in bed, pale pink and remote. The bed was painted white, a little girl's bed, clean and carved like a pastry and absurdly out of place in that small still room. Mabel lay with her eyes closed. Alexander stood beside her bed, mute and help-less in the face of her profound apathy. He took her hand and for a long time they continued there silent in the pale pink light of her room.

Suddenly, dazzling and light, her eye popped open and she fixed Alexander with a look. There was no one more ferociously alive, even then.

"Come on over here," she hissed. "Come close." Leaning over her body, he waited.

"There's not much time left," she dragged out, "and there's something I want real bad." Her eye was close now, Granma Watkin's eye. "Can you git me those earrings I like so much?"

"Which earrings?" he asked.

"You know," she snapped. "Sweetie Pie's lavender earrings. The ones she brought back from Hawaii."

"But how will I get them away from her, Mabel?"

There was a deep, wicked chuckle. "You'll find a way. I want those earrings before I die." Her eyes closed. He crept out of the room and stood in the narrow hallway talking to Loretta. Flodetta, Granma, Hetty and Barbara Jean were sitting in the living room silent, waiting; the Greek chorus, thought Alexander seeing them there, impassive, sorrowed.

"She's been like that pretty near all last week," Loretta was saying, "But now you're home . . . well, things'll get better, I guess." She smiled at him.

"Hey!" came a voice from the room. "Hey! You out there?" Loretta poked her head in the door. "Not you honey," her mother said. Loretta grinned. "That's the first time she's called me 'honey' since the day you left town," and she ushered Alexander back into the room.

"Well!" exclaimed Mabel. "So you're home. I didn't look to see you for a couple of years at least." She cackled her pleasure and tweaked at his jacket. "New?" she demanded. Then, "How was it?" She saw at once. She saw the tiny movement of his eye as, unsure, pained, it slid away and back again, veiled.

"Oh, you know, Mabel, Europe in the summer, full of tourists, the worst people . . . it's not nearly so nice as staying home, waiting for rain." He patted her hand.

"Huh!" she grunted. "Sit down". She poked at a place on the bed. "So it's no good . . . well, never mind. My honeymoon wasn't much either." She tried to laugh. "Can you imagine ole Orville out there trying to do the tango? He took me to Juarez for the weekend. Dancing. We stayed at the Side-Winder Motel on Laredo Street . . . God, it was awful," she reminisced. "But he's been good to me, all the same."

"Orville's special," said Alexander, hoping to get her off the subject.

"Yes," she brought out slowly. "Yes, Orville is all right." Exhausted, she dozed off.

She's going to live! he swore to himself, driving home. She's going to live, goddamnit, he swore through clenched teeth, and he pulled for her life as he had never pulled for his own. I'm not going to let go, she'll have to live.

Eunice, wearing a brown knit bikini, was standing next to the new pool talking to a brown-skinned man wearing a clean white short-sleeved shirt. She laughed at something and touched the man on the shoulder. Turning, she saw Alexander watching from the veranda door. "Oh," she smiled. "You're home. This is Mr. Espinoza. He's the pool man." She said something to Mr. Espinoza and he walked around the pool, writing things down, and then he left.

"Where were you?" she asked Alexander, coming into the living room and flopping down almost naked onto one of the red damask chairs. He remembered Alfonso Gaspari, brown skin on silk, and looked away. She saw the look and stroked her belly to anger him. Her belly was hard and flat but she liked to pinch up little rolls of flesh and squeeze them between her fingers. She was obsessed with her weight and constantly asked him if he thought she was fat.

"Out at the Truckstop", he answered. "Mabel's got cancer."

"God," she muttered, eyeing her leathery brown belly, "Look at this . . . a new roll. Do I look fatter to you?" She sucked her belly in.

"Yes," said Alexander, at last.

"You sonofabitch," she hissed, "I hope she dies," and Eunice walked out of the room.

Alexander spent most of his days out at the Truckstop. He took Mabel little things—a pincushion that had been his mother's, a negligée, armloads of magazines they laughed over, like *True Confessions, Modern Romance* and various movie magazines, and chocolate-covered cherries which she kept unopened, wrapped in red ribbon, near her bed. He took her a jelly roll that Marie made and her eyes glowed with greed, but several days later he saw it in her icebox untouched.

One morning Loretta telephoned him. "Mama's had a real bad night." She spoke quietly, as always. "They're taking her to the hospital. She's mad as a hornet and don't want to go. Maybe you can talk to her . . ." He heard an indignant crackle on the wire, Mabel's voice.

"I'm not leavin' here until I kin walk out on my own two feet, you hear? Tell them to call off the dogs!"

"Now, Mabel," he protested, "You go with them to the hospital. Please go. I'll come to you there." There was a silence and then he heard her put down the phone.

When he arrived at the hospital she was being wheeled down the hall for x-rays. "Tell this meathead here to watch what he's doin'!" she crabbed, greeting Alexander as the orderly rammed through the doorways with her chair. Alexander caught the orderly's eye.

The next day they operated on Mabel. Alexander arrived at the hospital and found Loretta, Ralph, Flo-detta, Granma Jenks, Hetty and Barbara Jean standing near the intensive care unit, waiting for news. There was a small, private waiting room and a meditation chapel, and thinking he could sneak a cigarette, Alexander went in.

Orville was sitting there in the half-light, smoking. He looked up and nodded his head but didn't say a word. In all the time Alexander had visited the Truckstop, he had never exchanged more than hello and goodbye with Orville. Alexander knew Orville was a man of few words, but all the same, as they sat there now in silence, he felt ill at ease.

Orville's big limp hands, cracked and blackened with work, lay slack and somehow useless on his knees. He was wearing new pants, hastily acquired for the occasion. Alexander saw he was crying quietly without moving. Finally, he spoke up and asked Orville what he liked to do in his spare time.

"I goes to swap meet. I likes to swap."

Alexander asked him what he liked to swap. Looking up, Orville took Alexander in. His eyes grew opaque and, after a furtive glance at the hallway, he attatched his gaze to a spot somewhere over Alexander's head. Then he said, "I only lets people think I goes to swap meet." Alexander waited. Orville's face grew pointed and after a while he added, "I robs graves." Perhaps he felt Alexander's responsive quiver, for after another long pause he told him, "Got me a gang of greasers. We's in it together." Orville grew silent and the two men returned to their mute vigil without exchanging another word.

Several weeks later Mabel got out of the hospital. They said they had gotten all the cancer and she was sent home. Alexander was out at the Truckstop one day visiting Mabel when Orville appeared in the hallway. "Sssssst," he hissed at Alexander, beckoning. "Come on in and take a look at some things I got." Alexander followed him into the room. Orville led him over to the corner and pulled back a curtain.

Tenderly laid out on the shelves there was a wonderful collection of treasures. Yacqui ceremonial masks, Seri baskets and pre-Columbian pottery of the rarest sort were laid out next to primitive Mexican religious paintings, ancient coral beads and pieces of gold. Mayan fertility goddesses, ancient flintstones, arrow heads—it was a breathtaking collection and amazed, Alexander stood and watched Orville lovingly finger each piece. Orville told him extraordinary stories about some of the pieces, and Alexander saw that he knew what they were, that he understood their value.

"Where'd you get such rare fine things?" he asked at last. Orville's eyes slid off and with a deep, satisfied sucking of his back teeth, he said, "swapped for 'em. Got 'em at swap meet," and he closed the curtain.

"You know," said Mabel, looking at him one day, "Loretta married a trucker." He was sitting next to her bed.

"Bud," he replied.

"Yes, Bud Cecil." she waited a moment. Breathing came hard since they'd taken away her lung. "It almost killed me," she continued. "Oh, I don't mean this," and she glanced down at her distorted body, wrapped round like a mummy, under the blankets. "It'll take a helluva lot more than this to kill off Mabel McPheeters," she chuckled, patting her belly with a weak hand.

"What I mean, about that other thing," she went on, referring to Loretta and Bud, "is that it broke something in me, way down inside. It was like a spring come loose in there. Something in me snapped. Do you know what I mean?"

"Yes," answered Alexander, "I do."

"He's all right, I suppose. There ain't no harm to the man, least not that I know of," she continued, thinking of Bud. "He's such an ugly brute though," she sighed. "Not like you." Mabel rolled an appreciative eye over Alexander.

"Do you suppose he'll be good to her? He's not one of us; he's not our kind." Rambling a little, she gave in to the pain.

"Mabel, listen to me a minute," he urged pulling her back. "Bud's fine. He's just what he ought to be."

"Uneducated," she mumbled. She was going to say "stupid" but changed her mind. After all, the man was her son-in-law now.

Alexander corrected her. "Bud's not uneducated in the way you mean. He knows things. He knows the road and the land."

"Not like we do!" Mabel spoke up.

"Different," explained Alexander. "He knows it in his way and he has a right to it; he's earned it, you know. He's part of these times, Mabel." She thought about this.

"He's still not good enough for my girl." She hated to give up the point.

"God, you're a stubborn lady," he laughed. "Nobody's good enough for Loretta, Mabel. But you wouldn't want her kind to die out, now would you?"

"No," relented Mabel.

"Don't you remember what I told you about the desert toads?" he asked, rubbing her soft hand.

"I've always hated them toads," she sulked. "God what a racket they make come rainy season."

"The secret is right there in those toads," he continued, amused by her resistance. "What do you suppose happens to a toad if the rains don't come? Or if the toad can't find his own species? It dies out. Its race is extinct and there's no one to pass on its genetic information . . . the end of the line," he trailed off.

"So?" she demanded, knowing perfectly well what he was talking about.

"So, that's why Loretta, that girl of yours, knew to marry herself up with Bud. She knew."

"Yes," said Mabel at last, "She knew all right."

"But you," she asked him, "what about you? Why didn't you fight to save your kind when you could?"

"Ah," he sighed, "My kind is dying out. There's no room for us here anymore."

"Hogwash!" Mabel rose slightly and glowered at him. "Then why did you marry her? Why didn't you fight to live? You can do it still! Git rid of her, send her back! Begin again."

Smiling, He rose to go. "It's too late. And besides," He laid a hand on her bandaged belly, "I've given up caring about what happens after I die . . ."

"Hah!" snorted Mabel as he left the room.

Mabel began to improve as the days passed, and by Christmas she was able to dress herself in a flame-red pantsuit and face Bud for the first time at the family table. He brought her an enormous monkey, four feet high, stuffed and glassy-eyed; he said he'd won it at the county fair.

"God help me, if that ain't the ugliest critter I ever laid eyes on!" She was pleased, all the same.

"I haven't got anything for you." And then, ashamed of her unfriendly manner, she softened. "That is, nothing but my girl. You can have her if you'll take good care of her." Seeing they were all moved and not wanting to become a sentimental old fool, she moved right on. "Soon as I can get up outta this chair and drive into town, I'm gonna buy you a proper man's suit. That is, if we can git anything that'll fit you . . . what size does a big hulk like you take, anyway?" she asked, eyeing his massive shoulders with something akin to respect.

"Aw, c'mon." He grinned. "I'd look like that stuffed monkey over there in a suit."

After Christmas Alexander gave a party to celebrate Mabel's getting well. She was so weak she had to be carried up the steps, but she looked wonderful in a new turquoise-blue outfit Orville and Ralph and Loretta had given her for Christmas. Her hair was as pale and gold as a new day and Loretta had done it up into a towering beehive. Mabel wore every last one of her diamonds.

"Arlene's going to be there wearing her pole cat and that hoity-toit Eunice will be sporting the latest, so I might just as well have

212

me some fun . . . what's the good of being a woman if you don't have a little fun with it?" she said to Loretta as she slipped on the rings.

Orville stayed home but Ralph, Loretta, Bud in his new suit and Mabel all went together in Mabel's Cadillac. Bud drove and Loretta sat in back with Ralph.

"Well, at least you can drive!" croaked Mabel as Bud took a corner beautifully.

"Which is more'n you can do!" he laughed.

It was the first time Eunice had received guests in the Snob Hollow house. As long as Mabel was sick Alexander had refused to entertain. Proud as Eunice was to show off her newly decorated house, she was angry that the party was for Mabel. But these days she found she had no power with Alexander even when she acquiesced. He shut her out.

Bud carried Mabel into the living room and placed her on a pale suede sofa. She looked around the room and saw everything was changed. Except for the tall portrait of Lily as a young girl, dressed in white, the room had been stripped of memories. Beige suede poufs and hassocks were scattered about the floor, and low chrome tables replaced the deep old mahogany of Eugene Dautremont's things. The room was filled with light and lucite, plants, flowers, cushions, new objects so transparent and clean they seemed to float through rather than exist in the room.

"This room's been embalmed," thought Mabel with a shiver, examining a bloodless, hollow lucite cube table at her side. Eunice, dressed in beige like the room, came up to Mabel bringing a young man. "Darling," she said to the slender young fellow, "this is Alexei's friend from the Truckstop. Mabel." There was an exchange of glances, a secret current between them. "And this," she continued, tearing her eyes away from the boy, "is Alessandro Davia. He did the house." She dangled an effortless hand toward the room, by way of demonstration.

"Look who's here!" Alexander came up bringing Viola, who rushed forward onto Mabel. "Well! Who would believe it!" hooted Mabel, surprised and happy. They settled down to talk, and pretty soon Arlene and Ed, Betty Rudd, Artie, Alma and Sweetie Pie came in and clustered around her. Artie, noticing Alessandro Davia, was smitten on the spot and rushed off in pursuit, but the others clung to her, and it was just like old times.

"Who's the darkie?" asked Arlene, meaning Alessandro who was almost black with the sun. Thin as a matador, he was wedged into beige velvet Levi's, a beige silk body shirt, unbuttoned to the waist, and a very large old concho belt.

"That's the New York decorator," said Mabel, rolling her eyes and pursing her mouth. Alessandro had his arm around Eunice, but he broke away to take Artie off somewhere and show him the house.

"Well, I guess we all know how *that's* going to end," smirked Arlene, riveted to Artie and Alessandro.

"No," contradicted Mabel. "It's a funny thing about endings. They sneak up on you when you're looking the other way. And they're all different . . ."

"It's time to go, Mama," said Loretta. She saw Mabel was tired. They drove Mabel home and Loretta helped her mother undress. She was turning out the light when her mother said, "Stay a minute. C'mon over here where I can git a look at you."

Loretta sat beside Mabel. In the months since she had been home, taking care of things, the intimacy of illness had been the bond, but the old closeness had gone, had given way to the tyranny of pain, of Mabel's struggle for life and Loretta's silence, the secrecy and silence of marriage. Sickness and marriage, they each have a way of changing people, and as if she felt this barrier, Mabel searched her girl's face for a clue to the truth about things. At last she said, "Are you happy, girl?"

"Sure I am, Mama," she replied, averting her eyes.

"You did what you wanted. You wouldn't listen," continued Mabel fretfully. She hadn't wanted to reproach the girl, not now.

"Mama, please."

"I won't always be around . . ." provoked Mabel. "There's never enough time. I could help."

Suddenly Loretta saw this was true. She had been so afraid her mother would die, that she would slip away, lost forever, and above all, Loretta wanted to spare her pain, to hold back the

214

confusions and truths that had come to her now at last, after years of growing in silence. It seemed terrible not to impart some piece of herself. "I guess I'm happy, Mama, but I don't know who I am any more. It's like someone pulled the plug in my brain and all those years are running out my pores. I never talked before. Things was fine. I just went along silent all that time, waiting for things to happen. Then Bud came along. He's a good man, Mama." she said fiercely. "I'm not going to find a better man. Not for me. It's just fine to want a *special* man, like you always did, but a person like me needs a plain man, someone strong. Someone who will be there. It isn't Bud that's gone wrong. It's me. It's like all of a sudden, these last months, I got trapped in the wrong body and I don't know who I really am. I'm like a note stuck down in a bottle just waiting for somebody to find me there, to read me . . . Do you know what I mean?" She faltered, almost afraid to look at her mother.

"I always knew who I was," Mabel protested. "You and Bud, you haven't had a fight? He ain't been fooling around?" she blurted out, her eyes bright as a hawk's.

"Mama!"

"Well. It never hurts to ask." She saw Loretta's eyes were full.

"Look," she persisted, almost gruffly. "There's no such thing as answers. Oh, I could say, Loretta, what you need is a home. A home and friends and a baby. A woman ain't much good without a home of her own. But there's more to it than that. There's no such thing as who you are, just flat out and simple like you was one height and weight, now and always, like you was a finished piece of goods. Why, you can be anything you want to be! You can have a dream and go after that dream; you can make yourself into whatever you want."

"It's what happens to you that makes you what you are," Loretta said in a flat voice.

"If you let it! You got to get a picture of yourself in your head; you've got to *make* yourself, like each day was the first day and you had a chance to get born all over again."

"What was your picture, Mama? Did it come true? What if no one else can see the picture you've got inside you?"

"Someone will see it. Sooner or later, someone will come along and see down there inside you; he'll see you standing there so fine and proud . . . I always had this picture," Mabel continued, excited, "of a white shee-fon negligée, dazzling and white as the moon. I kin see myself in that negligée, with little silver slippers. When I move, the smell of lilacs will float out, all around me, from inside my gown. Everything I wear will be soft against my skin. I'll be soft to touch, all over." Mabel's eyes were shining. "The one thing I always wanted was to meet a man who'd give me that white shee-fon negligée. I'd like to spend the night with him in a big hotel somewheres. Order up room service."

"Oh, Mama!" the girl cried. "How could you stand to *wait* all this time?"

"Wait? We all got to stand around waiting for *something*. It might just as well be that. It sure beats hanging around the Truck-stop, waiting for the trucks to come in, now don't it?" Mabel laughed. "It's like they say in the Program. You've got to take things one day at a time. One step at a time. But it doesn't hurt," she added, winking at Loretta, "to have a secret dream, to have a little plot tucked away in there," Mabel tapped her head. "Something for the future. Like money in the bank. Just in case that one-day-at-a-time business doesn't work . . ."

"You never got your dream; it never came true, did it, Mama?" Loretta's eyes spilled over.

"No." Mabel squeezed Loretta's hand. "But I had the dream, didn't I? I had that."

The next morning Mabel started bleeding and Loretta took her to the hospital.

When Alexander came to see her Mabel was propped up with pillows and there were tubes tied to her arms and coming out from under the bedclothes. A pale green hulking machine stood next to her, silent, like a bodyguard.

"Well," she barked, seeing him, "I'm still here." Then she turned to Loretta and finished giving her instructions. "I'm not dead yet, so don't look so blue. I just want to make damn good and sure that if anything ever does happen to me the government don't pick us clean. Now, you got it straight? Git my diamonds and them papers I told you about and every cent you can git your hands on into them safe deposit boxes. And if you ever tell those two old men where you got it hid, I'll take you for a fool," she admonished.

"Now, Mama," pleaded Loretta. "Don't go turning on Pa and Ralph. They're family. No need to hide the things from them."

"Family!" grunted Mabel. "They ain't McPheeters! I never met a Jenks yet you could trust with a dollar! Now you listen to me, girl. If anything happens to me, it'll be you out there running things. Don't let anyone git their hands on the books. Why, I've been writing the checks for close to thirty-five years now . . . I know what's there. I've kept my hand on it. You're my daughter. You've got to be strong."

She looked into Loretta, right down into her bones, and then, torn between satisfaction and the fear to let go, she demanded, "Fight for it, girl. Hold on tight. Let them know out there who's boss. Now you go hide my things."

After Loretta left, she turned to Alexander. "Tell that fathead doctor of mine to git these tubes and wires and things outta me. Goddamn city boy, how can he understand? They don't know anything." She glared at Alexander.

"Come on Mabel. Take it the best you can." He spoke low and with infinite tenderness.

"The hell with that!" she said bitterly. "I don't want to die. I refuse to die!" She lay there, her face to the wall, shutting him out. Then, after a while, she spoke again. "Don't you see? Them doctors don't know anything about dying. About the dignity of dying. I want to go home."

"Wait," he pleaded. There were things he wanted to say, things he had stored up, that he had to get out—but he saw, to his infinite regret, that she was asleep.

He drove home. Just as he was pulling into his garage he remembered something and, backing out, he went straight to Grunewald and Adams, the jewelery store. Picking out a pair of dangling gold earrings with a diamond and amythest-drop flower, he telephoned Sweetie Pie from the store.

"Sweetie Pie, I am wondering whether or not you would allow me to have those lavender earrings of yours?"

"What did you have in mind?" she asked, with a little giggle of excitement. She knew who he wanted the earrings for.

"I'd like to come see you," he replied. "I'm over here at Grunewald and Adams. May I come by now?"

"Why, sure," she answered, eager. When she opened the door he handed her the package. It was a blue velvet box wrapped in white satin. It looked beautiful, like a wedding ring, and for a moment Sweetie Pie entertained a thrilling hope. She opened the package and tried on the earrings. Standing before the hall mirror, she jiggled her head this way and that to catch the effect.

"Here," she said at last, handing him the lavender earrings. "They're not *real* of course. Not like these."

"It doesn't matter," he smiled, leaving. "They are just right."

He thought about driving back out to the hospital but decided to stop on the highway at a telephone booth and call Loretta first. He felt wonderful. It was four-thirty and the sun was still hot.

"Guess what?" he began, exhilarated. "I got the earrings. The lavender earrings!" Delighted by their brilliance, he held them up to catch the light, lavender drops of light. "For Mabel."

"We took Mama home," Loretta said. "She wanted to go home." Suddenly he felt the full violence of the sun. The highway leaped in blurred ellipsis, wet and hot, unsure. Two rigs thundered past, neck and neck, their horns sounding in careless challenge. The heat in the phone booth was intolerable.

"She wanted to die at home," Loretta continued.

"I know," he heard himself say, his eye following the rigs.

"She's gone," said Loretta.

"Yes," he said at last, and slowly putting the earrings back in his pocket, he watched the rigs clear the top of the hill, waver and then finally disappear.